SPLENDOR AND SPARK

ALSO BY MARY TARANTA

Shimmer and Burn

SPLENDOR
AND
SPARK

MARY TARANTA

MARGARET K. McELDERRY BOOKS
New York London Toronto Sydney New Delhi

MARGARET K. McELDERRY BOOKS

An imprint of Simon & Schuster Children's Publishing Division

1230 Avenue of the Americas, New York, New York 10020

MARGARET K. McELDERRY BOOKS is a trademark of Simon & Schuster, Inc.

For information about special discounts for bulk purchases, please contact Simon & Schuster Special Sales at 1-866-506-1949 or business@simonandschuster.com.

The Simon & Schuster Speakers Bureau can bring authors to your live event. For more information or to book an event, contact the Simon & Schuster Speakers Bureau at 1-866-248-3049 or visit our website at www.simonspeakers.com.

Book design by Sonia Chaghatzbanian

The text for this book was set in Baskerville.

Manufactured in the United States of America

First Edition

10 9 8 7 6 5 4 3 2 1

Library of Congress Cataloging-in-Publication Data

Names: Taranta, Mary, author.

Title: Splendor and spark / Mary Taranta.

Description: First edition. | New York : Margaret K. McElderry Books, [2018] | Summary: "Faris has her sister back but it's not the happy homecoming she imagined, and instead she must go once more into the Burn to help North find his father and inherit the magic that will allow him to reverse the Burn's hold on the kingdom of Avinea"—Provided by publisher.

Identifiers: LCCN 2018009925 (print) | LCCN 2018017313 (eBook)

ISBN 9781481472043 (eBook) | ISBN 9781481472029 (hardcover)

Subjects: | CYAC: Sisters—Fiction. | Magic—Fiction. | Plague—Fiction. | Social classes—Fiction. | Fantasy.

Classification: LCC PZ7.1.T383 (eBook) | LCC PZ7.1.T383 Spl 2018 (print) | DDC [Fic]—dc23

LC record available at https://lccn.loc.gov/2018009925

FOR AUDREY,

FROM SISTER TO NEMESIS TO SISTER
TO FRIEND

SPLENDOR AND SPARK

One

A HUNDRED YEARS AGO THE PALACE OF NEW PREVAST WAS BUILT FOR pleasure: four courtyards, an expansive garden with a hedge maze, two ballrooms, a swimming pool, and more than three hundred windows. It once hosted the royal family, a hundred servants, and a revolving guest list for three months out of every twelve. It was a summer home away from the bustle of the capital. An escape.

Now it's a prison.

A dozen servants, entire halls of empty rooms, shelves to the ceiling with no books or trinkets to fill them, peeling paint and saltwater decay on the wood and metal fixtures.

And a bastard prince who resents every inch of his opulent captivity.

It's suffocating, the way silence and anger ooze through the hallways and fill the ornate cornices of the plastered ceilings. The way they turn every meal into an abrasive symphony of silverware against porcelain, the grating click of teeth against crystal, and the low rumbling interruption of a cleared throat. At least back in the Brim, you could hear music in the dark when you couldn't sleep; you heard some proof that life existed, at least for somebody else.

In the palace all I hear is the ghostly whisper of the sea crashing against the rocks at the mouth of the harbor, haunting and full of loneliness.

Which is why almost every night, I escape to the roof, where I can see the stars and New Prevast and be reassured that someone somewhere is still breathing. Tonight my company is the flickering lights that come from the taverns crowded along the span of the Bridge of Ander, which connects the palace grounds to the city proper across the harbor.

In daylight the wilting buildings are shuttered up tight, while waterbirds sun themselves on the pilings below. At night vice opens its doors for a booming business, and the bridge is flooded with thieves and beggars and drunks. Any waterbirds still roosting become target practice for bottles that shatter against the rocks below. Pieces of colored glass eventually wash up on the black sand beach with the tide, worn smooth by the water. Terrible for holding magic or casting spells, but beautiful for collecting and lining the narrow windowsill of my bedroom on the second floor.

I hug my knees to my chest, balancing my chin on top, staring until my vision blurs and New Prevast loses its shape, becoming a generic smear of light and dark. The chill of the wind masks the briny scent of the sea, and for an instant I could be anywhere: the shallows of the Brim, the open fields of Avinea, the abandoned wagon of a traveling magician trying to save the world.

But then the window shutters open behind me and I hear the sigh that anchors me here.

"Locke," Captain Chadwick says, frustration warring with relief. I wonder how long he's been looking for me, or if I've become predictable. "You promised."

My fingers dig into the soft folds of my skirt. "I lied."

Another sigh, and I know the expression that accompanies it, the disappointment. A sliver of guilt worms through the chill, and I close my eyes. Poor Chadwick. As the captain of the Guard, his talents far exceed the role of unwilling babysitter, and yet, as the captain of the Guard, he follows orders from his prince.

"His majesty explicitly forbade you from the roof," Chadwick says, reciting the memorized spiel. "The tiles are slick—"

"And the courtyard is unforgiving of bodies and bones," I finish sourly, because it still hurts that his majesty told Chadwick to tell me, as if I were a servant unworthy of direct address. I open my eyes, biting the inside of my cheek, numb fingers circling the spell around my wrist.

I *am* a servant, I tell myself as I stare across the placid harbor, and his majesty hasn't spoken to me in weeks.

A third sigh, softer than those before it. "Faris, please," Chadwick says. "Not tonight."

Tears sting my eyes at the unexpected familiarity, and I fight them back with a savage fury. *Not tonight*, I repeat, but it's an impossible request. Tonight of all nights, promises have been broken.

Pulling himself out the window, Chadwick edges closer and sinks down beside me, adjusting the hilt of his sword out of the way. He's dressed in the ceremonial black and silver of Avinea: tunic, vest, and coat; too many layers for practicality but just enough for formality. He looks nice with his sandy hair pulled back and his beard trimmed to a mere shadow across his chin. He looks solid.

"The ceremony is over," he says softly. "It's done."

"And I survived," I say.

"As expected." He shifts his weight and cradles his hands between his knees. Glancing over, he says, "You did the right thing, Locke."

"Come on, Captain," I whisper with a forced, wavering smile, fighting around the dull ache in my chest. "Grant me a moment of self-pity."

He gives me a withering look, and I turn away, toward the glittering sea. I know what he's thinking and I know that he's right: I've had three weeks to wallow in my decision, three weeks to acclimate myself to its conclusion. When I walked away from the Prince of Avinea, I truly believed my feelings for him would fade, that our brief relationship had been nothing more than two lonely people clinging to each other in a moment of panic. He needed to focus on saving his kingdom; I needed to focus on saving my sister.

But for a moment we had needed each other.

I told Chadwick nothing of what had happened that morning in the monastery cellar when North offered me his heart and I refused it, yet Chadwick knows every detail anyway. There can be no secrets between a prince and his captain, and Chadwick knows everything that has happened from the moment I met North to the moment I turned my back on him.

I don't regret my decision. I can't afford to. But it still hurts sometimes, like a scab I keep picking off before it can heal.

Especially tonight, when I know Bryn—North's *wife*, I force myself to acknowledge—is being escorted to his bedroom in the eastern wing of the palace, where they will be supervised by members of the council. North's infected blood and Bryn's amplification ability prevent them from physically consummating the marriage, but sharing a bed and binding themselves through blood magic will suffice to prove the point until a true heir can be produced. Proclamations are already written, waiting to be sent to the few remaining strongholds left untouched by the Burn, and even beyond, to the nearest countries and potential allies scattered across the Havascent Sea. The Prince of Avinea has taken a bride and now has the means of finding Merlock, his missing father. Please send money and, if possible, men. While they won't arrive in time to help find Merlock, they'll be needed to clean up the mess he's made.

After twenty years of dying, Avinea is ready to live again.

I savor the way my envy burns through my blood at the thought of Bryn in North's bed, fueled by the traces of dead magic that still linger in my veins from an infection that nearly killed me. Allowing my vices such free reign is a dangerous, intoxicating game, and the court magician, Sofreya, will have my head for it when she sees I've been testing the limits of her protection spells again. Nestled in the crooks of my arms, the spells keep the infection pinned in place, away from my heart. But magic only runs skin deep; if I really wanted to succumb to my vices, the poison could easily be coaxed past the spells.

"So that's it, then," I say, and the ache in my chest sharpens, cutting the last threads of impossible hope I had buried inside me.

Chadwick squints toward the city. "*Wife* is only a title. No different from *prince* or *captain* or *king*." Looking at me, he says, "Respect the office, Locke. But don't assign it any more sentimentality than it warrants."

I bite back a snort of derision. It's more than a title; it's a guarantee that Bryn will always have power over North. Over me. And power to keep us apart.

"At least now we can leave," I say, my voice thick. Now that the wedding is official, Perrote, Bryn's father, will make good his promise to deliver clean magic to the palace, and North will be free to search the Burn for his father. Killing him is the only way North can inherit control of his dying country and its magic—thereby stopping the Burn at last.

"Locke."

I shake my head, petulant as a child, and Chadwick takes my chin in hand, forcing my face toward his. I avoid his eyes, staring instead at the thick scar on his chin, where the facial hair doesn't grow. He earned it years ago, he told me, playing swords with North when they were both boys being raised at the Saint Ergoet's Monastery. It was the first—and only, Chadwick was always quick to add—time North got the better of him in a fight.

"She's going to destroy him," I say, daring him to contradict me.

"No." Chadwick shakes his head, lips flat. "You and I will never let that happen. But if I have to defend him alone, I will do it."

"I don't—"

"You will be left behind if your only interest is in being a liability. Do you understand me? You have had two weeks' worth of training at best, when you actually put in the effort. You're not exactly an asset to the expedition."

I scowl more deeply. The magic spell my mother branded on my skin ten years ago is our best hope of finding Merlock. It acts as a compass through the Burn—and is the only thing our competition lacks. Without it, Chadwick would be wandering like a blind man, risking the lives of all who follow him, including his prince.

"North needs this spell," I say, with a hint of triumph at what that really means: He needs *me*.

"Prince *Corbin* will not risk Avinea for you again," he says, emphasizing North's real name with his teeth clenched. He loosens his hold on my chin, features softening as he grips my shoulders instead. Only twenty, Chadwick looks older these days, tired and spread thin. "He wanted you because you were strong," he says. "So be strong."

For a moment I resent him, but beneath it I recognize my indulgence for what it is: punishment, no different from the fights I used to stage at the Stone and Fern Tavern, when I would bloody a stranger's face for the chance to feel control over something bigger than myself. Wallowing in regret accomplishes nothing but wanting. Tears are not tolerated in the training barracks, and I can't afford them now. *Iron*, I tell myself. *You are stronger than this.*

"At least Cadence will be here tomorrow," I say. *Finally.* Perrote took her away from me two weeks ago without any chance of good-bye—without any chance of hello, really—when he returned to Brindaigel to fortify his holdings and to calm his people, who had only recently discovered that the world still existed beyond their hidden borders. Cadence was his fail-safe, a hostage to ensure North upheld his agreement to marry Bryn, to recognize Brindaigel as a sovereign state, and to grant Perrote a position on his council. Now, with his elder son, Rowan, left in charge of Brindaigel, Perrote is shepherding the entire Dossel family—Cadence in tow—back to the palace to celebrate Bryn's miraculous ascension from the daughter of a thief to the crowned Princess of Avinea.

They plan to stay for several weeks, ensuring Bryn settles herself as a permanent fixture in the palace and the shifting political landscape. And to establish themselves as well, I suspect: The parts of Avinea untouched by the Burn have been an open market of available landholdings and abandoned estates, ripe for the picking by those with the weaponry—or delusions of power—to defend their claims. The anarchy of the last twenty years will finally end; once Merlock is found and North is crowned king, North will finally have the time and the power to seize control of his fragmented kingdom and rebuild it to its former glory. No doubt the Dossels will all expect a piece.

Chadwick squeezes my shoulder. "Find comfort in your sister."

The comfort is small; my frustration is greater. Cadence arrives tomorrow, and I leave two days later. What kind of reunion is that? After months of being enchanted by Perrote's magic, Cadence woke up to find her whole world gone. She needs her sister, someone familiar to keep her steady on her feet. Instead she'll be abandoned all over again.

And yet I know I cannot stay behind, not even for her. *Especially* not for her. Going into the Burn with this spell is the only way I can help save this kingdom and ensure a future where she and I will never be separated again.

Chadwick watches me as I suck in a deep breath and then release it slowly. My fingers curl against the smooth stone tiles of the roof at my hip. At least with Cadence's return, North will fade from my thoughts the way he should have weeks ago.

"Don't let anyone see you out here, or it'll be my head," Chadwick says, turning back for the window and the warmer air inside.

I hide a small smile; ignoring my behavior is his awkward attempt at sympathy. "Of course."

"Locke." He pauses, features backlit into shadow. "You made the right choice."

Then why does it hurt, I want to ask, but I already know the answer.

Without another word Chadwick ducks through the window and disappears, but I linger, embracing the cold burn of the tiles through my skirt and the comforting sight of the breathing city across the water.

"I survived," I repeat softly. And now the real battle begins.

Two

Chadwick's admonishment follows me back inside, and I rise to its challenge, lifting my chin as I walk, straightening my spine. By the time I close my door behind me and remove my cloak, the reflection I catch in the mirror above my bureau is a cold mask, eyes half-lidded in silent appraisal, the way Bryn so often looks at me.

She will not beat me, I think; I will not be defeated.

Nevertheless, my mind strays to her empty bedroom, connected to mine by a shared parlor. There's a finality to the untouched bed inside that can't be denied: North and Bryn are married now, their lives inextricably intertwined. The bloodbound ceremony Sofreya performed links Bryn's heart to his, and from this moment on, Bryn is legally—and magically—recognized as an heir of Avinea.

By all rights North should have performed the ceremony himself, but his council has forbidden him from using magic. Anytime he does, the infection in his blood grows stronger, burrowing deeper toward his heart, threatening to turn him into one of the hellborne addicts who roam the Burn.

And he needs to be strong if he has any hope of finding his father.

As I prepare for bed, I allow myself a sliver of grim satisfaction in knowing that Bryn is not enjoying a night of wedded bliss but, rather, is counting down the seconds until sunrise when she can call her obligation complete and resume her real interest: exerting authority over the servants and visiting the nobles looking to curry favor and carve themselves a place in Avinea's future.

No one knows that I'm her prisoner; I'm explained away as a beloved friend with a wardrobe to match: fabrics and colored silks that elevate me above the servants, but not high enough to warrant interest for possible political alliance. It's exhausting, playing this game, and I crave the moment it ends, when the binding spell linking me to Bryn is dissolved and I'm free to take my sister and—

And then what? I never know what happens next. Do we stay here in New Prevast, like so many other refugees fleeing the Burn? Or do we sail for some unseen horizon, some faraway land neither one of us has ever heard of before? A new world, a new start, a new chance of finding the elusive concept of *home*.

Despite the hopeful promise of Cadence returning tomorrow, when I climb into bed, it's with simmering envy that no amount of self-reproach can banish, a slurry of vice as thick as dregs in my veins. *Wife*, I think again, and it hurts, like a blow to the stomach. *She's his wife.* My mother's spell aches across my chest, and I close my eyes, hoping to force my thoughts into silence the way I force the world into darkness.

Instead the world awakens.

Somehow I abandon my bed and fly, hurtling over New Prevast, led by a silver thread that mirrors the moonlit road leading out of the city and across the craggy lava fields below. A line of gold appears on the horizon, and I squint against it—the sunrise, already?—but as I draw closer, the air turns smoky and sour.

The Burn.

I barely have time to register the fact that my mother's spell is somehow dragging me out of my bed, before I land on my hands and knees in the square of a small village. The ash of the Burn instantly clears to the scorched earth beneath me, protecting me from the poisoned magic that soaks the ground, while the silver thread unravels further, tugging at me, begging me to follow. I hesitate, uncertain: I don't know where I am. Is it dream or reality? This has only happened once before, when I was caught off guard and unable to control the way my mother's spell unfurled. Since then, I've taken lessons with Sofreya to control its power. But they were based in theory alone, impossible to practice without the Burn to ignite the magic. So how did I get here?

The square itself is framed by the skeletal remains of a former marketplace; an empty fountain with a statue of some sainted virtue stands at its center, her features worn to grotesque anonymity. The square is eerily beautiful, even in ruins, and despite myself, I linger over the view, intoxicated by the breadth of so much destruction.

Past the broken roofline around me, I glimpse a great manor house sitting back from the village on a dune of rolling ash, amid lines of petrified trees. Dark arched windows and scorched stone walls are gilded with a flickering light from within.

I realize my mother's spell is still unwinding ahead of me, guiding me toward the manor house, which can only mean one thing: Merlock is inside.

Panicked, I grab the thread of the spell, trying to pull it back, but it tightens, turns taut, in danger of snapping. I release it with a flash, terrified of fraying the edges or somehow destroying it. It resumes its impatient tugging, and I stumble after it, scanning the ground around me for a weapon. The last time I faced Merlock, he was not happy to see me, and I doubt his opinion has changed.

Shadows shift through the petrified trees as I pass; something grunts, as if wounded. I pause, squinting, searching out the source. My mother's spell will attract hellborne addicts desperate for clean magic to cut through the fog of poison in their veins; standing still out in the open like this is dangerous.

The grunting repeats, then a pitiful mewl, raising the hair on the back of my neck. The air turns heavy, as though I'm being watched, and I hurry toward the gaping mouth of the manor house, pausing only to grab a chunk of broken stone from the long sweep of stairs leading up. There are other stones, stacked like a cairn, and the topmost stone catches my eye. It's still pale—full of magic that has yet to be consumed by the Burn. Did Merlock put it there?

Pushing inside the manor, I expect darkness and decay and an angry king. Instead the first thing I see is a small boy running through a marble hall, his leather shoes hissing against the slick tiles. He laughs, but the sound is distant, as though caught underwater. When he turns to beckon toward an unseen figure, my heart seizes. *North?* His features are there, but somehow rounded with youth.

A piece of painted plaster falls from the ceiling and hits the tiles, shattering like glass. Rather than getting hit, the boy—North— flickers and then fades, his colors dulling. The ruins of the manor house come into sharp relief behind him, cracking walls and broken columns and a ceiling that continues to fall apart.

Magic, I realize with a jolt. North as a child is merely a memory, and the spell that summoned him is being consumed by the Burn, feeding into the decay of the house around me.

Merlock. Too late I remember the thread, only to find its end, wavering above the heart of the missing King of Avinea.

Stunned, I drop the stone I grabbed outside. My breath catches in my throat and sticks. There are glimpses of North in Merlock's weathered face: the wide nose and black eyes, the olive color of his skin. But where North's edges are softened by kindness, Merlock is all cruel planes and sharp angles. The military uniform he wears is in tatters on his back, worn through at the elbows and knees, Avinean black and silver muted to muddy charcoal and smoke. Frayed epaulets hang from his shoulders in threads.

For a moment he ignores me, watching as North fades from view, with a kind of hunger I know too well. "I know you're there," he whispers in the dark, hoarse and uneven. "I can feel you. *Talk to me.* Set me free."

Did he even know North as a child? North told me he was raised by his mother, protected from his crumbling kingdom by the monks of Saint Ergoet's. And Merlock has been hunted since the Burn began. Waltzing into New Prevast to see his bastard son—giving *credence* to North's claim to the throne, legitimizing him and creating the means of destroying himself—goes against every cowardly action Merlock has taken since killing his brother.

And yet the yearning is nearly palpable, his bitterness evoking an overwhelming sense of pity.

As if feeling the weight of my gaze, Merlock finally focuses on me. His eyes slide to the thread that spans the distance between us and his hunger dissipates, replaced with a flicker of surprise that quickly melts into an air of boredom. "You are not who I thought you were," he says, lifting a hand to the spell, fingers skimming the thread. I feel each twitch of it, like a heartbeat jerked out of me.

I wet my lips and taste the sulfur of the Burn. "You expected my mother," I say, voice trembling. Is this real? Or am I caught in a dream, induced by the poisoned magic in my blood?

Merlock offers the barest ghost of a smile. "The tailor taught her well," he says, advancing toward me, still tracing the thread with one feather-light finger. "It's a magnificent spell. But useless in your hands, apparently."

The tailor? Does he mean my father? I open my mouth to ask, but find myself swallowing the question as he stops in front of me, head angled toward one shoulder.

"She was your age the first time she tried to kill me," he says.

His expression twists into something ferocious as he grabs me by the shoulder, igniting pain under my skin. All at once the spell retracts and I'm thrown back across the continent, slamming into my bed so hard I seem to bounce against the mattress. Heart racing, I stare at my curtained window before pain consumes me.

Biting back a howl, I reach for my shoulder, only to cringe away when I feel the scorched collar of my nightdress and the raw, gummy flesh underneath, where Merlock's skin touched mine.

Bile floods my throat, and I curl over the edge of my bed, dry heaving before throwing myself back against my pillows. With a shaking hand I touch my shoulder again, lightly, assessing the damage. What happened? Did Merlock just try to kill me?

Blood begins to soak my nightdress. Sucking in a deep breath, I force myself to my feet, yank aside my curtains, and flinch away from the sliver of dawn that greets me. Turning my back to the sun, I position myself in front of my mirror and slowly—grimacing—fold back the collar of my nightdress.

Mother of a sainted virgin.

The memory of Merlock's touch is burnt into my shoulder, ringed with a spreading shadow of poison. My entire collarbone is an angry violet-and-yellow smear of bruises. The poison he transferred into me dilutes like ink, spilling perilously close to my mother's spell, which still glows silver from being used. I stare at the damage, transfixed. Terrified. I knew that Merlock was a magician—inherently the most powerful one in Avinea—yet I also believed North had a chance to fight him. To *win*.

But if Merlock can do this with just a touch, what damage can he do casting an actual spell?

I begin to shiver as I lower my hand, spreading my fingers above my breast. Half an inch lower, and Merlock could have pulled my mother's spell out of my chest—

And then I realize with a sickening lurch: That is exactly what he intended to do.

Three

SOFREYA OPENS HER DOOR WARILY, DARK HAIR PINNED BACK FROM her face. When she sees me, her face blanches. I terrify her. Most people do. Plucked off the streets by Chadwick years ago, she was brought to the palace to help excise the poison North would invariably bring home after another fruitless search for his father. Now she views magic the way more of us should: as a danger.

I bite the inside of my cheek and uncover my shoulder, demonstrating the spreading infection. "I had an accident," I say.

Her eyes widen in alarm, but she dutifully steps back, allowing me entry into her study. It always reminds me of North's wagon, made stationary: shelves of books, drawers full of supplies, and jars and jars of rocks. Even Tobek, North's former apprentice, is here, tousle-headed and scowling as he pushes himself out of his cot and begins shoving his shirt back into his trousers. He doesn't acknowledge me, but as Sofreya leads me to a seat by her fire, Tobek begins slamming tea things onto the table across the room—loud enough to make sure I know he's ignoring me.

He's never volunteered the story of what happened after North and I left him with Bryn en route to New Prevast, the day her father intercepted them. But I know the end result: two cracked ribs, a broken leg, and a scar that runs jaggedly down his lower back. And I know another truth: that he blames me for all of it. After Bryn infected me with dead magic to prove a point, Tobek wanted to cut his losses and leave me to die. Instead North saved my life at the sacrifice of their mission, and that decision—that distraction—cost Tobek his apprenticeship. He answers to Sofreya now, trapped in the palace like all the rest of us.

"What accident could cause this much damage?" Sofreya pulls back the collar of my dress and sucks a breath in between her teeth, pressing gently around the breadth of the infected skin.

She's earned the trust of both North and Chadwick over the years, and yet I hesitate to admit the truth: that I have no control over my mother's spell when my anger runs deep, which is danger enough—and now Merlock knows I'm looking for him. More than that, he spoke of my mother with a familiarity that eats at me. Overnight I've turned into the liability Chadwick warned me against becoming.

"A moment of weakness," I finally say, avoiding her eyes. It's not a lie, exactly; more of a confession.

Her alarm sharpens, turns to rebuke as she rakes up my sleeve to see her protection spells, still sitting untouched in the crook of my arm. While she looks relieved that I haven't thrown away her magic, she still scowls as she drops my sleeve. "We can't afford weakness."

"Yes, Captain," I mutter.

Tobek slams a book onto his desk, his own form of rebuke at my petulance. It is a welcome glimmer of the boy I knew before. For the most part, whatever happened that day still haunts his eyes and flattens his smile and makes him quiet, and I accept his blame as a reminder of what happens when you stray from the course, when you let your heart triumph over your head.

"These are finger marks," Sofreya continues, fanning her own fingers in demonstration. "Did you go into the city? Were you *fighting* someone?"

I allow my silence to condemn me. Her hands hook into fists, and she begins to blink rapidly, as if holding back tears. "Prince Corbin needs this spell," she explodes at last. "Why would you even risk infecting it? What does that prove, Faris? That you're *strong*? This isn't one of your tavern brawls back home, and Prince Corbin isn't a drunk gambling a few copper tretkas on you to win. He's betting all of *Avinea* on you. If you're defeated out there, you don't get another chance tomorrow night. None of us do."

Her words cut deeply, for someone so meek. I work my jaw, struggling to come up with something to say in my defense, only to sigh. "I'm sorry," I say. "I know this is important."

"Then act like it," she snaps, stalking to the opposite wall and pulling a jar of white rocks from a shelf.

I catch Tobek glowering at me over three cups of freshly poured tea. Another silent barb. He knows I don't drink it.

"Lean back," Sofreya demands, shoving me hard against the chair. "Does Captain Chadwick know?"

Not yet, but he will, if Tobek's sudden smirk is any indication. "I'll tell him after—God Above!" I grunt as she begins excising the poison out of my shoulder and into the stone pressed to my skin. "A warning would have been nice!"

"A morning without having to see you would have been nice," she counters.

I tip my head back and grit my teeth. While Sofreya has never been as gentle as North could be when pulling poison from my veins, she's not making any effort at all today.

Almost an hour passes before we all hear the sound of wagon wheels on gravel coming from the drive outside. Tobek straightens, pushing aside the heavy curtains to peer out the window. All pain vanishes, and I sit up, ignoring Sofreya's protests, my mouth opening to ask what I already know from the way his expression mirrors my own racing heart.

They're here. The convoy from Brindaigel.

Cadence.

Any thoughts of Merlock or my mother fly from my head as I jump to my feet, nearly knocking Sofreya over in my haste for the door. She calls after me, frustrated, but she's excised enough of the poison that I can wait an hour or two before I need to return. It's reckless, ridiculous, and yet—it's Cadence. Nothing else matters.

I bolt through the halls, ignoring the reproving stares of the guards standing by, nearly giddy as I turn corners and cut through servants' halls.

After bursting out from behind a tapestry, I catch myself on the carved balustrade of the grand stairway that sweeps into the foyer.

An instant later, I'm racing down the stairs and out the wide front doors onto the veranda outside.

The council stands to the left—a trio of old men and one younger woman, all dressed in somber grays with high lace collars that went out of fashion when Merlock did. Guards form two staggered lines down the stairs leading to the gravel drive, where the carriages now stop, the Brindaigelian banners snapping in the sea breeze. Ducking between two guards, I smooth my hair with one hand, realizing—too late—that I should have brought a coat. The wind is bitter this early, hinting at the winter to come. But my adrenaline keeps me warm enough as I lean forward, staring hungrily at the first carriage door as a footman pulls it open and extends a hand to those seated inside.

Bryn's mother, Robetta, exits in a flounce of skirts and feathers, followed by Rialdo, Perrote's second son. Disappointed, I immediately dismiss the carriage and start eyeing the next one, fingers drumming an impatient beat against the balustrade.

The guards suddenly shift into attention behind me, and I glance over, double-taking as I see Bryn emerging from the palace, a vision of perfection in a dress of deep blue with silver trim, her dark red hair coiled around a gold comb. North stands at her side in all black, a slim shadow against her light. They're linked arm in arm, and while Bryn hasn't touched the binding spell that links us, her possessiveness stings deeply in the scars of magic around my wrist. She whispers something into his ear—he has to bend down to reach her. Whatever she said earns a forced, tired smile in reply.

Wife, I think, and it is still sharp as a knife.

Bryn scans the veranda before she catches my eye and arches an eyebrow in greeting, tightening her arm around North's.

I know better than to rise to her bait, yet my jealousy is an animal, vicious and uncaged. The poison still breeding in my shoulder ignites in warning, and my heart shudders once, as if struggling to pump my thickened blood. I force myself to look away, spreading my fingers against the cruelly cold stone of the balustrade.

It's only a title, I tell myself.

As Rialdo escorts his mother up the stairs, North starts down to greet them, only for Bryn to hold him back, her plastered smile never wavering. Let them come to her, she must be thinking. This is her palace, her prince, her crown. When her family greets her, it will be from one deferential step beneath her.

Even more Dossels emerge from the next two carriages: four elder sisters and a parade of spouses. Footmen stack mountains of luggage onto the drive, and I find myself tensing in annoyance. How many ball gowns do they think they need for only six weeks in a city too dangerous to explore, with barely enough noble families to fill one of the three dining rooms available here?

But no matter. Only one carriage left.

I edge closer to the stairs, weaving in between the guards, goose bumps from the cold alternating with chills of terror. What if she's not here? What if Perrote changed his mind and amended his agreement, demanding more in return for my sister? North can't afford concessions, and I can't afford much longer without her.

The final carriage door opens, and Perrote himself steps out, tugging down the bottom of his waistcoat before snapping the collar of his traveling coat. Seeing him awakens a ferocity inside me that feeds on the infection, a natural instinct to fight, to wound, to kill. He killed my mother, enslaved my sister, and withheld magic, enough to find Merlock, from its rightful master. I stare him down as he ascends the stairs, but he doesn't even glance my way. In my anger I feel the slight to be intentional, his dismissal a ruse. He knows I'm here.

Below, another figure emerges, running a hand through his dark hair. Alistair Pembrough. The king's executioner and another piece of the marriage treaty: a borrowed servant Perrote gave to North at my request. Like my sister, Alistair returned to Brindaigel two weeks ago, but now that he's back, he can fulfill the promise he made to me—that he'll find a way to remove the infection from my blood. From North's. Without needing more magic.

His expression bears the strained mark of a journey spent sharing a carriage with Perrote, but his face brightens as he turns back into the carriage, helping a third figure down. She moves hesitantly, looking to the palace with enormous eyes free of the spell that once shadowed them.

Cadence.

I start toward her, as an arm slides through mine. Bryn's smile doesn't waver, and she speaks from the corner of her mouth. "Slow and steady," she says. "My family feeds on weakness, and they see everything."

I straighten, free hand clenching my skirts in frustration. They've dressed Cadence like a handmaiden, in a plain but pretty dress that peeks out from beneath her dark traveling cloak.

She's a ray of sunshine in the gathering storm, a flicker of hope in my cracking heart. Despite Bryn's warning, I lift my hand, only for my greeting to wilt when Alistair offers her his arm.

How *dare* he try to touch her, after all that he's done to us?!
Don't take it, I think. *You can do this, all on your own.*

Cadence accepts his arm with a timid smile that makes no sense. How can she cling to Thaelan's murderer? What could he have possibly done to make her overlook his role in her enslavement?

As they move toward the stairs, Cadence flinches at every bray of laughter, dipping her face into Alistair's shoulder when a servant makes an unexpected movement. She's been too long lost to Perrote's magic, too long a mindless slave trained as a machine without capacity for expression. Now every thought, every feeling is painted brightly across her sweet face for the whole world to exploit. Alistair cradles her with a protective arm.

I want to kill him.

North excuses himself from the flock of Dossels who crowd him on the veranda, and quickly meets Alistair and Cadence halfway down the stairs. Alistair shakes his hand, and Cadence dips into a clumsy curtsy, staring at North as though he's made of starlight. North speaks to her, low and inaudible while bowing, and she flushes, hiding her face in Alistair's shoulder again. It's a newfound shyness, so sharply different from the bold, fearless little girl who argued with me over everything.

"Breathe," Bryn orders as Alistair relinquishes his escort to North with a forced smile. Only then does he scan the veranda, apparently looking for me.

My palms are slick with sweat; my heart is crashing like the waves at the mouth of the harbor. Ignoring Alistair, I stare as my sister approaches, drinking in every freckled inch of her, searching for any more damage inflicted by the four months under Perrote's enchantment. Is she really only twelve years old? She looks ancient, like she's seen more than any little girl should.

"Stop staring," Bryn says. "You'll terrify her, Faris. Good god, you look half-feral. Did you sleep at all last night?"

"I slept quite well," I say darkly. "And you?"

"No complaints," she says with a sly smile.

I can't bear it any longer. Breaking loose of Bryn, I shoulder through the line of guards, only to bump into one of Bryn's sisters. She turns, a reprimand framed on her lips, but it stalls.

Her name freezes on my tongue. Joyena. Third of seven in line for the throne, and Bryn's oldest sister. A widow now, dressed all in black.

I murdered her husband.

Stunned, I open my mouth, but what could I possibly say? That I'm sorry? That her husband's death still haunts my nightmares? That the smell of a candle snuffed out at night ignites a litany of memories that begin with a gun and end with blood? How can I explain that I had to choose between his life and my sister's, and I chose Cadence?

After all, I would choose her again if I had to.

Joyena's expression darkens as if she can read every incriminating thought in my head. She turns toward her mother, and a shared look is enough to relate my identity. She knows. Face burning, I ignore the first rule of the fighting ring and turn my back on them both, hurrying for the comfort, the safety of my sister.

North steps out of the way, and I throw my arms around her thin shoulders and hold as tightly as I can. "Cadence," I whisper, kissing the top of her head. "God Above, Cade, you have no idea how much I've missed you."

She wrenches back, as panicked as a cornered animal. I release her with a twinge of guilt. Of course. She's been through so much already, I need to move slowly. One step, then another.

"It's me," I say. "Faris." Then, terrified: "Do you remember me?"

She watches me warily. "Of course I remember you."

The cold creeps in, and I shiver, hugging myself. The whole world watches, even the servants who feign indifference as they continue stacking luggage on the drive. Smiling weakly, I reach for her again, but Cadence shakes her head and steps down, out of reach, wariness sharpening to something darker.

"I remember *everything*," she says, and venom seethes through her teeth. "Every single day at the workhouse, every single night. I was a slave, not a simpleton."

I reel at the implication. The steaming vats of lye; the hours of scrubbing linens until her fingers were chapped and bleeding; the greasy men who came looking for little girls to buy, who were not discouraged from touching their potential purchases. Four months of that torture, and my little sister was not asleep, just buried beneath a magic spell that muted her protests, her ability to scream?

I pivot, seeking out Perrote. Once again he ignores me, but I stare him down with a silent—murderous—promise all the same. There are monsters in Avinea, and I intend to destroy every one of them. Especially him.

"I saw you that day in the plaza," Cadence says, pulling my

attention back to her. "When the king called for someone to speak for me. I saw you, Faris. Just *standing* there."

"I'm sorry," I say. "But if I'd spoken for you, they would have killed me, and I needed to save you—"

"All you've ever done is save yourself," she snaps, features twisted. "*You* wanted to leave Brindaigel that night. And when Thaelan went back for you, you didn't even wait. You had already abandoned him." Her voice lowers to a whisper, wobbling. "Us."

I stare at her, stricken.

"*I* was the one holding his hand when the guards took him," Cadence says. "*I* was the one who stayed with him. But he still wanted *you*. Neither of you really wanted me, not when you had each other!"

This can't be real. Is she still jealous of Thaelan's attentions to me? Does she blame me for his death, and not the boy who slid the knife through his chest? Helpless, I look to Alistair standing two steps below. He rubs his mouth with his thumb, a cigarette tucked between his fingers. He doesn't meet my eyes, and I suddenly understand why she can cling to him for comfort now. He killed Thaelan, but only on Perrote's orders. He's just a prisoner, like her, whereas I walked away, free. The real enemy.

"Perhaps we should step inside," North suggests gently, gesturing, but Cadence doesn't move, staring at me as if in challenge.

Beneath my heartbreak awakens something bitter. Doesn't she know I would never have left Brindaigel that night without her? That I allowed myself to be bound to Bryn for *her*? That after everything I have done, everything still expected of me, Cadence was, is, and will always be the driving force behind my every decision? Even now, I would do anything for her.

Except, it seems, rein in my anger.

"He came back because you ran away from *me*, Cadence, and he didn't want you to get lost. You would have died down there. Don't you understand that?"

God Above, what is wrong with me? I cringe away from my own accusation as tears flood her eyes. Dimly I'm aware of the Dossels watching, and I chide myself for giving them any ammunition to use against me. Against her.

"I hate you," Cadence whispers, the sound barely there above the wind.

"All right," I reply, just as hoarse.

"It's been a long journey," Bryn says, brushing past me, curling an arm around Cadence's shoulders. "You must be exhausted. Shall I show you your room? I picked one close to mine, just like I promised I would."

Cadence breaks eye contact with me to look at Bryn. Her fury dissolves, and she stares like I might have, once: dazzled by the beauty, ignorant of the beast. They met briefly, before Cadence was returned to Brindaigel, and I have no doubt Bryn used every shared second to convince Cadence that she was a friend and not the enemy, not like her father. "You remembered?" Cadence asks, incredulous.

"Of course I did," Bryn says. "I've been so eager to see you again, Cadence. I hope we'll become as close as sisters while you're here."

Cadence returns Bryn's smile with a hesitant one of her own, accepting Bryn's hand. The threat I hear is as loud as a scream—

Bryn will take my sister from me just as she has taken everything else. I turn my head toward the sea, fighting back tears. What else did she promise Cadence in those stolen hours when I was kept away from her, unable to offer any protection?

"Faris."

I stiffen at North's soft address—the first he's spoken directly to me in weeks. He stands closer than I thought—closer than necessary, I tell myself, desperate for some glimmer of light. But seeking comfort in his company is as stupid as me guilting my little sister with Thaelan's death. I can't afford to be weak, and in this moment I feel in reckless danger of it.

Until I see the band of gold on his finger. A wedding ring.

"You have your magic now," I say. "We can finally find Merlock." Because the sooner we do, the sooner I'll be free. Standing still is going to kill me.

He sighs at my insistence on business. "Faris—"

"Corbin," Perrote calls, an edge in his voice. The others have gone inside, and now he stands alone on the veranda among the guards. "I suggest you join us, unless you wish me to play host in your own home."

Another thinly veiled threat.

North nods in acknowledgment but hesitates. "Don't stay out long," he says quietly, not looking at me, "and stay near the palace. We don't know how many men he's brought into the city."

My heart aches; he knows that all I want now is to run, but I can't even mumble thanks. He's already gone. Maids and valets appear now that the drive is clear, ready to direct the dispensation of luggage to the appropriate rooms.

"Any welcome for me?" Alistair asks, his smirk barely hiding the waver in his voice.

I slap him as hard as I can. Several of the servants pause their work to exchange amused glances as Alistair recoils, working his jaw as he rubs it with one hand.

"She needed a friend, Faris," he says darkly, "and it's either someone working with you or someone working against you. Which would you prefer?"

"She certainly doesn't need *you*."

"But you do. Your sister is a survivor, just like us, but we're not saved yet. You have to trust me. Just a little bit."

My shoulder aches and my blood hums, urging me to give in to my darker vices, to hurt him the way he once hurt Thaelan. But there's still enough of me left that sees the truth in what he says. I need him to find a way to remove the infection from my and North's blood without relying on Perrote's borrowed magic. Reluctantly, I concede that Cadence's trusting him is far better than her trusting Bryn.

There are enemies enough in the palace now: I can't afford to make more.

Alistair moves the hair out of his eyes. His cheek is a bright and angry red, and I glean some small satisfaction from it. Exhaling softly, he tucks his cigarette back between his lips.

"It's good to see you," he says.

I turn on my heel and storm back into the palace. Everyone lingers in the foyer, admiring the crystal-and-glass chandelier looming overhead, fitted with two hundred ivory candles taken from other, more useful rooms in the palace. North looks visibly ill at

Bryn's promise to have it lit for dinner, wasting precious resources simply for show. The Dossels' arrival costs money he doesn't have, money that would be better suited to fund his struggling army.

Instead Bryn insists on dinner and dances and hired servants to attend her family and demonstrate her success. She stands in the center of them all, Cadence still clutching her arm. As much as I loathe this game of politics and polite conversation, I'm tempted to invite myself into the fray, if only to stand more closely to Cadence again, when Chadwick materializes, blocking my view.

"We need to talk," he says, voice low. His eyes fall to my shoulder, and I inwardly curse Tobek for ratting me out already.

"It's nothing," I say. The party heads down the hall, to where drinks will be waiting prior to everyone retiring to their rooms to refresh. I take a step to follow.

Chadwick holds me back. *"Now."*

Another rule of the fighting ring: Know when you're defeated. Holding back my sigh of frustration, I nod my head. "All right," I say. "Now."

Four

THE ROOM ECHOES WITH FOOTFALLS, BOOTS SQUEALING SHARPLY against the polished tile. The narrow windows along the back wall are unshuttered, showing an approaching storm outside, turning the room muddy with shadow.

The smell of sweat fills the room; grunts bounce back from the ribbed ceiling, noise enough to mask my conversation with Chadwick from any potential eavesdroppers. *Lunge, parry, block, and thrust.* Thaelan keeps tempo in my head as I hear the shouted orders of the officers overseeing the recruits.

Chadwick marches to the far end of the training room, and I follow, self-conscious in my silk dress. I'll never become proficient with a sword in the short time before we leave for the Burn, so my training is not with the others but instead with Chadwick himself every afternoon, honing the skill I already have: hand-to-hand combat, either barefisted or with a variety of smaller weaponry.

This special treatment has not endeared me to the other recruits. The sons and daughters of merchants or farmers or street rats, with no better alternative in the city, they volunteered for the meager wage of a soldier—and the promise of a potential land grant if North succeeds in saving Avinea. To them I'm a pampered lowborn noble, my presence here no more than the indulgence of a foreign princess. Like the binding spell that links me to Bryn, my mother's spell is a carefully guarded secret, and the others treat me like a transient distraction

"What happened?" Chadwick demands, arms folded across his chest.

I chew the inside of my cheek, debating how much to say. But withholding information puts more than just me in danger. "I saw Merlock last night."

He stares at me. "What? Where? Here in the palace?"

Sighing, I edge closer, lowering my voice as I explain what happened. He listens, incredulous, then tugs back the collar of my dress to examine the damage himself. "I thought Sofreya was teaching you how to control this."

"It happened while I was sleeping," I say darkly. "It's not like I just wandered into the Burn."

"Is the spell damaged in any way?" He presses at the discoloration of my skin.

"It's fine," I say, annoyed at his priorities, pulling out of reach and jerking my collar back into place.

"This spell is our only lead to Merlock," Chadwick reminds me. "We can't risk this happening again before we reach the Burn. This needs to be excised before it spreads farther."

"Yes, Captain."

He scowls at my sarcasm. "Does Corbin know of this?"

"He's been preoccupied this morning."

"Good." Chadwick nods once, emphatic. "This is between you and me, Locke. He fails to see reason when it comes to you."

"I don't think hiding this from him is a good idea—"

But Chadwick isn't listening to me. He's looking past me. I realize the room has fallen silent, and I turn to see the soldiers all kneeling in respect to North, who stands on the balcony above us with the Dossels flanking him on either side. Cadence is among them, inexplicably still wearing her traveling gloves. Their dark leather clashes with the shortened sleeves of her pale dress, and she picks at the fingers nervously, standing close to Bryn and Alistair.

North's eyes briefly meet mine before they settle on Chadwick with a touch of acrimony. Chadwick scowls and steps away from me, loose hair escaping his ponytail and framing his face.

"Is this the extent of your army?" Perrote spreads his hands along the balustrade, surveying the sweat-soaked recruits with an amused smirk. "So few. So *young.*"

"These are just our newest volunteers," North says without missing a beat. This is not his only army, is what he means. New Prevast—*Avinea*—is well protected. It's a bluff, and not even a good one. If North had an army, Avinea would have some semblance of order. At best he could say he has allies in some of the remaining cities, where those who assumed power are willing to acknowledge his status as prince.

At worst, this is it.

Rialdo joins his father, and grunts in disapproval. "Will more come?"

"We've sent word to the south," North says. "But the weather is turning. And there's only one safe pass through the Kettich Mountains. Travel is slow."

Rialdo exchanges looks with his father. "If you need men, I'd be happy to send for some of my own to assist," Perrote says smoothly. "You do not want your kingdom left unguarded."

"A generous offer," North replies. "But unnecessary." He turns to lead the way out of the room, and after another survey of the soldiers, Perrote turns to follow.

I watch them go, holding out hope for a second glance from Cadence, but she disappears in a sea of skirts without acknowledgment. I am not forgiven for what I said outside, and I feel myself wilting.

Chadwick frowns. "Wasn't that your sister?"

Her *I hate you* echoes through me, head to toe and back again, cold as snowmelt. It isn't the first time she's said it to me, but this wasn't a burst of frustration at my refusal to yield to some childish plot. This was whetted to a sharpened point for months, memorized and recited for hours on end. For the first time, I don't mourn that it's only two days we share until I leave for the Burn. Right now, I can't escape soon enough.

"Yes," I say, and stalk away before Chadwick can reply.

That night I'm awakened by a familiar burn around my wrist. Bryn, calling for me, as if I'm not only the length of a parlor away from her own bedroom.

Unless she's in North's rooms again.

I roll onto my stomach and pull the pillow over my head, ignoring the summons. Despite having spent the afternoon under Sofreya's tutelage—and having received deserved admonishment for running away—I approached bed warily, terrified that I would lose control of my mother's spell once I closed my eyes. As a result, I fought off sleep for hours, an iron poker clutched to my chest to tamp down the spell until exhaustion prevailed. A part of me half-hoped I would lose control again anyway, giving me another chance to face Merlock, to ask questions about my mother. The more realistic side of me knew that he would not suffer my curiosity a second time. If we met again, one of us would end up bleeding, and it wasn't going to be the most powerful magician in the kingdom.

The summons inches up my arm, into my shoulder, my teeth. The longer I ignore it, the more painful it will be. Growling into my mattress, I throw the pillow aside, then stand and yank my door open. The parlor is lit by thin slivers of moonlight peeking through the curtains, but light also spills from under the door of Bryn's room, which is a small relief: She's not with North after all. I knock and she calls for me to enter.

Bryn sits in a silk robe at her writing desk, a sheaf of ink-scrawled papers in hand. She shuffles through the papers with a frown, a quill dangling between two fingers. But my eyes are drawn to Cadence, who sits cross-legged on the edge of the four-poster bed, also in her nightclothes. I tense, bracing a hand on the doorframe. Is she planning to sleep in here tonight? With *Bryn*?

"Yes?" I ask.

"I'm thirsty," Cadence says. "I want some coffee."

SPLENDOR AND SPARK   37

I look at her briefly before my eyes fall back to Bryn. So this is how my torture begins: while my sister watches at two thirty-eight in the morning. "Did you need something, your majesty?"

Bryn looks up from her letters. "She wants coffee," she says.

Cadence demonstrates a pocket watch, and I understand the warning implicit in the gesture. Three minutes, Bryn told me once. That was as long as I had to come when she summoned me, or she would mete out punishment in blood.

I stare at my sister, dubious. Drinking coffee this late was clearly not her idea, but it gives me one of my own. "So then we'll go get coffee," I say, forcing my voice brighter, coaxing. "Have you been to the kitchen yet?"

She wavers, torn. Exploring the palace this late at night is far more appealing than sitting in a bedroom while Bryn writes letters, even if she's angry with me.

"The kitchen is for servants," Bryn says coldly.

Cadence flinches, and then straightens, lifting her chin. "And I'm not a servant," she whispers fiercely, clutching at the watch.

Bryn shifts in her seat, glancing toward me. "But you are," she says. "Two cups of coffee."

"Ticktock," Cadence adds, and beneath her crowing smile is the slightest flicker of apprehension. Will I actually do it? Will she get in trouble? The sister within the lace and cotton nightgown is barely visible beneath this goading little monster. How far can Bryn push her?

How far will she go on her own?

Cadence swings the pocket watch in warning, and I turn numbly into the hall. A guard jolts to attention only to gape at me in my nightclothes, but I ignore him, shoving aside a damask tapestry and ducking into the servants' hall beyond. Within the first few days of arriving at the palace, I learned the layout of the halls out of necessity, memorizing the fastest ways to each of the rooms Bryn was likely to visit, in case of something like this. With the wedding and other preoccupations, however, this is the first time I've actually needed them.

The kitchen should be empty this time of night, but when I step inside, a figure is seated on the island, back to me, feet hanging several inches off the scrubbed stone floor. The fire is banked too low to offer much light, but the small tiger begging for scraps is identity enough.

North.

He doesn't look over as he extends a piece of meat to the tiger, Darjin, and I spin on my heel with a flash of adrenaline.

"I see you still don't sleep at night," he says, stopping me mid-retreat.

I pause with my back to him, hands framed on the doorway as I stare down the darkened servants' hall and debate whether or not to just keep going. Yet returning to Bryn's room without coffee would be begging for retribution—something I refuse to let Cadence witness if she's already this eager to emulate Bryn. Reluctantly I turn back into the kitchen. "I was just coming for some coffee."

He pushes himself to his feet, brushing crumbs off the front of his trousers. He's still dressed, shirtsleeves rolled to his elbows. While he's always been thin, preparing for Perrote's return and the subsequent expedition into the Burn has taken a toll, leaving him more gaunt-faced and shadowed than usual.

"Bryndalin?" he guesses, hands sliding into his pockets as he leans back against the island, hooking one ankle over the other.

Darjin pads over to me in search of more scraps, and I crouch, scrubbing at his flank, grateful for the excuse to hide my face, and my surprise. Of course North's on a first-name basis with Bryn. He can't call his wife "Miss Dossel" for the rest of their lives. "Cadence, actually," I say, standing again.

North arches an eyebrow. "She's certainly acclimated to palace living quite quickly." His eyes briefly lower, and I remember I'm in my nightclothes. I fold my arms over my chest, and he blushes, dropping his gaze to the floor between our feet. When he scratches the back of his neck, I catch a glimpse of a dark mark along his throat, some new spell I don't recognize. A burr of envy catches in my stomach at the bitter reminder that we're practically strangers now, and the only thing we share these days is the roof over our heads.

At least I know the spells exposed on the flats of his wrists: the doubled crosses that were part of the council's decision to forbid him from practicing any magic until he can find his father and secure the throne.

"Why aren't you sleeping?" I ask.

He sighs, hair falling forward as his chin dips toward the floor. "There's been another golem attack in the south," he says. "Just like the last one. They made it as far as the Corsant city limits before imploding."

Chills race down my back. "They carried infected magic?"

A slight rise of his chin confirms my guess. "The Burn has consumed over a hundred acres in less than a week. The city has evacuated, but . . ."

But I remember the map he once drew me, of the kingdom of Avinea and all the dark places where the Burn had taken hold, leaving only broken bits of land in between. Avinea is running out of sanctuaries. And if New Prevast is any indication, even a sanctuary becomes a prison when too many people crowd its walls.

Swearing under his breath, North slams his palm against the island behind him and straightens, raking his hair back with both hands. "Why is he doing this? Why *now*? He's had twenty years to destroy Avinea if that was his intention. What changed?"

"Are you sure it was Merlock?"

He gives me an impatient glance. "Baedan wouldn't waste the resources on golems. Now that she has my blood, she has a chance of inheriting everything. Expanding the Burn right now isn't her priority."

"Baedan is not the only hellborne in the Burn, your majesty," I remind him wryly. But he's right: as our only real competition for finding Merlock, Baedan wouldn't waste time on petty attacks, especially if she's heard that North plans an expedition soon. "If news has gotten out that you got married and now have magic and the means to hunt Merlock, thereby destroying the Burn and everyone who lives in it . . ." I trail off, shrugging. "That's incentive for any hellborne with half a practical thought in their head, don't you think?"

A ghost of a smile crosses his lips as he glances over. "Fair enough," he concedes.

I catch myself smiling back, only to remember myself. I look away.

He straightens. "Right," he mutters to himself. "I apologize, Miss Locke. You have your own concerns."

"North—"

"North is dead," he reminds me tightly, and I wilt with the rebuke, feeling useless in the face of his frustration. An uneasy silence stretches between us, but my wrist continues to throb, reminding me of my task. I strike a match on the stove to start a flame before filling a copper kettle. Behind me North wordlessly pulls a tray from under the island and sets it on top, then crosses to the adjacent pantry. He returns with a small burlap sack of coffee and a sunken sieve that he sets into the kettle.

"Thank you," I mumble.

He crosses to the doorway without looking back. "Good night, Miss Locke."

He doesn't even wait for a reply. I bite my lip to keep from calling after him, focusing instead on the dark coffee grounds until they blur into meaningless shadow. When footsteps return, I twist toward them, hopeful.

"Almost forgot," he says, stepping back into the pantry. When he emerges, he offers me a small covered dish. "The most important thing."

I accept it warily. "What is it?"

"Sugar," he says, and my heart cracks with the memory of that night in his wagon, when he made me a cup of hot water sweetened with sugar and drew me paper flowers to replace the one I had lost in the woods.

Don't, I warn myself, but my blood warms to the thought of a different night in the wagon, when I slept curled against his side and woke to the feel of his skin ghosting across mine.

North watches me, expectant. Despite the weeks of silence

between us, a single word could close the gap now, a single step. My fingers hum with a need to pull back the collar of his shirt, to explore the unknown spell that lies hidden at his throat. Sofreya may have excised the poison from my blood, but my heart will always be greedy and it sings its desires now: *more*.

No one would know, I tell myself: We're all alone down here in the dark, with no one to witness our weakness. But I hear Chadwick, see his disapproving face. And I feel Bryn in the burn at my wrist, Cadence hanging on her every move.

North made his choice and I made mine. If I had wanted to be a mistress, Thaelan would still be alive.

"Good night, your majesty," I say.

He doesn't answer.

Ten minutes later I nudge Bryn's door open with my hip. I set the rattling tray on an ottoman in the center of the room, sloshing coffee in the process.

Cadence grins, hanging over the edge of the bed, her long golden curls spilling down to touch the carpet. She regards me with upside-down eyes as she brandishes the pocket watch.

"Twenty minutes and thirty-seven seconds," she announces.

"Well." Bryn picks up the tray and shoves it at my chest. Coffee, sugar, and cream spill over the edge, soaking the front of my night-dress and the weave of her carpet. "Take it back to the kitchen and we'll try again."

Five

BREAKFAST IS TORTURE.

The routine developed over the last few weeks is maddening: Sit, be served, wait for all to finish, second course, repeat. I can't refill my own water from the blown-glass pitchers in front of me; if I want salt, I have to ask it of whoever sits beside me, who then continues the message down the row. When it arrives, a servant dispenses it, as if I'm too simple to know how much salt my eggs require. And when I'm finished and want to bolt back to my room, or better yet, to the training barracks to spar with Chadwick, I have to sit in silent abjection until North or Bryn stand, dismissing us all.

I used to believe Thaelan had freedom. I used to envy him the lifestyle that afforded him nice clothes, guaranteed meals, a life free of fleas and cracks in the windows. But this is no better than life in the Brim.

At least down there you could run.

The only ones immune to the torture this morning are the Dossel children, who chase one another through the cavern of the dining room, voices ringing to the arches overhead. They clamor beneath the table, knocking into our knees in a game of tag, using the stoic-faced servants as their touchstone bases.

The game soon morphs into playing Burn, where the dark veins of the marble floor become rivers of poison they must avoid as they race to reach the safety of a curtained alcove—Brindaigel. When a child succumbs, their anguish is vocalized with shrieks and dramatic pitching, as the others dance out of reach with expressions of morbid delight and a barrage of questions: Does it hurt? Are you bad now? Do we kill you? Will you kill us?

Cadence pretends not to notice the game, feigning dignity that mirrors Bryn's, even as her eyes slide back again and again with a shadow of wistfulness clouding her face. She used to be the fastest runner in her pack of Brim rats, but there was no running at the workhouse. There was no Perrote watching either. And while he ignores her the same way he ignores me, Cadence is not so indifferent to him, flinching at his voice, staring at her plate when he moves. *She needs a friend,* Alistair echoes, and it infuriates me to think that that is why he chose the seat on her other side. Playing the hero. Earning her trust while I'm still waiting for a simple acknowledgment.

Sol, one of the boys, rolls across the floor, rumpling his clothes. "I'm dying," he wails. "Cut my heart out, quick, or I'll turn into a monster!"

His cousins shriek with horrified delight. "Better yet," one of the older girls says, "let's give him a crown and call him the King of Avinea!"

"All hail the withered king," the others chorus.

Despite myself, my eyes slide toward North at the head of the table, who eats while scanning a handful of council reports at his side—damage reports, no doubt, from the golem attack he mentioned last night. He pretends not to hear them, but when the children begin an elaborate coronation, a muscle in his jaw tightens and doesn't relax.

"I'll play grandfather," someone calls, rushing back to their make-believe Brindaigel. "Here, we must have war!"

"Those children are beasts," Bryn says mildly, her own uneaten breakfast pushed away from her, hands clasped across her stomach.

"Wait until you have your own," her mother says with a knowing smile, shared by all the women at the table.

Bryn's returning smile is glazed with ice. Her eyes settle on North. "Children are not born monsters," she says. "It's a skill inherited from their parents. *If* I have children, they will not scream at the breakfast table, because they will be taught better than that."

They will be taught how to be cold and calm and calculating. There's no surprise in the attack if everyone hears you coming.

"Cadence is less than a year older than Sol, and yet she conducts herself like a lady," Bryn says, sitting up, leaning forward. She reaches out and strokes Cadence's loose curls before squeezing her shoulder. "Ideal, I think. I would be happy with a daughter like her one day. Or a sister." Her eyes cut slyly toward me.

Cadence blooms more brightly than a rose beneath her attention.

She's wearing her traveling gloves again, and it occurs to me suddenly that she doesn't wear them because she's cold or finds them fashionable. She wears them to hide her reddened, work-roughened hands, so unlike the soft, spoiled hands of those around her. My little sister is ashamed of her past, and that, more than Bryn's taunting, is what deflates me.

"You have sisters enough already," I say sharply to Bryn, pushing my chair back, throwing my napkin onto the table. "How many more do you need?"

"You have not been dismissed," Bryn says, fingers still resting on Cadence's shoulder.

"It's only breakfast," North says, annoyed, without looking up from his reports. "Why should she be forced to sit here with the rest of us if she's already finished?"

Bryn's frigid gaze transfers to him. "Oh," she says. "I didn't realize Faris belonged to you."

North stares down at his paperwork, but everyone watches me now, to see what I do, whose side I choose. Even Cadence openly stares, a flicker of concern filling her blue eyes. I latch on to it with a desperation that surprises me. My sister is still alive, buried beneath gifts of silk and satin; maybe she's not entirely against me.

Not yet.

A sudden clap startles the awkward silence. "The Stone and Fern Tavern," Rialdo says. "I *knew* I recognized you!" Grinning, he waggles a finger at me with mocking admonishment. "I lost money because of you!"

Beside him his wife stiffens. "I beg your pardon?"

"If you lost money," Alistair says drily, his first words of the meal, "it's because you bet on the wrong girl."

Rialdo barks a laugh, twisting toward Alistair. "That's right! I was with you that night! You told me she was a sure win, but I bet on the other one instead, the little wiry one."

His wife looks scandalized; Perrote looks annoyed. My skin begins to tighten uncomfortably, and I look to the door behind me, tensed to leave.

"Sit down," Bryn says coldly. She balances a silver butter knife along the table's edge with a careless grace. She won't use it against me, not here. There are too many witnesses and possible spies among the servants to risk exposing the spell that binds us together. And while Cadence might find a late-night request for coffee harmless fun, I can't imagine that the workhouse has inured her to cruelty—or the knowledge that Bryn's father is the one who put her there. If Bryn wants my sister's continued adoration, she has to show mercy.

"Do you still fight?" Rialdo asks.

"Of course not," says Perrote. "She has no reason to."

"You underestimate me, sir," I say flatly. And then, defying Bryn's order, I stride out of the dining room, back straight and chin raised—until I'm out of sight. Only then does the adrenaline force me to pause, breathless at my own nerve. Perrote is not my king anymore and I owe him no loyalty, and yet for sixteen years he was the dark shadow cast over my life, cutting off the view of the sky around me. Talking back to him carries an inherent fear of retaliation, even though here his power is limited, his role relegated to that of a mere guest.

Chairs scrape back in the dining hall, and I quickly straighten, hurrying for my room to avoid anyone catching up to me. Only with the door shut safely behind me do my nerves unfurl again, and I cross to the window, staring out at the harbor beyond. We sail tomorrow, and it's both too soon and not nearly soon enough. I expected these final two days to be nothing but Cadence and catching up; when I left, it would be with a proper good-bye and a promise to come back—something I was cheated out of in the dungeons six months ago. Now I don't even know if she wants me to come back, or if Bryn has already replaced me.

The sea beyond the harbor is an endless, placid gray, mirroring the thin-spread clouds above. It would have snowed in Brindaigel by now, and despite myself I feel a pang of longing for the home I knew, where Cadence and I were still allies.

I can't leave like this, full of anger and regret. She needs to know what I've done, and why. If she still hates me, then at least I tried.

Decided, I turn back into my room, and pause, surprised. A slender letter sits atop a wrapped book on my bed. My eyes swing to the closed doorway, as if to find a courier there with an explanation, but whoever delivered it must have done so during breakfast. I overlooked it in my nerves.

Warily I sink onto the edge of the mattress and pick up the letter first, tracing the generic wax seal on the back before snapping it open with my finger. Inside, the thick paper shows an address and a name. Dimitr Frell. My mother's contract.

A shiver racks my body. Ever since discovering a coded list of coordinates and names denoting my mother's contacts within Avinea, I've been determined to track down Dimitr Frell listed here, in New Prevast. But her coordinates were ambiguous, and his name worthless without proper city records. Chadwick caught me examining old council documents for more explicit answers, and North became suspicious of my motives, so he decreed I was forbidden to leave the palace.

But now I have his address. Who else knew I was looking for him?

My eyes fall to the book. *North.* He used to leave books for me in his wagon. Recommended reading, he called them, when really they were gateways to conversation—to friendship. Is this a token of peace to smooth the start of our journey, when we will have no choice but to share close quarters as we head into the Burn?

But the book that accompanies the letter is a medical text, its pages worn thin, dog-eared, with notes in the margins. Inked diagrams and illustrations are preserved beneath sheets of vellum, marked with careful notations and discoveries tabulated for future reference. Why would North want me to learn medicine? Usually the books he offered were historical or geographical; this is just—

Oh.

There, on the inside cover, a delicate bookplate edged in fine scrollwork, framing a familiar family crest. This book belonged to Thaelan. And only one person in Brindaigel would have known that.

The boy who killed him.

Picking up the address again, I consider the implications. Alistair knew my mother's plan to escape Brindaigel, to hunt down Merlock and stop the Burn. And as much as I loathe admitting it, his father played a pivotal role in her attempted escape. Since then

Alistair has always known more about my mother than I have, maybe even including who her contacts are, and where they live.

Only Alistair would believe he could earn my forgiveness through a bribe of information.

Still, energized, I ball Frell's address in one hand and listen at my door to ensure Bryn didn't return to her room after breakfast. Hearing only silence, I slip back into the hall and head straight for the servants' stairwell. Chadwick will be expecting me in the barracks for one last training session, followed by an all hands meeting before lunch, which gives me two hours to track down Dimitr Frell—and finally get the answers I need about my mother.

Like most of the palace, the library was stripped bare long ago by savage nobles exploiting a missing king—and then a child prince with no power—selling off whatever was valuable for passage off the continent to escape the Burn. While most of the shelves now sit empty, the bolted ladders rusted into place, North's travels across Avinea have yielded a small crop of maps and books. With the library's broad tables for paperwork and heavy doors for privacy, Chadwick has been using the library as an impromptu war room. Most of our mandatory meetings have been spent detailing how to carve poisoned hearts from under unyielding ribs—the only way to kill a hellborne—or how to stem the flow of an infection through the use of tourniquets when Sofreya's spells no longer hold. Even swallowing pills pressed into shape by the palace doctor. Harmless powder here in the palace, but out there in the Burn, the real ones will stop our hearts before the Burn can transform us into monsters. Five days is all it takes to do so, ten with Sofreya's spells. But

SPLENDOR AND SPARK 51

with North's blood already infected, we've given ourselves seven.

One week to save the world.

With Chadwick in such high demand this morning, I assumed the library would be empty, everything already packed away for the journey. Instead I find North at a far table, maps spread around him. And in a chair pulled close beside him, hunched forward with a grim expression, sits Alistair.

They fall silent simultaneously as North tenses, leaning back, his hands dropping into his lap. Alistair grabs something off the table and slides it into his jacket pocket as he stands. His chair catches against the threadbare carpet and twists out of position. He corrects it with one hand, watching me warily even as he forces his trademark smirk.

My surprise at seeing them together dissolves into suspicion. What business could Alistair possibly have with North? "What are you doing?"

Alistair's eyebrow arches. "Nothing."

"Doing nothing is a waste of time," I say, folding my arms across my chest. "Why aren't you in your laboratory? You claimed you could figure out a way to cure the infection."

"I've only been here one day, Faris—"

"You've had two weeks in Brindaigel."

His expression darkens, smirk vanishing. "I had other responsibilities to attend to in Brindaigel." A hand rakes through his hair before falling back to his side. "I am still the king's executioner."

Frell's address digs into my hand—and a needle of guilt stabs low in my belly, demanding my tolerance, if nothing else. But Alistair awakens the worst in me, a primal need to attack first.

"Then I guess you're already two weeks behind," I say.

Swearing beneath his breath, Alistair faces me fully, eyes flashing. "A hypothesis is useless without experimentation. I need blood if I'm going to remove poison from it. Are you volunteering?"

North avoids my eyes, but his fingers tug at his sleeve, as if to hide what might lie underneath. Temper flaring, I storm toward Alistair, reaching for his pocket. He tries to stop me from retrieving what's inside, but I block his defense, my dress straining at the seams with the motion. Alistair relents, and I withdraw a glass syringe from his jacket, still warm, filled with a dark, viscous fluid peppered with flakes of gold and violet. I've seen infected blood before, and yet it still makes my stomach sink to see North's. This is what lies in his veins, thickening beneath the skin. Killing him.

"If you need blood, you take it from me, not him," I say, voice shaking.

Alistair doesn't flinch from my stare. "I need several vials. Half a dozen at least."

"I have blood enough for that. You need only ask."

He shakes his head, lip curling. "Of course," he says sardonically. "Forgive my oversight. I nearly forgot that I'm only here on your good grace, Faris Locke; I will henceforth post all requests through you." Glancing to North, Alistair nods his head in acknowledgment before turning lazily toward the threshold. Halfway there, he starts to whistle, then pauses once he reaches the threshold. "You know where to find me," he says to me with all the arrogance he once demonstrated in Brindaigel. "You don't even have to knock."

I scowl after his retreating backside.

"I can spare a vial of blood," North says, drawing my attention back to him. He begins rolling up his maps, his movements stiff, jerky. He's in an overcoat—on his way out the door, no doubt, for one last look at the *Mainstay*, our chartered ship. With Merlock's last verified location being in the capital of Prevast, deep in the heart of the Burn, we'll save time—and magic—by sailing around the kingdom instead of riding through it.

"You can't afford to take any risks," I say. "And letting him slide a needle through your skin, into your veins—if he'd gone too deep, or not deep enough—"

"You sound like Benjamin."

I bristle at the comparison. "Captain Chadwick understands what is at stake."

"And I don't?" North snorts, sliding several maps back onto a shelf behind him. "I've been fighting this war long before you had any reason to, Miss Locke, and I'll be fighting it long after victory carries you into the sunset."

I bite the inside of my cheek, wounded by the callous implication. Yet it's true: The moment he takes his throne and dissolves the spell binding me to Bryn is the moment I take Cadence and run, far beyond the reach of Bryn's family. I might become free, but I will not be forgiven.

Yet my daydreams of faraway places are only that: dreams. In truth all I know of the world is contained on the maps in this room.

"You cannot guilt me for wanting my freedom," I say.

He groans, hands scrubbing at his face. "Faris—"

"Baedan almost killed you for less blood than this," I snap, brandishing the syringe at him, sickened by its weight, its warmth. "You're being reckless, and it is not like you."

His expression sharpens, turns brutally cold. "Pembrough is here on your request, you may recall. I would have thought that came with some degree of trust in his efforts—"

"He has a loyalty spell above his heart," I interrupt. "Perrote says the word, Alistair hands this blood over, and Perrote forges his own weapon to kill Merlock. Now you have two competitors, not to mention a bloodbound wife who will certainly fight."

"I'd like to see Perrote drag himself into the Burn to hunt for my father."

"He doesn't have to. He has an army and magic enough to send in his place."

And North does not. A wedding gift of hand-me-down magic and a small contingent of new recruits is abysmal protection against a tyrant, no matter how confidently North lies about more volunteers coming before the winter. Avinea is too fragmented, its unpoisoned cities too few and far between, most operating under their own rules and self-proclaimed leaders. Travel is dangerous, and the truth is, no one would make the journey for an infected prince that no one believes will succeed.

Even after North kills his father, the fight for Avinea will have only just begun.

Neither of us speaks, but as North gathers up his remaining maps, I tent my fingers on top of them, pinning them in place. "I'll put them away."

North stops, suspicious. "What are you looking for?"

It's like its own kind of fistfight, the way we keep circling each other with our words, exchanging blows. I know him, but he knows me too, and knows that my motives are more than simple housekeeping. It's these small reminders that threaten me far more than accidental meetings in a darkened kitchen.

"You're expected at the *Mainstay*," I say.

He wants to argue with me but resists, dropping his chin and exhaling softly. He releases the maps. "Don't be reckless," he says at last, his anger broken, replaced with resignation.

"Likewise." I pointedly offer the syringe to him.

"Keep it," he says, brushing past me. "You may need it one day."

It isn't until he's gone and I've settled myself at the table that I realize what he meant. Giving me his blood now is a contingency plan in case he fails, so someone other than Bryn or Baedan can inherit.

He's already preparing himself for failure.

Six

THE ONGOING COMMOTION WITHIN THE PALACE IS COVER ENOUGH for me to slip past the milling servants unchallenged. It took longer than I wanted to pinpoint Dimitr Frell's address on North's outdated maps of the city, and I have less than an hour for my questions before my training with Chadwick. The lack of time is both infuriating and a relief. I want answers, but I don't know how many I can handle, when I'll have to leave in the morning without the chance to pursue them further.

Despite my rush, I slow as I near the harbor and its labyrinth of crates and fishing tarps. There's something sharp in the air, just beneath the usual brine of salt. Expectation, maybe, or hope. From here the city, the kingdom, and the Burn all lie behind me so that all I see is open water and a wider world than I ever expected to find. Like when I would sit on the roofs of the Brim and frame the stars between my hands, the ocean pulls at my stomach with a heartsick yearning for more than I've been given.

Most of the ships docked here are smaller doggers meant for fishing, with the occasional larger vessels that exchange news and meager supplies between the coastal cities of Avinea when the weather is good. The *Mainstay* is one of the former, captained by a woman named Davik and crewed by her two brothers. They were the only ones willing to risk sailing beyond the safety of the harbor this late in the season.

I catch a glimpse of Captain Davik now, face tipped to the sun while her brothers carry crates up the gangplank, the sleeves of their woolen sweaters pushed up to their forearms, exposing a tangle of tattoos—all ink, no magic. While other captains wanted payment in spells, Davik asked for money. "Something useful," she said.

Guards appear on the gangplank, North safely shepherded amongst them, and I quickly continue on before anyone recognizes me. The city itself is not nearly as hopeful as the harbor. The people here are mostly displaced from other areas of Avinea, but their hope for a safe haven has been worn down to a more basic hope for survival. The Burn isn't the only thing destroying the kingdom; its people have also been corrupted by years of reliance on magic, followed by years of hardship without it. Guards maintain the peace where they can, but even they were raised on magic spells and easy answers, and have as little patience as those they protect.

The address Alistair gave me leads me to a narrow alley off an empty street in one of the many abandoned quarters of the city. Some areas were decimated by a coughing disease one frigid winter years ago, after mercenaries stole the spells protecting the inhabitants; other areas teeter on the brink of becoming small pockets of the Burn after spells were stolen recklessly, without finesse, leaving fraying threads of magic that no one, not even North, will risk trying to salvage. I don't know the cause of this street's desolation, but I feel it, a dark, rotting history entrenched in the very cobblestones.

The address leads me to an abandoned storefront half-collapsed into ruins, and I scan both it and those around it with mounting frustration. I have no pocket watch, but I hear the seconds ticking at the back of my mind as I search for some clue that Frell—that *anyone*—lives here. But then, in an alley between two buildings, I come to an age-stained door that has warped out of its frame and now hangs loosely off rusted hinges. Despite its decrepit appearance, however, it swings open silently at the press of my hand, revealing a staircase leading to the apartments upstairs, with broken furniture blocking the way. At first glance this building seems like another dead end, but the air lacks that squalid feel of the other buildings around it, and the furniture is too neatly placed, with enough room to maneuver if you know where to step.

I set enough traps outside my rooms in the Brim to recognize this one. Frell must be here, and he doesn't want company.

For the first time, I reconsider what I'm doing; not from fear of Dimitr Frell, but fear of the answers he might give. For ten years my mother has been a mystery to me, her past cobbled together from memories and stories and the occasional surprise discovery. To label her a hero or a villain was entirely based on my whim, and a selfish part of me wants to keep that small measure of control over her. Once I know the truth, there's no escaping it. I'm a realist, after all—a survivor. Dimitr Frell lives alone on a forgotten street in a city that keeps no records. He did not escape Brindaigel to the bright new life of freedom that Thaelan and I always planned for ourselves. He's still hiding, but from what?

Yet I've come this far, scarred inside and out. Who else can tell me who my mother really was, what she expected of me? If she tried—and failed—to kill Merlock herself, what made her think her six-year-old daughter could do it? What is really buried beneath my skin? A spell? Or a vendetta?

An ounce of your strength, I think to myself, and start up the stairs.

I pick my way over the furniture as the entire building seems to crack and sway around me. The wallpaper is worn thin in a visible line up the wall—shoulder height, as if someone has spent years leaning against it for balance.

Two doors stand opposite each other on the landing above: one closed tight and the other broken down to reveal an empty apartment beyond. My heart lurches unexpectedly, and I dry my sweaty palms along my skirt. Touching the small dagger I carry beneath my cloak calms me, and I knock firmly. "Dimitr Frell, I need to speak with you."

No reply.

Hesitation turns to frustration. It never occurred to me that he wouldn't be here, and despite moments ago wondering if I even wanted to see him, now that there's a possibility I won't, I refuse to accept it. We leave in the morning, with no clear promise of return. I don't want this stone left unturned while I'm out in the Burn, with no guarantee I'll have another chance.

Decided, I twist the doorknob, and am surprised when the door swings open with an eerie screech.

This is madness, I think, even as I duck through the narrow opening. "Mr. Frell?"

There are two windows ahead of me, with curtains drawn against the light. An oil lamp sits on a crooked side table adjacent to a battered love seat stacked with books. A tarnished sword lies unsheathed on top of them, and empty spools litter the floor. Overhead, intricate woven designs hang from the ceiling. Several have begun to fray, and loose threads dangle, wafting in my wake. Fascinated, I reach out, trailing my fingers through the threads. The entire room feels like an untold story.

"They're beautiful, aren't they?"

I spin, heart slamming into my throat, as I squint into the murky darkness. A middle-aged man with glasses and thinning dark hair watches me from a doorway across the room, barely distinguishable from the shadows. Thin, knobby, he wears threadbare clothes and stands with a permanent slouch—one I recognize from my own father, earned from hours spent over tedious needlework. He's a tailor, then, or was once.

Is this the tailor Merlock referred to? It wasn't my father?

"Dimitr Frell," I say, recovering my voice. I retract my hand, returning it to my blade.

"I have not been called that name for many years."

But he doesn't deny that it's his. Emboldened, I take a step closer, the floors creaking in warning. "My name is Faris—"

"Locke. You look like her."

"So I've been told," I say slowly. He knows who I am—even

seems to have been expecting me. My pulse races, a drumming beat in my chest, but I force myself to stay steady, to not rush into this and lose my way. My chin points toward the threads above us as I struggle to keep my excitement in check. "What are they?"

"Spells," he says, his own face tipping to the ceiling. His expression changes into something reverent, like a doting father amongst his children. He caresses one gently, fingers deftly sliding across knots and braids.

Of course. Without magic to use, he had to rely on something more readily available. Dimly, I wonder what my mother's spell would look like on display like this, or the binding spell. Then, more concretely, I wonder what kind of madness drives a man to go to such efforts.

"So," he says with a weary sigh, forcing my attention back to him. "You've brought me the spell."

My chest tightens as I study him warily. It surprises me how easy this is; I expected opposition, denial, riddles, and more questions. Yet Frell doesn't look like he has any fight in him. "How do you know about that?"

"The timing cannot be coincidental. The prince's marriage has brought magic back into the city, and you seek me out on the eve of his departure into the Burn, with the spell he needs to save his kingdom." He smiles, but it is creaky, as though it's not often used. "Based on your mother's last letter, I expected you ten years ago. Or, at the very least, I would have thought she would come herself, gloating, for all I doubted her ability." He looks beyond me. "Is she here?"

"She's dead," I say, marveling that I almost feel sad to say it, rather than angry.

Emotions flicker across his face before his expression slackens. "Oh."

"How did you know her? Did you teach her how to weave magic?"

But he shakes his head, turning into the dark room behind him. "You don't have time for such irrelevant questions. Come. I may be rusty, but I'm not useless yet."

Despite my interest, I refuse to be denied basic facts. "Are you from Brindaigel? Did you escape? Did my mother help you?"

Another tired smile spreads across his face as he opens his hand toward me. "Give me the spell," he says, "and I'll forge the weapon. Beyond that, I have no need for company. Or questions."

"What weapon?"

An eyebrow arches. "She trusted you with her spell but not her plan?"

"I was six years old," I say darkly, pulling back the collar of my cloak to expose the knotted spell beneath my skin. "It wasn't a matter of trust so much as she was being hunted and needed somewhere to hide her work."

Frell's mouth falls open, shock registering across his face. "You're the vessel? But the blood—"

The exterior door to the building slams open below, and Frell tenses. "Did you tell anyone you were coming here?"

"No." I lean into the hallway, catching sight of three of Perrote's guards, already flinging aside the broken furniture, followed by a man in a beaked metal mask—the uniform of Perrote's council. And there, bringing up the rear at a more sedate, unhurried pace, is Perrote himself.

Panicked, I withdraw back into Frell's apartment, shutting the door and fumbling with the dead bolt, aware that it is merely a moment of protection. When the guards reach the landing, they begin slamming against the door. It gives in its damaged frame, and I scan the room around me for something heavy or more useful than my small blade, but the tarnished sword looks heavy, and my training with one is incomplete. "Is there another way out?"

Frell stares hard at the door. His fists are clenched, his expression oddly defiant. "It appears the hunt is far from over."

The door splits down the center. Swearing, I tear aside the curtains and struggle with one of the windows. But like the door, it's been warped out of its frame and sticks, useless. Even if it could open, the broken cobblestone street is too far for me to safely jump.

One of the guards shoulders through the crack in the door and unlatches the dead bolt. Grabbing my dagger, I stand in front of Frell—a meager apology for bringing destruction to his door—but Frell pushes me aside, picking up the tarnished sword from the love seat. With one sweeping blow, he cuts off the guard's arm.

The guard screams, recoiling back onto the landing, and I openly stare, rooted to the spot. Who *is* this man?

Whoever he is, whatever training he must have had makes for an impressive stand when the other two guards kick through the door, followed by the councilman. Yet while Frell fights well, I am erratic, confused. Despite the dagger, my instinct is to use my fists, and my blows are clumsy, easy to avoid. When a guard nearly slits my stomach open, I finally snap out of my haze and launch myself forward, throwing an elbow into his throat before ramming my dagger into his chest. His eyes widen in surprise before his body slumps into me, blood spilling over my hands.

All at once I'm thrown back to a night not long enough ago when Bryn ordered me to a kill a man and I obeyed. That was different, I tell myself; he was unarmed, begging for mercy. *This* was self-defense.

Even so, my guilt costs me my attention long enough that the second guard grabs me by the arm and twists it back until I cry out in pain. The first guard collapses to the floor, my dagger still buried to the hilt in his blood.

Across the room, Frell is likewise cornered by the councilman, his glasses half-hanging from his nose as he struggles to catch his breath. Inexplicably, he's smiling.

"It has been a very long time since I've done that," he says.

His smile infuriates me. How can he make jokes when everything I've worked for now hangs by one of his fraying threads?

The councilman edges toward the doorway and shouts, "Clear!" Only then does Perrote enter, expression mildly amused as he scans the dank apartment before settling on Frell. "Dimitr Frell," he says. "The legend himself."

Frell spits at him.

Perrote sighs wearily, snapping a handkerchief out of his pocket and mopping the saliva from his face. "Your mistake, Mr. Frell, is your arrogance. You believed yourself safe once you escaped Brindaigel. But I know how to hunt down rats."

"This rat knew your labyrinth far better than you ever did," Frell replies. "Well enough to ferry news of Avinea to those not too blind to believe the truth. You put your own ear to this rat's mouth more than once, or so I'm told. God Above knows your shadow crows never brought you news of anything."

A flicker of annoyance crosses Perrote's face, a hint of wounded pride at his lackluster ability to cast spells with any merit. "And yet I caught this rat all the same."

At his nod, the councilman releases Frell, shoving him forward. He stumbles a step, scowling as he adjusts his glasses. "How convenient that you found another crown to steal so quickly after losing your first."

The councilman kicks the back of his legs, and Frell buckles at the knees, hitting the hardwood floor with a crack that rattles his furniture.

Perrote's expression sours. "What you and Miss Locke have both forgotten is that you are still citizens of Brindaigel, and that I am still your king." He pauses, deliberately folding his handkerchief and replacing it in his pocket. "And as my loyal subjects," he finally continues, "you still fall under my jurisdiction. I am your judge, jury, and executioner. Hiding in this city for twelve years does not absolve your sins."

"Thirteen," Frell says. The councilman cracks him on the back of the head.

"Miss Locke, I'm being rude." Perrote gestures me forward. "I've interrupted your conversation. You came for a reason, and I encourage you to continue."

I stare at him, bemused. I came for answers about my mother; Perrote clearly believes my motives to be more than that. With Frell having expected me—or at the very least, my mother—perhaps they should have been. But even with my arm pinned and a sword at my chest, I only want one thing, and it is not any kind of weapon.

"Why did she try to run that night, and not any night before?" I ask. "What news did you bring through those tunnels to prompt her to finally leave?"

Frell gives me a pitying look. "The last news I brought to Brindaigel was of Corbin being named a legitimate heir of Avinea by the monks raising him," he says softly. "But that was nearly twelve years ago. Your mother didn't need an heir to act, not like those monstrous fortune hunters hoping to be rewarded for finding Merlock; she needed *that*"—he nods toward my chest—"perfected before she would risk leaving that much magic behind in Brindaigel. She wanted guaranteed victory. Nothing more, nothing less. Your mother did not leave on my account."

"Guaranteed victory of what?"

But there's no answer, only the gunpowder crack of a pistol and the gaping hole that opens in Frell's head. I jerk forward at the noise as the councilman withdraws, smoke still clinging to the barrel of his gun. Frell pitches forward, and Perrote shoves the tip of his boot under his shoulder and rolls him limply onto his back.

I struggle against my captor, fury boiling like fire through my blood, testing the limits of Sofreya's protection spells. A litany of apologies to Frell runs through my head; this is my fault. Perrote must have followed me from the palace, and in my haste for answers—and my desire to go unnoticed by Chadwick—I didn't even consider the possibility. How could I be so reckless, after chastising North for being the same? And now a man is dead, his blood spreading at our feet. And with him, any hope of answers about my mother.

Perrote sighs again, wiping a fleck of blood from his coat as the councilman grabs a chair and arranges it to face me, just out of reach of the spreading pool of blood. Perrote settles himself in the chair, folding one leg over his knee, picking at invisible lint on his trousers before pressing his hands together. For a moment he says nothing, and simply watches me with his head cocked and that supercilious smile plastered across his face.

"Faris Locke," Perrote says. "At long last we find ourselves with an opportunity to speak unobserved and uninterrupted."

A thousand rebuttals flood my mind, but I bite my tongue. With a sword still pressed to my stomach and an arm tightening around my throat, rising to Perrote's bait would leave two bodies on the ground.

"Please." He gestures to the sagging love seat. The guard clamps a hand on my shoulder and pushes me down, fingers digging into the pad of bandages to the blistered skin underneath. I force myself to meet Perrote's eyes, to be the ironhearted girl my mother tried to make me ten years ago when she perfected this spell to find Merlock. But there has to be more to it; finding Merlock would not guarantee victory. What weapon was Frell talking about? The sword? It lies discarded at the councilman's feet, too tarnished to be anything more than scrap.

"I'm told you have none of your mother's many abilities," Perrote says, interrupting my thoughts. He inspects the back of his hand and rubs at his knuckles. "Or our tragic rat's."

"What do you want from me?" I force bravado even as I fruitlessly scan the room in my peripheral vision for this so-called weapon. Attacking Perrote is worthless, because of all the protection spells he wears. The guard behind me is the easiest target, but he's twice my size, and well trained; not to mention the councilman standing between me and the door, pointedly reloading his pistol.

My eyes stray back to the body, and I feel myself wilting, the need to fight draining. Did Frell always know it was only borrowed time? Did he remember that one inescapable truth?

Nobody leaves Brindaigel.

"I'll extend to you the same offer I gave your mother," Perrote says. "Give me the spell and I won't kill you. Or your sister." He spreads his hands. "That's all I ask."

My dagger. It's still leveraged in the guard's body, but within reach, yet Perrote's threat gives me pause. Cadence has always been my liability as far as Bryn was concerned, but this is the first time Perrote has used her against me. And unlike Bryn, he has no reason to show me mercy.

"You'll have to fight Bryn for her first," I say, mind spinning.

"That spell"—he levels a finger toward me—"was cast from magic that belongs to me."

"This magic belongs to Avinea," I say, body tensing. "And you were never a king. You have no power over me, not while North is alive."

"Corbin cannot save you," he says. "He cannot even save himself from what's to come. The sooner you accept that, the less painful it will be." Exhaling, he rubs his palm across his short-cropped hair. "Skin her," he says.

I lunge for the dagger and yank it free. The guard moves to

stop me, but I twist and bury the dagger hilt-deep in his shoulder, forcing him to stagger back. With my heart racing, I then grab the oil lamp from the table and slam it into the startled face of the councilman. He gags against the noxious fumes, wrestling off his mask, and I duck, throwing myself onto the landing outside, nearly tripping over the body of the third guard.

The stairs, the road, the palace. I map them in my head as my blood beats with one simple fact: If Perrote is willing to threaten her, Cadence is in danger, and I've left her unprotected. Again.

Behind me the guard and councilman give chase, one of them grabbing my cloak, knocking me off-balance. I yank the cloak off and hit the door hard at the bottom of the stairwell—emerging outside, breathless.

The cold cuts through me like a knife, but I barely feel it as I run for the nearest cross street. The door slams open again, and I risk a glance back to see both men close behind, expressions fierce. My distraction costs me, and I trip over a loose clutch of broken cobblestones, skinning my elbows when I land on all fours. Grunting, I gain my feet and keep running, but not fast enough. They catch me, one taking my arms and the other my feet, sweeping me up off the street, without breaking their stride.

They carry me into an abandoned storefront, kicking the door off its rusted hinges and shuffling me past broken glass cases and walls emitting the scorched-wood smell of rotting magic torn apart too carelessly. After dropping me to the mildewed floor, the guard pins my arms above my head, and the councilman sits on my legs, ripping back the collar of my dress to expose the scar above my chest and the spell threaded like ink around it. With his eyes still watery from the kerosene, the councilman wipes his face dry and unsheathes a narrow dagger, spinning it in hand.

"Hold her steady," he says.

A moving target is always harder to hit, and I begin to struggle, to no real avail. The councilman is undeterred as he slides his blade beneath my skin with a glimmer of heat that cuts through the clouded fog of my panic: He's going to peel my skin off, and my mother's spell with it.

The mercantile door slams open and two figures enter, their faces hazy. The councilman releases me and stands, but the guard is slower to act; he's yanked back and thrown against a shattered display case. I push myself to my knees, teeth clenched against the swelling pain. How far did he get? I'm too scared to look, too scared to see a hole in my chest and my mother's spell ruined, cut apart at the seams. Grabbing the torn collar of my dress, I hold it closed and stand. The room spins out of focus around me.

Iron strikes iron; iron strikes flesh. I hear grunts, cries, the sounds of a body hitting the ground, and I smell blood being released into the air. Someone begs for mercy—the guard, I suspect. No doubt he was pressed into service by the noble nature of his birth and now acts on orders out of fear, his loyalty to Perrote guaranteed only by the spell woven above his heart.

Flattening a hand to the wall, I suck in a deep breath as my vision begins to settle. The guard lies cowering on the ground, hands up in terrified defense as a woman holds a sword to his throat. She takes a step forward, angling for the kill, just as a third figure frames the doorway.

"Don't," Chadwick says, a low and gravelly warning.

The woman glances back. Dark hair frames her eyes; her cheeks are flushed with color. I don't know her; she's not a part of Chadwick's hand-selected team heading into the Burn. "Sir?" she says.

"They are not ours to condemn," Chadwick says.

"Sir," the woman repeats, more pointedly, loath to forfeit the win.

Chadwick shakes his head once, swift and subtle, a signal. But the councilman grins around a bloodied mouth, pinned to the wall by another Avinean soldier.

"Diplomatic immunity," he crows, only to choke on his laughter as the soldier pinches him more tightly around the neck.

"Release them," Chadwick orders. The soldiers exchange dark glances but dutifully comply, and Perrote's men waste no time in scrambling out the door, disappearing into the lengthening shadows of the street.

"I don't understand the clemency," the second soldier, a young man, says, sheathing his sword.

"Return to the palace immediately," Chadwick says in that same, flat tone of voice.

"Sir—"

Chadwick gives the woman a look that refuses argument. Frustrated, she sheathes her sword and glances at me before storming outside, the man at her heels.

"It was Perrote." The accusation comes out as more of a shout, and I close my mouth, color flooding my cheeks.

Chadwick finally looks to me, concern warring with disappointment. "I know. Contrary to what half this city believes," he says,

"I did not become captain of the Guard because I was friends with the prince. I *did* earn this position, Locke. Grant me some credit."

"Then why let his men go?!" My fury is making me shake, and my words spill out in a mess. "I am sworn to the Prince of Avinea, and Perrote has no right—"

"You belong to Bryn," he interrupts, eyes flashing. "Who is allowing her husband to *borrow you* for his expedition. How could you be so stupid, Faris?!" He launches into a pace across the floor. "You were told not to leave the palace! You've risked everything in frivolous pursuit of—I don't even know what!"

"Dimitr Frell," I say softly. And then, with a pang of heartache: "He was possibly my last link to my mother."

Chadwick presses his hands over his eyes. When he speaks, it is carefully enunciated, each syllable weighted. "And who told you where to find this man?"

"Alistair Pembrough."

"Alistair Pembrough," he repeats. "Perrote's executioner—his daughter's ex-betrothed. A boy who is magically bound to be loyal to his king. And you decided to pursue this lead alone, with no protection, against strict orders."

It is an echo of the words I spoke to North, and yet, when directed at me, they chafe. "Alistair—"

Alistair told me where Dimitr Frell lived, but Perrote knew where to find me too. A possible payment from a loyal servant to his master?

No. Alistair abhors Perrote nearly as much as I do. But if he were under a spell, acting on orders . . .

"We cannot risk unbalancing an already precarious alliance,"

Chadwick continues. "Perrote is withholding the remaining balance of magic promised to Corbin until our departure in the morning. Killing two of Perrote's men or accusing him of any hand in this will guarantee his withdrawal of resources. None of this"—he lowers his hands and meets my eyes—"ever happened. Do you understand me?"

"A man is dead, and I was nearly skinned. Does that not warrant any reaction?"

"No," Chadwick says flatly. "Because we need him more than he needs us."

The injustice of it infuriates me. Nothing has changed since I left Brindaigel: Perrote can still kill with impunity, and no one will dare stand up to him.

Livid, I storm out of the building, Chadwick at my heels. When I turn right, back toward Frell's apartment, Chadwick stops me with a hand on my arm. "The palace is *that* way," he reminds me.

I shake him off. "Frell's body—"

"I'll send a man to dispose of it."

"He's not garbage to be floated out to sea!"

Chadwick closes his eyes but nods once. "I meant, I will send a man to bury him. He will be attended to."

"There's also a weapon," I say. "It has something to do with my mother—with *this*." My palm hovers over my bleeding chest. "I have to find it before Perrote's vultures pick the apartment clean."

"You are not the only one leaving for the Burn tomorrow," he explodes. "I have thirteen other people back at the palace, relying on me to ensure that everything is ready and we're as prepared as possible. I am not wasting more of their time hunting down mythical weapons from your mother! We had a plan before Corbin ever met you, and that plan would still hold merit if we were to lose you. If you want to stay behind, so be it. But that is your choice, and you make it now."

We stare each other down, our breath frosting in the frigid air.

"We leave tomorrow," Chadwick says, more gently this time. "We give this one to Perrote. But it's a long game, Faris, and I assure you that I intend to win."

"And if he kills me before then?"

He has the decency to look me in the eye when he says, "You were never my priority."

Seven

"ONE DAY," ALISTAIR SAYS, CUFFING HIS SHIRTSLEEVES, "WE'RE GOING to have a conversation that does not involve any spilled blood."

Against Chadwick's wishes, I insisted on seeing Alistair upon our return to the palace, instead of the palace doctor. Because of the risk that my blood-soaked clothing would be noticed by the servants while I stood in the palace entryway and argued, he finally relented. Now I sit on a table in the infirmary while Chadwick stands guard by the door, arms folded and expression murderous. There are even more guards posted outside—on order from their captain. Until we sail tomorrow morning, I am to be escorted everywhere. His one concession to me was that Cadence would be watched too, though far more discreetly. It's a modicum of relief, so long as I don't allow myself to remember Chadwick's warning in the city. If Perrote were to attack my sister, Chadwick's guards would be powerless to stop him.

But North would retaliate. She's safe so long as North remains within the palace walls. But after tomorrow when both he and I leave, her life is in Bryn's hands. Can *she* stop her father?

Maybe I *should* stay. But what good would I be, haunting my sister's every step when I have no power to stop Perrote from hurting her? If anything, it might drive her further into Bryn's clutches. And without me, North may lose time trying to track his father. If he died in the Burn, our future would die with him.

"Stitches," Alistair announces gleefully, jerking me back into the moment. I frown at his enthusiasm. After years of studying books, he finally has a chance for practical application.

Dark hair falls over his eyes as he assembles his tools, and I openly stare at him, trying to determine whether or not this is the Alistair who first offered me a chance at freedom—or a puppet masterfully controlled by Perrote to lead me astray. When he leans forward to retrieve a bandage, I grab his arm and yank back the collar of his shirt, to reveal the loyalty spell branded above his heart. Black, like ink. If it were in use, it would glow silver.

Alistair clears his throat, eyebrow arched. "Can I help you with something, or are you just enjoying the view?"

I release him, slumping forward. Tears of frustration and a growing paranoia needle at the back of my throat, and I press the heels of my hands to my eyes, fighting them back. Whose plan is this, Perrote's or Bryn's? Making me doubt everything and everyone I know?

The door slams open, and North storms in like a god of war. He turns to Chadwick first, and then to me, the bloodied mess wearing only my chemise on the table, a blood-soaked dress balled up beside me.

"She's fine," Chadwick says, catching him by the shoulder before he can thunder over and disrupt Alistair's work.

I meet his eyes and nod: I'm fine. He sags back in relief, but then his anger returns. "I made it perfectly clear she was not to leave the palace grounds for any reason."

"And I am not a governess," Chadwick replies, ice-tipped steel. "I trusted Locke on her word; I can't be responsible if she lies. I've already wasted half a morning chasing her through the city."

I cringe, and Alistair pulls a face as he presses a damp cloth to my chest, cleaning the wound. "Say the word, and I'll give the order," he whispers. "Silence and bed rest for the invalid."

I half-snort, gratified by the offer.

"What happened?" North demands, pacing a short line in front of the door, hands on his hips.

"There was an attack," Chadwick says, with a warning look to me.

"They knew about the spell," I say, parroting the lines we agreed upon. "They tried to skin it off me."

North's hands drop, and he pales. "Who?"

"No harm done," Alistair interrupts, threading a horrifying, hooked needle. "A few stitches and she'll be fine."

"A few stitches? She's been burnt!" North approaches, staring down at the scorch marks on my bare shoulder, the bandage removed so Alistair can work more freely.

Alistair makes a face and looks away. He can't help me with that one.

"I didn't recognize them," I say tightly, barely a lie. "I don't know who they were." As Alistair threads the needle through my skin, I make a fist and hit the table, hissing through my teeth.

"Sainted virgins," I growl, "you could have warned me!"

"Sorry," Alistair says with a wicked grin. "That's the executioner in me."

North spins on his heel and stalks to the opposite end of the room, where he picks up jars of ointment and salves from the bookshelves, only to replace them again. His annoyance permeates the room and thickens the air, until he finally turns back toward us, fists clenched at his sides. "Bring me Sofreya," he says to Chadwick.

"Locke has already been excised, and Sofreya is busy," Chadwick snaps. "The magic Perrote graciously donated to our expedition is full of knots and needs to be unraveled."

"What were you even doing in the city?" North ignores Chadwick. "What possessed you to be so reckless?!"

He should know the answer to this, because it would be his answer for this morning's blood experiment: desperation. And while my brief conversation with Dimitr Frell answered one question, it inspired a dozen more. What is buried in this spell that guarantees victory? Dimitr was surprised that I was the vessel; his first concern had been about blood. My blood? Was he worried I had somehow damaged the spell? Have I?

North frowns at my expression—my lack of a ready reply—and I look away, guilty.

"I don't care how busy Sofreya is," North says at length. "Miss Locke cannot safely carry this burden anymore."

Chadwick begins to protest, but I jump in. "I've never been safe, not even here in the palace." I glare toward Chadwick. "With so many *enemies* waiting to attack."

"They only wanted the spell," North says, not looking at me. "It would be better suited to someone—"

"Expendable?" I challenge. He frowns, and I bite back my frustration. "Don't try to save me," I say. "We both know Sofreya can't dismantle something this complicated, especially not in the short time we have. My mother wove caveats into her spells, and this one's been buried ten years deep. You're going to lose the only advantage you have. It is selfish to sacrifice the whole—"

"Don't. Don't you *dare*." North levels a finger at me. "You are not the few, Faris!"

My name silences the room as North realizes his mistake. Chadwick lowers his head, fists clenched across his chest.

North straightens. "I want Sofreya," he repeats.

Chadwick speaks to the floor. "Your majesty, listen to me—"

"NOW!" North slams his palm against the wall, rattling the sconces. Chadwick stares at him before he turns hard on one heel and storms out of the room, slamming the door behind him.

Alistair works quickly, silently, finishing his work and wiping the stitches clean while North prowls the small infirmary. Eleven crooked lines that sting like a sunburn. I resist scratching at them as I push myself off the desk, reaching for my bloody dress.

"Don't treat me like a prisoner," I say, tugging it back on. "My mother died for this spell. It is mine, North."

"Faris is right."

North spins, expression unreadable as he sees Bryn standing in the doorway, eavesdropping on our argument.

"Then I'll leave you behind," he says to me, still looking at her.

"You will not." Bryn folds her arms across her chest. "This is my kingdom now too, and you do not make state decisions on your own anymore, my darling." She spits the endearment like the curse it's meant to be. "Not even you could unravel that spell in less than a day. You're wasting time even debating the option. The sooner you find your father, the sooner we ensure our undisputed reign."

North's sarcasm scorches. "Mine or yours?"

"Our hearts beat the same now," Bryn says with that same icy smile. "Surely we're beyond semantics."

North stares her down, but it's a battle already decided. And while the victory is in my favor, I can't help but be suspicious. "Why are you agreeing with me?" I ask her. If North finds his father, her reign is far from secure.

She snorts, as though my question is too ignorant to be answered. "When Corbin inherits, *I* inherit," she says. "And the only thing keeping my father from killing me for that inheritance is the blood he needs to forge the blade."

Of course. Perrote cleverly kept a vial of all his children's blood back in Brindaigel for his own macabre—likely murderous—reasons, but Bryn's was needed for the bloodbound ceremony. She can't bleed otherwise, not while I'm bound to bear her wounds, and Perrote needs more of her blood to link himself to the crown.

"So you will return—success or failure, Faris—not just for me. Cadence will also be waiting for you."

And therein lies the threat: We can succeed, but not without cost. She's befriended my sister so that if North tries to deny her power . . .

Chadwick's words return, haunting, wrong. I am not a liability.

But because of me, North might be.

"Why not come with us if you're so concerned with our success?" I ask darkly. "Your amplification abilities would be far more beneficial out in the Burn than here in the palace."

"You drag me out into the Burn, and my amplification abilities will poison you within hours."

"Your father has enough magic to protect all of us."

She rolls her eyes. "My father's magic is the only thing giving him the upper hand right now; he won't waste it on *me*. And Avinea can't afford to lose both its monarchs. One of us must stay behind." Her eyes cut toward North. "If you leave Faris here, he'll try this again and you will lose your only advantage over him."

North stares at her, understanding dawning across his face.

Chadwick returns, Sofreya in tow. She looks more frazzled than usual, with violet shadows bagging beneath her eyes. "You needed me?" she squeaks.

"It was Perrote who tried to skin Faris," North says flatly to Chadwick. "Were you going to tell me that?"

"Of course he wasn't," Bryn says, "because he knows you can't do anything about it." Smiling, she glances over her shoulder at Chadwick standing frozen in the doorway.

North lowers his head, fists clenched tightly at his side. Tonight he will be forced to toast the man who made his mission possible— and the man who tried to destroy his greatest weapon. It's an insult, and he's powerless to retaliate.

"Sir?" Sofreya looks ready to burst into tears.

"My apologies, Sofreya," North growls. "There's been a change of plans. Go back to your work."

"Good." Bryn claps her hands. "So we're settled? Secure? Is everyone happy?"

Far from it. I adjust the hem of my dress and rake my hair back. The room lurches, and I lean against the table as Alistair offers me a steadying hand.

"Not too fast," he cautions. "You lost a fair amount of blood."

And I owe him even more, if he's to continue his experiments. "I'm fine." I straighten, pushing his hand away.

"My father will have need of his executioner this afternoon," Bryn says suddenly. "I suggest you find him as soon as you can, Pem."

Alistair stiffens. "What?"

"There is a fine line between loyalty and anarchy, and the two men who attacked Faris this afternoon must be held to that standard. Don't believe that because you're here on palace invitation, you are excused from your other obligations."

Alistair blanches, and for half a heartbeat I pity him.

"Now," says Bryn, clapping, "the real concern. We need to finalize our seating arrangements for tonight's dinner. What unmarried noble should we throw toward Joyena?" She extends her arm toward North, but it is not an invitation; it's a threat.

Slowly North slides his arm through hers and allows her to lead him out of the infirmary. Chadwick inclines his head in respect, but it's forced, a meaningless act of ceremony. He watches them down the hall before he shakes his head and turns in the opposite direction, toward the barracks. I'm tempted to follow, to challenge him to a one-on-one sparring match, so that we can pour our silent screams into the floor. But his careful schedule has already been upended because of me. I'm the last person he'll want to see—and he's the last person I'd want to fight when he's this angry.

Instead I glance toward Alistair, still pale as he wipes down the table. I open my mouth, but what could I possibly say? Even in Avinea, he's a prisoner to Perrote.

We all are.

Eight

A SLURRY OF VOICES RISES FROM THE FOYER, BOUNCING TOWARD THE domed roof. A colorful pageant is reflected in the crystal chandelier and its two hundred lit candles that brighten the room. The doors of the palace are thrown open to the dark night outside, to allow colder air into the stuffy, crowded room, yet the smell still lingers: sweat and perfume, ambition and greed.

One hundred and thirty guests, and tonight is the first time most of them have ever stepped foot in this palace, or paid their respects to its prince. They were lured here with the promise of opulence and splendor, the likes of which haven't been seen—haven't been afforded—since Merlock destroyed the capital twenty years ago. The crew of the *Mainstay* will be on display, along with the six soldiers hand-chosen by Captain Chadwick to execute our expedition tomorrow. He couldn't afford to choose more, not with the limited magic Perrote offered. Not with Perrote staying behind, with an undisclosed amount of men possibly lurking in the city.

But the nobles don't seem to care who stays and who goes; so long as there's any chance that Avinea is going to survive, these are the men and women who want to be first in line to say they were there when it all began.

Clutching my shawl more tightly across my bandaged shoulder, I peer over the balustrade, my stomach twisted with nerves. North is easy to find, dressed all in black near the doors, clutching a glass of wine while staring wistfully outside. Chadwick stands discreetly to one side, dressed in his ceremonial uniform again.

Perrote is also easy to find, centered in the middle of the foyer, his voice cutting over everyone else's gentler hums. He commands attention and wields authority, his silver circlet flashing in the candlelight, reminding everyone who he is and how powerful he must be, with silver to wear and magic enough to spare for a dowry. Lords and their wives flock to him eagerly and hang on his every word. They ask questions about Brindaigel and exchange looks of amazement and surprise at the perfect picture he paints of the kingdom nobody even knew existed. That nobody connects it with Corthen's rumored stronghold is pure luck—or a conclusion swallowed by those playing politics.

The very sight of him makes my skin crawl.

Perrote looks up suddenly, as if drawn by the weight of my loathing. His eyes lock with mine and he arches an eyebrow—so like his daughter. Head cocked, he lifts his glass of wine in my direction, as if in invitation. The people around him all crane to see what's drawn his attention, and the whispering begins.

I can't do this.

Decided, I slink back down the hall and cut through the servants' stairwell, dodging serving trays and kitchen staff in an effort to shake off the guards still dogging my steps. The servants are unaccustomed to parties of this size, and their nerves are contagious, thickening the air with a suffocating anxiety. It's a relief to leave it behind for the silence of an empty hallway, and I catch my breath, steel my nerves.

Alistair opens the door when I knock, baggy-eyed and rumpled, his shirttails loose, his vest unbuttoned. He's too surprised to say anything, and I flush beneath the weight of his gaze as he studies me in my dinner gown.

"Yet another conversation over spilled blood," I say by way of explanation.

He frowns, almost distractedly, and then my meaning sinks in. "Oh. Right. Of course. You leave in the morning."

"Bright and early," I agree, pushing past him, inviting myself into his study.

He closes the door behind me, leaning against it. There's a strange, eerie finality to the sound.

I ignore the way he watches me, and examine his room instead. North spared no expense. His bedroom is on the second floor like all the others, but his laboratory—a repurposed study—is on the first floor, tucked into the eastern wing of the palace, as far from the ballroom as possible. There are windows overlooking the sea, shuttered and closed now, but with slants of moonlight that steal through the clapboards. A heavy desk littered with glass and metal instruments takes up the right side of the room; an entire wall is shelves, mostly empty except for a handful of books that sit forlornly in one corner. Medical texts, some in a language I surmise to be Terelese, the language of the Northern Continents.

A leather chair sits at the desk, and I sink into it, pulling myself closer to the structure of Alistair Pembrough's thoughts, avoiding the questions in his eyes. I tip a box of pumice toward me, jostling the contents, before letting it fall back again. There are notes, neatly stacked and in impeccable penmanship, diagrams and questions and new ideas scrawled in the margins. Empty vials sit cradled in a velvet case, waiting to be filled.

There's something missing between Alistair Pembrough, the king's executioner, and this, the mind of an intelligent man who was going to be a doctor before duty called him to the dungeons of Brindaigel. Some hidden secret I have yet to discover.

But do I really want to know?

I slump down in the chair, rolling a chunk of pumice in my hand. "It's an improvement over the dungeon," I say.

He snorts. "It wouldn't take much. Do you want a drink?"

I nod, and he moves toward another shelf, empty save for a glass decanter full of dark liquid. I stare at him as he works. Now that I'm looking, I notice there's a gauntness to his face that wasn't there in Brindaigel, deep-pooled shadows and a faint scrub of facial hair.

"Conclusion?" he asks, after filling two glasses.

"What?"

"Scientific process," he says, handing me one before he leans back against the desk, cradling his own glass to his chest. "Start with a theory, form a hypothesis. Execute an experiment, and examine your conclusions. You were staring. I wondered if you had reached a conclusion."

"My conclusion is that you're still a prisoner like me," I say softly.

Whatever happened this afternoon after he stitched me closed fills his face, darkens his eyes, leaves its memory in his motions as he brings his own glass to his lips. He hesitates, then downs the drink in one gulp. "I hate magic," he says.

Snorting, I raise my own glass in halfhearted agreement.

"But science will prevail." His eyes meet mine before he looks away, thumbs tapping the rim of his glass. "It has to."

"So you can leave Brindaigel?"

"So I can prove I'm not the monster you still think I am."

I lower my drink, startled.

"*And* so I can leave Brindaigel," he adds, with a tight, humorless smile.

It strikes me once again how much this boy and I have in common. Under other circumstances—in different lives—maybe we could have been friends. But Thaelan's death still hangs between us, and while my head can separate the boy from the order he was given, my heart still finds footholds of accusation. Thaelan didn't die from lack of a survival instinct, as Alistair once said.

He was murdered, and I can never forget that.

I lift the glass to my lips; the alcohol smells smoky and bitter and sweet. It tastes terrible, and I welcome it greedily.

"I'm sorry," Alistair says at length. "I should have assumed you would be followed this morning. I thought—" He breaks off, eyeing his empty glass with some regret. "I thought I was helping."

"Did you know who he was?"

"No. Only that he was a watchtower here in Avinea, relaying news back into Brindaigel. Did you speak to him at all?"

"Barely. Cryptically. At the very least, I now know why my mother chose the night she did, and that I wasn't her intended vessel for this spell. But"—after draining the last of the alcohol, I grimace and set the glass on the edge of his desk—"desperate times, desperate measures." Clearing my throat, I softly add, "Thank you for the book."

Alistair nods. Dark hair falls forward, hiding his eyes. "I doubt you have much of Thaelan's."

"Nothing," I say.

He opens his mouth but hesitates, pushing away from the desk and returning to the decanter. "There was a ring," he says, his back to me. "He had it with him the day he died, and he asked me to give it to you."

My heart seems to stop for one hard moment. "Where is it?" I ask, as if I don't know, as if I don't remember the moment Bryn pulled it from her finger and used it to pay North to bring us to New Prevast. The triumph on her face, the *smugness*—

"She took it," Alistair says. "She knew it had value to me, so she took it. And I couldn't say no, not then. I needed her the same way she needed me. But not anymore." Returning to the desk, he changes the subject. "Do you know how I met Thaelan?" When I shake my head, he says, "I caught him in the tunnels."

"He never told me he got caught."

"Of course he didn't, because practical Faris would have made him promise not to risk his life again, and that would have been the end of escaping." His smile cracks. "My father was still alive at the time, but everyone knew who I was. What I would become. Most of the recruits down in the barracks were afraid of me, but

Thaelan was different. Where others already saw a monster, he saw potential. And so the bribes began."

It hurts to hear Thaelan starring in a story different from the one I knew, yet I find myself leaning forward, eager to hear more.

"It was entirely mercenary at first," Alistair continues, lost in the memory. "I had no formal education, but Thaelan's family did. So he brought me books. And then he brought me stories." He gives me a pointed look, and my stomach tightens. I always believed myself to be Thaelan's secret, buried beneath the rugs, hidden behind locked doors. Yet Alistair knew everything about me, except my name. Thaelan trusted him—but not entirely.

"And finally," Alistair says, "he gave me hope that escape was actually possible. I had something to look forward to, something to plan for. Until my father died."

I roll the edge of my glass along his blotter. "Why did he keep us both secret? Had I known you were on our side, that whole night could have been rewritten—"

"Because Thaelan was never a saint, Faris," Alistair says with an edge to his voice. "Escaping Brindaigel isn't nearly so impressive if you have someone holding your hand and marking the way. He never told me your name for fear of implicating himself. Names are power." He swallows hard and looks away, profile outlined by the fire behind him. "You would have destroyed him if anyone had ever discovered your relationship. And that fear was enough to hold his tongue, even with me. If you hadn't tried to run that night, he would have married Ellis, and you know it." He starts to take a drink but stops, setting the glass on the desk instead. "He loved you, but he always had a contingency plan."

His words are needles, sharp and itchy under my skin, and yet—it is their honesty that burns the most. Thaelan *would* have married Ellis. To pretend otherwise is pure self-indulgence. But we always understood that: It was a part of who we were. Two separate worlds, trying to find somewhere to coexist.

"To be fair, I don't fault him too much," Alistair adds wryly, lifting his head to look at me. "I fully intended to leave Brindaigel without Faris Locke if the chance ever arose, no matter what I swore to my father."

A few short months ago I was too naive to appreciate strength born of necessity and honesty. But I value it now. "I would've done the same," I say.

He moves his hair off his face. A touch of arrogance returns as he regards me with bright blue eyes. "Liar."

I don't answer, leaning forward so that my shawl shifts, exposing my bare arm across his desk. An unspoken invitation.

Alistair dutifully loads a glass vial into the iron bracket of his syringe. Prior to drawing blood, however, he traces the raised lines of magic around my wrist, pressing at them with a clinical analysis that is oddly endearing. "Does it hurt?"

"Only if I ignore her when she summons me."

"What happens if you never answer?" He bends forward, pinching my skin, sliding the needle deftly into my vein.

"The pain just gets worse," I say, mesmerized by the sight of my blood, brackish and cloudy, filling the vial. "I imagine that eventually something would happen, but I've never tested it that far."

"You have terrible scientific method." He gives me a withering look before resuming his work, removing the first vial and replacing it with an empty one.

We fall into a strange silence, not uneasy but not quite comfortable. With my eyes trained to the moonlight slanting through the window, I say, "I met Thaelan when I was nine. I saw him stealing apples from a street vendor. He made it look so easy. I didn't realize part of the trick was being a nobleman's son—that privilege breeds its own kind of invisibility. So when I tried it, I got caught and he didn't. He paid for my apples, asked for my name, and made me promise to never steal again."

Alistair half-smiles, focused on his work. "Did you?"

"Of course," I say. "We were poor and hungry and I had Cadence to consider. But that was Thaelan. He saw potential where others saw nothing."

Alistair corks each of the vials of my poisoned blood. Seeing them laid out in a neat row in his velvet box sparks a new wave of guilt for how reckless I've been with Sofreya's spells. It would not take much to poison my heart.

Alistair hands me a bandage for my arm and then carefully closes the lid to the box. Before I can stop myself, I ask, "Are you all right?"

He looks over, bemused. "What?"

"Hypothesis," I say. "If you were to roll back your sleeves, there would be new rungs on your ladder."

His expression tightens at the allusion to his self-inflicted battle scars. For a moment he doesn't move. "It's a sound theory," he says at last. "Based on prior research. I can't fault your logic."

Without thinking, I touch his arm. We both freeze in surprise.

A simple kindness can be cruel, and yet I don't pull back. "I see potential in you too, Alistair Pembrough."

He gives me a troubled smile. "I see too much whiskey in you, Faris Locke. But thank you anyway."

The door flies open, and Cadence bounds inside, breathless and grinning and still dressed for dinner, with her curls sliding across her shoulders. Darjin trots in at her heels. She's always had a way with animals, and a magic tiger was apparently irresistible. He's been her newly adopted shadow since she arrived.

"Pem! You weren't at dinner, so I brought you dessert!" She brandishes her gloved hands—dinner gloves tonight, no doubt a gift from her new benefactor—clutching two thick slabs of fruit bread wrapped in a cloth napkin. Then she notices me, my hand on Alistair's arm, and her grin evaporates, the fruit bread faltering.

"You look beautiful, Cade," I say with a painful ache, because Bryn can deliver what I never could: dresses and gloves and perfect curls, a life in a palace, and enough food to fill her belly and still sneak some for later.

"Bryn was right," she snarls. "You're a thief just like our mother! Do you have to take *everything* from me?!"

"No, Bryn is all yours," I retort, before I can stop myself.

She throws the fruit bread at me and scoops up Darjin, bolting back down the hall.

I stand to follow, but Alistair holds me back. "You'll never find her," he says. "Corbin's former apprentice has been teaching her the secret passages in the palace; she'll be somewhere in the courtyard by now."

I sigh, sinking back into his chair, resenting that he knows her more than I do now. "All I can think about is Bryn's sixteenth birthday, when you and her rode through Brindaigel in that ridiculous carriage, throwing out flowers to celebrate your engagement. Cadence took hers home, and it died overnight. She was devastated." I suck in a shaky breath. "What happens when this bond with Bryn dies too, and she realizes that the beauty is only skin-deep? She's suffered enough disappointment already."

"She's a Locke," Alistair says with a bracing smile. "She'll survive."

"Why can't she just live? Why must everything be a battle, with winners and losers?"

He shrugs helplessly, and I briefly close my eyes, suddenly drained. "Too much whiskey," I mutter, standing. He moves aside, but as I step past, I pause, grappling with myself. I've had weeks to prepare for tomorrow, for saying good-bye to Cadence so soon after our reunion, and yet, in my delusion I imagined it would be with Cadence waving from the arched courtyard of Saint Ergoet's, where she would be protected by the monks until my return. The monastery's reputation would keep Perrote and Bryn from any outward attack, to avoid the risk of alienating themselves from the city. But now she'll be here, burrowed into Bryn's hip.

"I have no right to ask—I don't even know that I should, but . . ."

"I'll keep an eye on her," Alistair says. Then, more quietly, "Come back alive."

"I will," I say. I have to, for Cadence. Whether she wants me to or not.

Nine

I WANT NOTHING MORE THAN TO BURY MYSELF IN BED, BUT MY NIGHT is far from over. Chadwick paces the hall outside my bedroom door, ignorant to the furious looks of the guards trailing me down the hall, having finally found me again. He looks up on my approach, relief warring with something else.

Dread settles in my stomach, cutting through the haze of Alistair's whiskey. "What's wrong?"

He starts to speak but stops, glancing at the guards. "We need to talk."

"Of course." Bypassing my bedroom door, I walk him into the less scandalous parlor instead, closing the double doors behind me with a rise of unease. "Is everything all right?"

Ignoring my question, he does a cursory check of both bedrooms and our shared bath to ensure no servants are lingering, before he finally looks at me.

"Kill him," he says.

My hands flex around the doorknobs at my back as my heart slams painfully against my ribs. I picture Perrote at the dinner table, silver circlet flocked with blood, and feel my stomach tighten. "Who?"

"Merlock," he says, and a for a moment I feel disappointed. "If you have the chance tonight, kill him."

In my dreams, he means. I'll have to let my vices overrun me until there's enough Burn in my blood to activate my mother's spell.

"It's a risk," he says, running a hand through his hair, mussing the carefully combed ponytail. "But if it keeps Corbin out of the Burn . . ."

Then he would be in a better position to defend his palace and his city from Perrote's inevitable coup.

Exhaling softly, Chadwick reaches into his jacket and retrieves a blade sheathed in cracking leather, the hilt tarnished with age and wrapped with thread. He hesitates, weighing it in his hands, before offering it to me.

I accept warily. "What is this?"

"One of only two blades that were forged with Corbin's blood," he says grimly. "Three, if we count Baedan's. They were given to me so that if he and I became separated in battle, I would have the means of killing Merlock even if Corbin wasn't with me."

I unsheathe the dagger an inch. The blade is polished brightly enough that I catch a glimpse of my frightened expression reflected back. "You would inherit the magic?"

"Ideally, when a king dies, the heir is present to perform the blood ceremony which will bind the king's heart to his heir's. But if the king were to die in battle, or without the heir on hand, a proxy could bind the heart to their own until the heir arrived."

Fear simmers, low in my belly, at the hesitation in his voice, the missing warning. "But . . . ," I prod.

Chadwick lowers his head, guilty. "The heart of a king is not an easy burden to bear," he says. "Magic needs a heartbeat to survive, and it will latch on to whoever holds it. But if the carrier does not have royal blood, the magic will destroy him. Or her. Proxies are simply vessels, Locke." He bumps his shoulders in helpless apology, looking uncharacteristically tired. "The only way to release the magic again is by stopping the heart that holds it."

Oh.

"A proxy," I repeat. "A polite word for *sacrifice*." Is that what I am now, with my mother's spell locked under my skin?

Chadwick takes back the dagger and unscrews the rounded pommel, revealing a slender vial of blood hidden inside the hollowed hilt. "Use the blade to cut through the spells Merlock wears. Once they're gone, he's like any other hellborne."

"And the only cure for a hellborne soul is a carved-out heart," I recite in a dull tone.

He nods in approval. "Remove his heart and bind it"—he touches the dark thread around the hilt—"and then protect it with the blood." He shakes the vial to illustrate. It's clean, a dark, uninfected red. How long ago did North have this blade made?

After screwing the vial back into the pommel, Chadwick hands me the dagger. "And then come back with the heart as fast as you can before it takes hold of your own."

"And if it's not fast enough? If something goes wrong? You know North won't kill me to release the magic."

"I will," he says.

I make a face to hide my fear. "Could you maybe hesitate half a second first?"

"Locke, if you can't do it, I understand—"

"I didn't say that." I clutch the dagger to my chest, out of his reach. "Does it work on anyone? Could I cut past Perrote's protection spells and kill him with this? Or even Baedan?"

"It'll only dismantle the spells of those with shared blood. One cancels out the other, so to speak. So no. It won't work on anyone who doesn't share North's bloodline—anyone who can't inherit if he dies."

"Bryn could."

Chadwick knots his hands behind his neck. He watches me, eyebrows furrowed. "Yes," he says at last. "You could destroy the binding spell and kill Bryndalin with that."

It steals my breath, and I regard the dagger with newfound admiration.

"But," Chadwick says, and I know what's coming.

"But Merlock first," I say flatly. If I fail, North will still be dependent on Perrote's magic. Killing Bryn would undoubtedly sever that alliance. And if I succeed . . .

Chadwick's desperation is unsettling, a contradiction to the stoic taskmaster I've come to know. He's not asking me as North's captain of the Guard but as North's closest friend, who knows that the odds are against us, and who will take anything that may tip the scales in our favor. "You wanted to fight," he says. "You wanted to protect the prince, no matter the cost. Sometimes that payment is made in blood."

"I wanted to fight," I agree, "but that often implies a chance of success. Even slight odds are better than none."

Moving away from the doors, I sink onto a love seat, crinolines and silk kicking up in a frothy cloud around my legs. I clutch the dagger to my stomach, the leather warm. I understand the request and I don't resent him for it, and yet I can't help but feel trapped. How can I say no when I'm the only one who can get to Merlock from the safety of the palace?

But then I think of my sister and wonder, how can I possibly say yes? For so long, it's been her and me, alone against the world. Only—I have to admit—she's wanted more than me for years. First with Thaelan, now with Bryn. For all I claim to be my mother's daughter, with an insatiable heart that always craves more, I never considered that Cadence was the same. Would she even care if I died, or would her hate preclude any grief?

"What happens to my sister?"

Chadwick kneels in front of me, expression fierce, hands firm on my knees. "I swear to you on my life, no harm will come to Cadence. I'll see to it. Once Corbin inherits, Bryndalin will be an heir. She'll need protection from her father if she doesn't want to be murdered in her bed with one of these." He touches the dagger, and it feels heavier in response. "Cadence will no longer be used as leverage."

"And if North doesn't inherit?"

Chadwick has never been one to spare my feelings. "Then we're all dead anyway."

I am not a hero. For me, fighting in the Brim was a way to make money, not a way to save the world. I wanted Thaelan and marriage and family: safety, security, and a place to call home, a place that was free. I still do. If there were no Benjamin Chadwick or bastard prince or missing king to intervene, I would be a coward.

Or would I?

Ten years ago my mother cut me open and made me stronger. I didn't want to be a fighter, but I became one from necessity—a consequence of her choice for me, which means my choice is simple.

There are monsters in Avinea, and I have the ability to stop them.

I look Chadwick in the eye, the dagger clenched tightly in my hand. "Be ready with your knife when I come back."

Despite my conviction, sleep eludes me an hour later as I lie on my bed, dagger clutched to my chest. Earlier, Sofreya removed my protection spells without question, though her eyes chided Chadwick in silent remonstration before she disappeared back down the hall, back to her study to unravel more knots.

I'll probably be the only one sleeping in the palace tonight.

I force myself to close my eyes, only to open them again with a sudden shock of adrenaline—and fear. I try to rationalize my decision; I was never guaranteed a return from North's expedition. It makes no difference if I die in my bed or die in the Burn.

But it makes a difference knowing that one is only a possibility and the other, guaranteed. I want my chance, slim as it may be.

Without the protection spells, I can feel the poison in my blood more clearly, thick and swollen in my veins. I try to coax it higher in small steps, focusing on my anger over Perrote, my heartache over Dimitr Frell—even my continued frustration with my mother and her breadcrumb trail of clues. The poison warms but doesn't seem to spread beyond a faint hum, as if it knows my hesitation.

And then I hear it. A muffled laugh, cutting across the shared parlor and into my room, where it settles over me like a veil.

Cadence. Spending the night in Bryn's room. Again.

All at once the poison flashes through me as if ignited, but I bolt upright, heart sliding into my throat with a shot of terror. The dagger clatters to the ground, and I clutch at my coverlet, sweat breaking out across my back.

Anxious, I launch myself off the bed and drag my hands through my hair. I'm trembling as I pace at the foot of my bed, alternating between relief at having postponed the inevitable, and a fierce reproof for my being a coward. How am I supposed to kill a magician? A *king*? A blade forged with blood is only half the equation. I still need to be strong enough, fast enough, to pierce it through his skin.

Am I even capable of this?

Another laugh cuts through the room, but this time it's Bryn. I stare at my door, shoulders still heaving, flooded with an envy so bitter, it dries my mouth and thickens my tongue. I can't imagine leaving Cadence to this. Even if North succeeds and Bryn is eviscerated, Cadence will suffer the loss of another friend, however false she may have been. I can't bear the thought of my little sister turning cruel beneath Bryn's care, but I also can't fathom her turning cold, afraid to trust anyone because everyone has disappointed her—including me.

I can't leave her behind again.

Sofreya doesn't say a word when she opens her door to find me standing there, miserable and chilled. Inside, Tobek watches from his cot as she replaces the spells in the crooks of my arms. When our eyes meet, he rolls over, shoulders hunched against my gaze. He was not considered essential for the expedition, and I know it hurts, to go from being North's only companion for months on end to being here, another haunted face in the halls, trapped by circumstance.

"You never taught me how to fight," he says to the wall as I prepare to leave.

I stop, startled. "Did you still want to learn?"

He rolls back to face me, scowling. "Yeah. Yeah, I want to learn."

"As soon as I get back," I say. From his expression, he's ready to fight the whole world, and I can't blame him.

I'm halfway down the hall when I run into Chadwick exiting the library. Candles cast dim shadows through the partially open door, and I catch a glimpse of North, Darjin sprawled at his feet. My assumption was right: Nobody's sleeping tonight.

Chadwick's eyes widen, and he reaches for the knife at his hip with a questioning look, but I shake my head, staying his hand before he can cut out my heart. "I'm sorry," I say.

He deflates, chin sinking toward his chest. His hand drops and he nods once, dismissing me.

Ten

THE PALACE IS A BATTLEGROUND THE NEXT MORNING, OVERRUN with servants and guards and last-minute supplies to be carried to the palace dock where the *Mainstay* has been moored. An undercurrent of panic hums in the air, the sharpening taste of anticipation.

A crowd of people has formed a buffer between the palace guards and the *Mainstay*, craning their necks for a glimpse of the prince—or better yet, of his bride. After years of wanting, the entire city seem greedy for the memory of what New Prevast once was, what it might one day be again. Their lust for magic is almost tangible, as is their desire for a return of the spells that once made New Prevast a prosperous trading post. Spells to navigate to the best fishing spots off the harbor, or spells to draw fish to waiting nets; spells to keep streets from clogging with snow, or spells to keep thieves from local businesses. They want it all, and more:

They want protection from life, and recourse for those who have lost property—or loved ones—to the Burn.

It's clear from the crowd's attentions that Bryn and her family embody everything beautiful about the past, whereas North is everything Avinea has become—gloomy in all black, gaunt and shadowed at only nineteen from years of searching, which the crowd knows nothing about. They dismiss him entirely.

Sofreya joins me on the palace drive, clutching a jar of pale rocks in the crook of her arm, each carefully threaded with magic to be unraveled and dispensed as needed.

"Look at them," she says bitterly. "So many of them fled the Burn out of fear of being poisoned, and yet they still crave magic as if it will end their suffering. What other kingdom do you know of whose people refuse to work if they don't have a spell to make it easier? Or who refuse to protect their city if it means actually fighting, but expect protection for themselves?"

I don't know how to answer her, and she continues walking toward the ship, still muttering, leaving me to scan the sky anxiously. The light is an ominous gray, and the *Mainstay* looks tiny against the span of the Bridge of Ander behind it. While I know that the ship's size is beneficial for dodging the rocky shoals of the coastline, I can't help but feel it is inadequate protection against such a vast, unyielding sea.

Tobek appears, juggling more supplies. Darjin darts between his feet, and Cadence chases after the tiger, giving Tobek a side-glance that turns his ears a bright and telling pink. He pauses to get a better grip on the crate he carries, eyes tracking Cadence as she catches up to Darjin. She scoops the animal into her arms, hugging him with his paws dangling over her shoulder. She watches the crowd warily, startling when North approaches and touches her other shoulder.

"Darjin is your responsibility while I'm gone," he says. "If you don't mind watching over him?"

Cadence hesitates, looking toward me. She wants to accept, but she also knows that I've agreed to follow North into the Burn, which makes him my ally while she remains my enemy. But her love of animals outweighs politics, and she shifts Darjin's weight in her arms. "Can he sleep in my bed?"

"Of course. But he hogs the blankets," North says, eliciting a laugh from her. He wets his lips and seems to bend forward in the wind. "May I ask one more favor of you, Miss Cadence?"

Wariness returns. Was Darjin only a bribe? "What?" she asks slowly.

North glances over his shoulder at me, but then nods toward Tobek. "Watch over him, too. He's the same as a tiger. They both need food and fresh air and a friend."

Tobek clutches at his crate as the pink of his ears floods into his face.

"Only, he does not sleep in your bed under any circumstances," I say, with a pointed look to both of them.

Cadence scowls at me; clearly I have ruined the moment.

North smiles and offers her his hand. "Do I have your word?"

After shifting Darjin over her other shoulder, Cadence shakes his hand. "Will you bring me back a souvenir?"

"Of what? Ash? Rubble? The skin of a hellborne?" Bryn snorts as she joins them, skirts lifted in one hand to avoid dragging them across the icy gravel. "I'll buy you much better presents in town."

Cadence wilts, embarrassed, but North winks at her, and she immediately brightens, hugging Darjin even more tightly.

"Good luck," Cadence says as North gives Darjin a farewell scratch behind the ears.

Bryn turns to me, folding an arm around my shoulders as she pulls me close for a hug. Her chin is sharp against my throat. "I'll trust you with my husband, and you'll trust me with your sister," she says softly.

"Is that a threat, your majesty?"

"A promise," she says, releasing me. "And a warning. Find Merlock and hurry home."

"Are you that eager to lose your crown?"

Her smile is as hard as the gravel we stand on. "There's more than one crown in this kingdom."

What does that mean?

She links her arm through North's, and they lead the procession to the dock. All at once the fear of what I'm doing hits me hard in the stomach, and I'm overcome with doubts and second guesses. So many lives at stake—Chadwick and his soldiers, North, Sofreya, even Davik and her brothers. Is it selfish of me to risk them when I could face Merlock alone? Or is it foolish of me to believe I could defeat the most powerful magician in the kingdom with only a dagger?

Cadence hangs back as the rest of the palace crowd follows North's lead. I lag behind as well, searching the gravel at my feet for the right words to say. She watches me from the corner of her eye, mouth thin, shoulders tight.

"Can I say good-bye?" I ask at last.

"Why bother?" Then, more savagely, "I hope you won't leave Prince Corbin behind if he gets lost."

Wounded, I watch as she speeds up, drawing level with North and Bryn. Bryn welcomes her with an arm draped possessively over her shoulder. With Darjin, they could be the perfect family portrait.

But she's mine, I tell myself, although her words sting. Bryn can have a lot of things, but she can never have Cadence.

Perrote follows us on board, surveying the small vessel with a curled lip and an arched brow. He tests the strength of the railing and tips his head back to appraise the sails. "Perhaps you should say a few words," he says, looking at North. He gestures toward the crowd, the servants, the city. "News of the recent golem attacks have unsettled them. And now that you're leaving, they need strength."

North's expression darkens: News of the attack was leaked from the palace against his express wishes. If the city is unsettled, it was by design.

"I'd be more than happy to speak for you," Perrote says. "If it helps."

Scowling, North ignores the barbed offer and approaches the ship's railing. He studies the faces below him and wets his lips again—a weakness. I can see the way Perrote revels in it. Then North begins to speak of his father and the growing Burn, and of a new plan to find Merlock.

"We are not yet defeated," he says. "I know that I've spent too long fighting this battle alone, allowing my people to believe me a coward hiding in a palace, waiting for his father to come to him.

"But my way of thinking was incredibly selfish," he continues, "and more than that, it was unfair. I shouldn't hide the hope that I have. You need to know it exists, and that I will fight for this kingdom as long as I can. But I cannot continue to fight this alone. A kingdom is built by its people, and to not include you in its future was a mistake I will never make again. I owe you an apology, and I offer it, sincerely. Avinea was never mine to save; it was ours."

There is unsettling silence from the crowd. North waits, rigid with nerves, and then, resignation. It's too late. Instead of acting as the prince—and the hope—his people needed, he hid his identity to search for his father unimpeded by obligation. His choice was made years ago, and now his people make theirs. Avinea could still be saved, but not by this gaunt young man who can barely stand straight in the wind. Instead they turn, expectant, to the man who appeared like a miracle, armed with magic and an alliance that could save them all.

"Brindaigel pledges its support," Perrote says, buying into their attention, barely concealing his grin. His voice booms—a thunderbolt where North's voice was a soft wake in the harbor.

North looks over, stricken, as Perrote approaches the railing, displacing him. "My daughter has brokered peace between our kingdoms, and Brindaigel will honor that sanctity with the protection this kingdom needs. An army," he says, turning to North. To most, this gesture would look like an appeal, a doting father-in-law bequeathing a belated wedding gift to a beloved son-in-law.

But most don't see the threat in the curl of his smile, or the battle strategy in the arch of his brow.

"We will protect this city in your absence," Perrote says, turning back to the crowd, "and we will protect this kingdom, so that my daughter's heirs will have a land of their own. So that *her people*"—he lets the moniker settle over them like a mantle of velvet that they pull more tightly for warmth—"have a future."

With a dramatic flourish he spreads his hands wide with a flash of sulfur, a shimmer of magic. A shadow golem emerges—not the birds or the rats he was so skilled at producing in Brindaigel, but a full-grown man in shadowed armor, holding a shadowed sword. It's not a complicated spell, but it's impressive to a crowd of people who haven't seen magic of this size in years.

The figure tenses, preparing for battle, and then lunges toward the crowd, sword striking against the railing of the *Mainstay*, sending sparks and embers flying. The crowd gasps before pressing forward, eager to see more clearly.

My heart lurches into my throat, and I want to scream "Traitors!" at them all. Magic destroyed this kingdom, yet, as Sofreya said, its people still crave it. They're caught up in long-ago memories of a better time and a better world, when magic poured freely from the king's touchstones, and his provosts dispensed spells to address any and every problem they had.

North was right when he said his people don't want to fight for their survival; they just want to be saved. And Perrote is proving he can be the one to do it. They'll never know he's not a king, that his magic was stolen, that it is finite.

The skill is in cheating.

North stands by as Perrote's golem runs through several more paces before Perrote presses his hands together and the soldier disappears in a trail of fading embers. How is North supposed to compete with that?

He can't. Not unless he comes home with his father's heart.

He watches his own people cheer Perrote like he's a hero, a savior—the one who stays behind to protect them while their own prince abandons them the way his father did.

"To ensure your success, my son, I offer you a parting gift." Perrote now turns to North, who straightens at the attention, dark eyes flashing. Perrote smiles widely, extending his hand down the gangplank. "My beloved son, Rialdo, who has earned his place in my own army, and now seeks to earn his place in yours."

Rialdo saunters on board in his Brindaigelian army uniform, a pack slung over one shoulder. His wife and two young daughters trail behind him, expressions stony.

Bryn stiffens, and I glance over at her, surprised. Is that concern for her brother, or concern for her husband? We only have magic enough for ten of us to enter the Burn; Rialdo puts us off-balance. He hasn't trained to fight the hellborne—or himself, should the poison enter his blood—and he will be a stranger among soldiers who have known one another for years. Like me, he is a variable to be viewed with distrust.

North's expression remains carefully guarded. With so many witnesses, to deny Perrote's offer would be an act of hostility, and he can see which way the crowd is leaning. He has no choice but to accept with a tight incline of his chin. Another grateful beneficiary of Perrote's unparalleled generosity. But, like me, he seems bemused by the offering. What does Perrote hope to gain by sending his son into the Burn?

"This should be interesting," North says beneath his breath as he heads belowdecks, leaving Bryn to stand alone, unacknowledged, on the deck.

Perrote offers her his arm, and she takes it stiffly, eyes locking with mine.

Her husband, I think. My sister.

Nobody is safe in this new game of war.

Sailing does not suit me.

Within an hour of our leaving the harbor behind, the sea turns violent. The *Mainstay* dips and bucks with a stomach-churning variability that keeps me pinned to the deck as my breakfast taunts me with a game of will-it-or-won't-it make a triumphant return.

The only relief is the spray of cold water against my flushed face, but it doesn't take long for the water to harden into chips of ice in my hair. There's snow on the horizon, and in my panicked state I imagine it to be an omen of Rook, God Above. Or perhaps punishment from Tell, Goddess Below. We left the earth behind, and she is warning us to go back where we belong.

My misery is compounded by how little the weather seems to affect anyone else. Chadwick and his men run through training exercises on the crowded deck while Rialdo watches from above, cigarette dangling from the corner of his mouth. Bront, one of Davik's brothers, is at the helm while Tieg, the other, secures the ropes around the crates of supplies.

Davik herself maneuvers around the soldiers with a lithe grace that belies her strength. Despite the chill, she only wears a sweater, with the sleeves punched up to her elbows, showing off a map of tattoos and scars wrought from a lifetime of charting her own freedom. I've gleaned her story from the few visits she made to the palace to speak with North. She salvaged the *Mainstay* when she was my age, facing a similar story: younger siblings to feed, dead parents, and no other easy way to make money. But where I found Bryn, Davik found freedom.

My envy is almost palpable.

"I never cared for the water." I stiffen, hugging the railing as North joins me, hands shoved into the pockets of his overcoat. The wind snaps his hair across his forehead, and he absently brushes it aside, only for it to fall forward again. "It doesn't hold magic at all; it doesn't seem to hold history. Not like the earth."

I hesitate in my reply, not wanting to encourage him in conversation, and yet eager for a distraction from the rolling horizon. Behind me I can feel Chadwick's disapproving glare burning into the back of my neck.

Shifting my weight, I search for safer—less personal—topics. Tipping my chin toward Rialdo, who is still watching the soldiers through a haze of cigarette smoke, I say, "Do we know why he's here?"

"His father is an optimistic bastard," North says, almost cheerfully. "Rialdo certainly can't kill me before I kill Merlock, and he's not my heir so he can't do it after I inherit, either. But that doesn't mean he can't *steal* Merlock's heart and ferry it home to his father. After that, it's just a matter of Perrote killing you to get to Bryndalin's blood, killing her, and *then* killing Rialdo to release the heart. Like magic, he inherits the world." A wry smile crosses his face. "I imagine at some point he'll find the time to kill me as well."

My stomach somersaults at his flippancy. "Rialdo's a proxy?"

"Yes," North says, surprised. "You know about proxies?"

I force a smile to hide my guilt. "He's willing to die for his father?"

"His father is willing to kill him, and Rialdo can't argue." He taps his chest, above his heart, where Rialdo—as a member of Perrote's army—wears the same loyalty spell that Alistair does, linking him to his father's every command. The idea of so much murder is a chilling prospect, and I shiver, unnerved by the cold ambition so rampant in their family. Then again, Perrote had seven children, and he only needed one heir. All the rest are redundancies, and they know it.

North leans against the railing and studies me with a slight smile. "Don't fear for me, Miss Locke. If I die a king, it will be at my wife's hands, not her father's. And fortunately, she has no reason to kill me, not while she still has bargaining power."

Me. He means she would use me as a bargaining tool against North's magic.

"I'm sorry," I say. "I never intended to be such a liability."

"Don't apologize," North says with a hint of bitterness, shaking his head. "It was my decision alone that put us in this position."

"Sir." Chadwick clears his throat, and North turns toward him, eyebrows raised in question. Chadwick's eyes cut toward me. "It's time," he says.

North nods and straightens, glancing back toward the diminishing city behind us. "All right, Miss Locke," he says. "The hunt begins."

Eleven

CHADWICK LEADS US BELOWDECKS, THROUGH A NARROW HALL HUNG with nets and ropes. His soldiers eat in the galley kitchen to the left; our bedrolls lie waiting in the cargo hold on the right. But we bypass both and reach the captain's quarters, where he knocks once on the heavy wooden door, before it swings open in invitation.

It's a small room, but cozy, with a built-in bed that reminds me of the bunks in North's wagon, a narrow desk, and a bureau. Even without windows to see outside, I feel the water levels rise and plummet. My stomach follows suit.

Davik stands at the desk, studying a map that's laid out and weighted down by navigational equipment. Sofreya sits perched on the edge of the built-in bed while Chadwick closes the door behind us and takes his usual stance, arms crossed.

"Merlock was in Prevast when you saw him with your mother's

spell," says North, approaching the map and tagging the capital. "But the Burn stretches from the sea back to the Kettich Mountains. We need to know where he is now, to know where to dock."

"Oh," I say. "Of course." My eyes stray toward the door and the thought of miles of water around us, with no access to the Burn to ignite my mother's spell. With North still ignorant of my ability to find Merlock by encouraging my own vices into action, I tentatively ask, "How . . . ?"

North grimaces and runs a hand through his hair, spiking it as Sofreya flinches and stands, forcing a smile. She holds out a small jar full of rocks.

Black rocks.

My heart thumps painfully in my chest with leftover fear from the night before. I look to Chadwick in accusation: It's his fault that North doesn't know another way. "Oh. You're going to poison me."

North won't meet my eyes. "Only a little. It'll be localized. I'll transfer it into you, because Sofreya has never been infected. But then she'll excise it immediately, using a buffer. It's risky, but Avinea is huge; we need to narrow it down as much as possible."

My eyes fall to his wrists, hidden beneath the sleeves of his coat. "Does the council know you're performing magic?"

"The council isn't here."

What am I afraid of? I knew to expect this; it's why I came. And North isn't asking me to cut out his father's heart, only to pinpoint Merlock's location. Yet fear lingers, like cold fingertips pressed against my spine. Perhaps it's not fear, but shame that North is willing to sacrifice so much for his kingdom, and I'm not.

"Miss Locke, you are not obligated—"

"I know," I interrupt. I meet Chadwick's gaze in challenge. Shrugging out of my coat, I fumble to unbutton the collar of my soldier's uniform and expose the clean black tunic underneath. Sofreya directs me to the bed, and I sit, briefly closing my eyes as the boat bucks again.

"So how does this work?" Davik asks, inching closer. "Will you magically vanish into the Burn?"

I force a smile to hide my growing unease. "It's almost like I become two people. One stays behind and one wanders off."

"It's a scrying spell." North takes a seat beside me. The bed is narrow, and there's no room to be polite; our legs collide as he angles himself for a better position. "Only instead of needing water, it requires poison to work."

Unlike the shadow birds or rats that Perrote's guards used to spy on us in Brindaigel, I project my entire body with the spell—including all its human weaknesses. Shadow rats could still bite. And I could still die.

Davik shakes her head and rubs her arms, muttering under her breath about defying the gods. She's Chadwick's age, and only has memories of what magic can do when left to fester. Like Sofreya, she views magic as a danger.

I can't argue with that.

The spells at North's wrists have been removed, but this close, I can see the finer details of the spell at his throat, perpendicular lines intersected with circles and dots.

"What does that one do?" I ask.

North cuffs his shirtsleeves back. "Gives me strength," he says.

"And how does that work?"

The edge of his mouth quirks into half a smile. "Magic."

Sofreya hands him the jar, and the stones click together as he curls one into his fingers. I rake the collar of my tunic back to expose the puckered, stitched skin above my mother's spell, and he sucks in a deep, steadying breath.

"I'm so sorry," he says, pressing the stone to my skin.

The first time the infection entered my blood, it was amplified through Bryn, and the pain was bright enough to burn the stars from the skies. But like this, with North guiding the poison, it's more of an ache, like too much wine or too much wanting. The poison calls my vices out of hiding, and a tiny worm of desire inches through my stomach at North's proximity. This close, I see him for who he really is: barely nineteen, and not nearly as confident as he pretends to be. Same as the first time I met him, he's in need of a shave, but it suits him, with his serious eyes and his parted lips and his total concentration on the task at hand.

And then the spell ignites with a flash of warmth and a tug behind my heart, and I'm flying over miles of water, over the jagged coastline of Avinea, past abandoned cities and empty fields and campfires demarking tribes of hellborne surviving in a vast expanse of nothingness.

But I'm moving too fast to see anything concrete, to recognize any landmark I might be able to match against North's maps. Panic begins to claw at my chest, digging into my throat, and I fight the spell the way Sofreya taught me, trying to slow it down, to give myself time to breathe.

As suddenly as I began, I stop, dropping to a dune of ash as tall as the building beside it. I gain my feet, breathless as if I raced here instead of flew. I'm standing in a wide street with the ruins of wealthy townhomes on either side. There are mountains ahead of me, hazy in the distance, and the remnants of an enormous church behind me. The roof has collapsed, and all that remains are arches and walls and the frames of broken windows.

And a circle of small stones, stacked in offering along one of the rotting sills. As previously, some have turned black while others are varying shades of gray, indicating how long they've been exposed to the Burn.

Bemused, I reach for the one closest to me, slender, pale—*warm*.

Something inside the church creaks, and I drop into a defensive crouch, inwardly cursing myself for hiding Chadwick's dagger deep in my bedroll for the journey, out of reach for practical use. I'm not ready for this, and already the fear of my last encounter with Merlock clouds my thoughts, makes me frantic. Another crack sounds, and as I press myself against the half-wall beside me, one of the remaining arches breaks loose of its moorings and collapses into a cloud of rubble and dust. Shadows flicker; I hear muted voices, as though caught underwater. Two men, arguing.

Coughing, I back away from the church, eyes watering from displaced ash. One of the voices is Merlock's, but the other one I cannot place. Does Merlock have an ally here in the Burn?

Without warning, the ground dissolves beneath me and I'm thrown back into my body on Davik's cot, gasping as my heart hits my spine and bounces back against my ribs.

North is there, concern etched across his shadowed face. "Are you all right?"

I'm sprawled on my back. I scramble to sit up again, only to see the others staring at me as if I'm a ghost. My tunic is soaked with sweat and my chest hurts, as if I were dealt a strong blow from a worthy opponent.

"I'm sorry," North says. "I didn't know how else to bring you back. . . ."

He's holding a knife, the blade slick with blood. *My* blood.

Still panting, I examine my arm and see the shallow cut he made. "You were in a trance," he explains, his voice full of self-recrimination. "I thought perhaps pain might wake you up."

I force a smile. I swallow hard, fighting to control my breathing. "You were right. Thank you."

Chadwick clears his throat. "Did it work?"

"How could it?" Davik looks skeptical as she hands North a clean bandage. "She was here the entire time."

"She's glowing." Sofreya looks like she might cry. "Look at her, lit up like starlight. It's a gift from the gods."

"So where are we going?" Chadwick asks, moving to the map.

I press the heel of my hand to my temple as North gently binds my bleeding arm. It is a risky move, to have his skin so close to mine, and yet I'm not in a state to care.

"It wasn't Prevast," I say, watching him work. "It was somewhere smaller. Near the mountains. A village, maybe."

"The mountains?" Chadwick exchanges skeptical looks with North. "There are no mountains in Prevast."

"He wasn't *in* Prevast," I repeat.

"Are you sure? It's a big city."

"I'm positive," I say, seething at Chadwick's patronizing tone.

"The mountains are on the southern edge of the Burn," says North with a frown. "Was it the Kettich Mountains or the Heralds?"

"I don't know."

"We don't have enough magic to cross the entire Burn looking for him," Sofreya says. "If he's moving, we need to know where he's going, not where he's been."

"What else did you see?" Chadwick demands.

"There was a church. Or at least, what was left of one."

North presses his thumbs once against the bandage, soft as a kiss, before standing and joining Chadwick at the desk. "What type of church?"

"I don't know," I say. "It had . . . church things. Arches. Windows. There was a waterfall behind it."

"Oksgar," North says with complete conviction, pressing his finger to the map. He repeats the name beneath his breath. A spark of excitement lights his face, and I stare at him greedily, hungry for more of this forgotten North, where enthusiasm outweighs obligation. "Here. If we dock in Bresdol—"

"There's no harbor in Bresdol," Chadwick interrupts, shaking his head. He points higher up the map. "We're safer in one of these fishing villages. The hellborne will have no interest in them, with the cliffs preventing the dead magic from seeping into the ground. If Merlock is really strolling through the Burn, we can't risk sailing too far south or we'll miss him."

"Come on." Sofreya takes a seat beside me, already armed with a stone buffer to excise the small amount of poison North transferred into me. "We don't want that to fester."

I turn to face her more fully, and something drops from my lap in the process. North glances over, then startles. "What is that?"

A stone. I bend for it, then roll it across my palm. "It's from the Burn."

"That's impossible." He takes it from me. "A stone this size would be consumed with dead magic. But this is still warm."

"There was a whole pile of them, stacked like—" I break off, darting a look to North, whose expression has become impossible to read. "Like the shelves of your wagon," I finish softly. And the windows of the rooms he once lived in at the monastery.

Like father, like son.

"You brought something tangible back from the Burn?" Davik reaches for the stone, and I offer it to her, but North edges away from me as if stung.

"North?" I start, but he yanks the door open and stalks outside, letting the door slam shut behind him.

Awkward silence fills the room until Davik clears her throat. "Ben? An explanation, please?"

Chadwick hangs his head and sighs. "Merlock and Corthen went to war, but they were still brothers despite it all. Whenever one of them wished to speak to the other under a banner of truce, they would leave a cairn of stones."

Davik exchanges puzzled looks with me. "So what does that mean?"

"I can only assume it means Merlock knows we're coming," Chadwick says, looking toward the door. "And he wants to talk."

Twelve

THAT NIGHT I FIND NORTH BACK ON THE DECK, BUNDLED AGAINST the cold as the dark coastline unfurls ahead of us. The skies have cleared and stars brighten them, but we're long past the start of the Burn. Thick smoke hovers against the shore and spills across the water. Fragments of abandoned cities slip in and out of view, along with brighter pockets of gold fire and red embers as the Burn eats afresh through the earth.

I lean against the railing, finding a star low on the horizon, and fix my sight upon it, a trick Davik suggested, to keep my stomach calm against the battering skips of the prow as Tieg steers us toward the northwestern edge of Avinea.

"Chadwick thinks Merlock knows we're coming," I say at last.

North sighs. "Of course he does." He glances over. "I was seven years old when the monks legitimized me," he says. "My mother was livid. She would have raised me a bastard, my blood a weapon, and my mission a secret. Instead I was made a prince. The monks thought I would be a beacon of hope, a possibility of a future in which Merlock could be killed. Instead they made me a target, an excuse for all the anarchy since I was just a child. I was forced to hide in the palace to avoid being hunted like my father, either by the hellborne hoping for a widespread Burn, or by the people still hurting from his betrayal." Sighing, he drops his chin toward his chest. "But I didn't even know if my father knew I existed until recently."

I watch him from the corner of my eye, mulling over his speculation. I wonder if I should mention what I saw the other night, Merlock watching a flickering memory of his son playing in the hall, asking North to speak to him and let him go. "I think he's always known," I say. "And maybe in some twisted way he's just trying to save you."

North snorts, derisive. "By killing Avinea?"

"By warning you that even kings are mortals," I say, "and mortals were never meant to wield magic. Apparently no one's seen him since the Burn began—"

"Because he couldn't bear to face the consequences of his choices. He's a coward."

"You said yourself, the Burn originally spread because fortune hunters got infected and poisoned the earth where they were buried." Giving him a pointed look, I say, "Merlock was never the one expanding the Burn, and there has to be a reason. Maybe that reason was you."

North shakes his head. "You give him far too much humanity, Miss Locke."

Perhaps he's right. After all, my mother tried to kill him—more than once. And while the mystery of my mother has been unraveling thread by thread, slowly reshaping the way I once saw her, I'm still too close to see a pattern. Between her and Merlock, they can't both be heroes, and a selfish part of me wants my mother to be right, for Merlock to have always been the enemy.

I wonder if North feels the same in reverse.

We lapse into silence. Then North shifts, pointing ahead. "There it is."

I frown, seeing nothing but shadow. But then it appears, like one of Rook's mythical giants, hunched on the cliffs overhead: the castle of Prevast. Built of dark stone, it rises from the earth, stretching toward the stars with dozens of towers and spires. A veranda juts out over the water, supported by arches carved from the cliffs themselves. One of the castle towers rises higher than the rest. A watchtower.

"It's beautiful," I say.

"It's dead," a voice says flatly behind us.

I stiffen as Rialdo saunters up to the railing, flicking ashes into the water below.

"There's dignity in death," North says, "when the alternative is to suffer."

"Dignity?" Rialdo scoffs. "Almost a million people lived up there and Merlock left them all to rot. How many of them died with grace? How many were Burned alive?"

"Too many, and all innocent," North says, dipping his chin into the collar of his coat. "The city was protected by magic for years without fault. Yet as soon as Corthen began stealing that magic, the provosts said the spell was weakening because the king was weakening. The cowards who believed them fled. Those who remained loyal to my father stayed." He shakes his head, lips twisted in distaste. "Merlock was a hero once, but his people abandoned him because he wasn't infallible. And in his fury he Burned them all, even those who would have fought for him."

"He was complacent," Rialdo says. "His brother was a threat, but he refused to acknowledge that until it was too late."

"Like your father refused to acknowledge Bryn until she became more powerful than him?" I ask.

He straightens, eyes flashing, but North cuts in. "Merlock knew Corthen never had a chance," he says softly, his words nearly torn loose by the wind. "Like most second-borns, Corthen was a mere shadow of his brother. War was the only way he would ever earn glory."

Rialdo rolls his eyes at the implication that he, too, is merely a shadow of his father, or now, of his youngest sister.

North watches the castle recede back into the night with a rawness in his expression that hurts. "People are impatient," he says. "Their temperaments are fickle. When Merlock returned from the war overseas, ready to embrace the people he loved, he found a city that had turned its back on him in favor of his brother and the promise of something more, something better."

"*Was* Corthen better?" I ask.

North shrugs. "Corthen was a thief and a liar," he says. "He had no magical abilities of his own, and yet he managed to convince the kingdom that Merlock was weak and defenseless. He appealed to Avinea's insatiable greed by promising egalitarian access to magic he didn't even have. No more provosts, no more touchstones. Magic everywhere, for everyone."

"Then you don't blame Merlock for destroying everything?"

"I didn't say that," he says. "Merlock didn't have to kill his brother to keep his crown, but he did it anyway, to prove his power to the people. And it poisoned his heart. That he blames Avinea for making him do it, rather than accepting responsibility, is entirely on him."

I shiver, hugging myself. "Showing mercy could have saved him."

Rialdo flicks his cigarette into the water and pulls away from the railing. He smirks, but it barely conceals a newfound tightness in his expression. "Mercy is for those who lack conviction."

North waits for Rialdo to disappear belowdecks, spreading his slender hands across the railing. "Mercy is often the more difficult choice. Sparing Corthen's life would have made Merlock look weak. And more than anything, he was afraid of looking weak."

I shove my hands into my coat pockets. "I think Merlock wants to be found," I say again. "Maybe after all these years he's looking for your mercy. Or forgiveness."

North grunts in derision. "Then he's going to die a very disappointed man." Glancing over, he forces a smile. "Thank you for your help this afternoon."

"Of course. That's why I'm here."

"Of course," he repeats, but his smile drops as he lapses into silence, staring out across the inky sea.

After another miserable day at sea, it's almost dark again by the time Davik calls out the warning that we've reached our destination. There's no harbor ahead, only a small alcove carved into the cliffs, with decimated piers half-crumbled into the water. Not broken from the Burn but from the sea and a lack of maintenance. We've passed a handful of fishing villages like this already, safe pockets of land protected by the rocky walls around them—like Brindaigel kept safe in the mountains, but in miniature. Villagers fled years ago out of fear of being trapped, but a few houses remain, elevated on stilts, emerging from the thickening fog. Other houses, farther back, are built into the cliffs themselves, their roofs green with moss, and white from the ash that falls from above like snow.

No one speaks as we navigate closer and drop anchor a safe distance away from any possible shoals or rubble unseen in the water. Adrenaline hums through me as I realize that this is the moment that changes everything. For all Chadwick trained his men against the hellborne, there was little he could do to prepare them for the Burn. If Sofreya's spells don't hold, we'll all be poisoned slowly, potentially without notice, until we're too far inland and too infected to turn back.

Davik and her brothers remain on board, but the rest of us drop rowboats into the water, loaded with enough supplies to drag our back ends lower into the water.

The fog thickens as we strike sand. The six soldiers begin unloading cargo and stacking crates inside one of the cliffside houses. Its door is warped out of its frame, the window glass is splintered but still holding strong, and inside is warmer than expected, despite hard-packed dirt floors and damp walls that have sprouted with moss and small mushrooms. Rotting fishing nets hang from the walls, slick with algae and a crusty buildup of salt.

"It's only temporary," North says with a bracing smile, eyes catching mine.

I shrug off his apology. "You've never seen the Brim," I say. "This is luxury."

Nobody else seems to agree. After the tidy barracks of the palace, dirt floors and damp walls are hardly appealing, and some argument ensues over who gets to lay their bedrolls on the two bed frames remaining, and who is relegated to the floor.

"We won't be sleeping here," Chadwick finally says, ending the disagreement before it turns physical. "Catch your breath and say your prayers, because we leave in a few hours."

"What, in the dark?" Rialdo asks, concerned. Even those of us raised in Brindaigel know the horror stories of what happens in the Burn after dark—when the hellborne are far more active. Far hungrier.

"In the dark," Chadwick agrees. "The ash we unsettle won't be as easy to see, making us harder to track."

"And won't that precaution be negated by the magic spells we're all wearing?" Rialdo asks darkly.

Nobody replies, but it's an understood possibility the soldiers have prepared for, evidenced by the weaponry they strap to their backs and hips. It is not so much *if* we fight the hellborne, but *when*, and how many.

Due to my limited training, Chadwick refused me a sword, allowing me a matching set of daggers instead. But I have my own unique armor: a breastplate with hammered iron in the front and a leather holster in the back, intended to mute my mother's spell and keep me from being dragged across the Burn by accident. The breastplate will also keep the spell from potentially draining too quickly. We have no idea how long it will last.

I feel foolish pulling on the armor while the others are all dressed smartly in their matching leather tunics and boots, but it's my own fault. North wanted me to learn how to control the spell to unfurl it more slowly, but like my training with Chadwick, three distracted weeks with Sofreya produced unsatisfactory results, so here I am.

While the others double-check their packs and eat a quick meal, I duck outside to the empty beach, eager for a moment alone and room to breathe. My nerves are beginning to fray from such close quarters, and I need them to be steady before we enter the Burn, or my anxiety will pull the poison through my blood even faster.

The water is barely visible through the fog, but as I draw closer, the waves fall into focus, washing ashore with white ribbons of foam. Stones and a thick layer of broken seashells are left behind, and I crouch out of reach of the tide and pick through the sand, unearthing an unbroken snail shell colored sunset orange and pearly pink, a shock of color against the faded world around me.

A souvenir for Cadence.

I didn't cry when Cadence told me she hated me, and I refuse to cry now, not with the Burn waiting at my back. And yet, cradling the shell in my hands, I once again acknowledge that I may not be the one to give it to her, that I might not make it back alive. This fact has always been a worry, needling at the back of my mind, but now it feels more definite, unarguable. Our final words to each other were far from forgiving, and I inwardly chastise myself for not trying harder, for not pushing further, for leaving her to Bryn—

"You shouldn't wander away from the others."

I startle as Chadwick emerges from the fog, armed for battle. "The fog is thick," he says, "and plays tricks with your eyes. There's old magic in the ground above us, Locke. You can't always trust your senses."

I nod and pocket the shell as if it's a promise, stepping past him toward the camp. We haven't spoken since the night I failed at becoming North's proxy, and I can't help but feel like he blames me for being weak. Compared to his six soldiers, fully trained, ready to die, I feel like a fraud.

"Locke." He stops me, a hand on my arm. "You don't have to do this. I asked too much of you the other night; it wasn't fair to expect that sacrifice. If you need to be back in New Prevast with your sister—"

Ostensibly it sounds like a token of peace, an easy out for me and one that sings to the ache in my heart. But honestly, it's the same concern he voiced at the palace: If I'm going to be a liability, I'll be left behind. It would be insulting, if he weren't so practical.

"We all have obligations in life, whether we choose them or not," I finally say. "Finding Merlock is apparently mine. Cadence will survive until I come back."

Chadwick nods and thumps my arm once in a gesture of awkward truce; I'm gratified he doesn't remind me that the odds are stacked against us ever coming back. Lies are easier to believe when left unchallenged. "The others are waiting," he says.

When we emerge from the fog, I see North standing at the center of a loose circle of Chadwick's handpicked soldiers—Gideon,

Terik, Jarrett, Cohl, Elin, and Sull, all of them with more than five years of training. But with the addition of Rialdo to the party, Sull, the youngest, will stay behind to guard the supplies. Like Tobek, he doesn't take the new assignment well, glowering at the others, who share a nervous energy.

While North is not dressed in uniform, he still looks imposing, regal, like a leader. His eyes meet Chadwick's and he nods once as he takes a breath.

"Here it comes," Rialdo mutters.

"I want to thank all of you," North says, looking each of us in the eye. "What I ask of you is not easy, and is not guaranteed. That you're here in spite of the risks is a testament to your courage and your dedication to restoring Avinea. Such sacrifice will not be forgotten."

The soldiers murmur acknowledgment but Rialdo audibly yawns, earning a reproving look from Chadwick. Yet unlike the tepid reaction at the harbor, North's words seem to energize the soldiers.

Still, the procession up the cliff is quiet, solemn, each of us lost in our own thoughts—our own doubts. By the time we reach the top, my nerves have sharpened into dread, and I survey the Burn spread ahead of us. Even knowing my limited role in this expedi-tion, I feel exposed, vulnerable.

The feeling seems to pass through the group, as everyone fully realizes what we're doing. We are not the first contingent to enter the Burn to search for Merlock. Years ago, when the Burn was still new and Merlock still more man than myth, rich nobles— both from Avinea and from other power-hungry continents within reach—funded expeditions to find Merlock and reclaim the magic the kingdom so relied upon. Avinea's best soldiers crossed into the Burn, believing themselves invincible and their king a weakened coward, easy to find, easy to kill.

None of them returned.

There are no surviving journals or notes from these failed expeditions for us to study. No warnings for us to heed. Our plan is reliant entirely on whispered rumors and educated guesses. Yet this isn't a riot in the city, or a hellborne attack on a farming village, which are small, easy to manage battles. This is the Burn, a plague born of corrupted magic, and our only defense is more magic, provided by a king that no one had even heard of until three weeks ago, dispensed by a woman with barely any training.

In this moment we all realize: Plans are easy in the safety of the palace. Faced with reality, even a solid strategy can begin to fray. And if nothing else, every one of us knows the danger of loose threads and frayed edges.

With embarrassed glances several of the soldiers check and double-check the spells Sofreya cast across their forearms. Even Rialdo is strangely quiet, pale as his hand rests on the pommel of his sword.

"Locke." Chadwick gestures me forward.

Moment of truth. The others shift, curious as I unbuckle my breastplate and set it at my feet. Drying my hands against my trousers, I step forward, shoulders back and chin raised, defiant of Chadwick's limited expectations of me, defiant of the soldiers' distrust of my role. Sofreya stands by, ready to intercede if something goes wrong, but the ash gives way to the earth below. Grass springs forth, and, emboldened, I take another step.

The familiar itch starts beneath my skin, a strange, welcome heat that spreads from my heart throughout my body. And then the thread of magic unspools and I surrender myself over miles of misshapen terrain, toward a watchtower that rises from the ash like a skeletal tree. I quickly note an abandoned settlement at its feet, and a campfire somewhere near the tower, flickering shadows across barren walls. The mountains are far to my right, no more than black peaks against the starry sky.

Satisfied, I withdraw one of my twin daggers and pierce the pad of my thumb. The pain slams me back into my body, and I stagger into Sofreya's waiting arms.

"Well done," she says.

"Did you see him?" Chadwick asks.

"Let her breathe!" Sofreya shoots him a scathing look as she buckles my armor back into place and then forces a canteen into my hands. I dutifully take a sip, but quickly press it back to her, trying to ignore the way the others look at me, a mixture of curiosity and fear.

"What just happened?" Gideon asks, but North overrides him, map already open.

"Watchtower," I say, describing the scene as best I can, ignoring the way the others' eyes prickle my skin.

"Is she hellborne?" Elin asks.

"Just a magician," Jarrett says.

"None of us are magicians," Gideon cuts in, eyeing me skeptically. "That's the point. So we don't steal the magic and disappear with it."

"Then what *is* she?"

"A valuable asset to the expedition," Chadwick says, silencing his soldiers with a scowl.

"Dorrent is northeast of Oksgar," North says. "It's the closest watchtower within range."

"So he's still on the move." Chadwick frowns over the map, tracing a line between Oksgar and Dorrent.

North nods grimly, folding the map closed. "You were right," he says to Chadwick. "If we had sailed to Bresdol, we would have been two days behind. From here we can move northeast and we might have a chance of intercepting him."

To his credit, Chadwick doesn't even gloat. Instead he shoulders his role as captain and takes the first step forward, to join me in the Burn. There's no dramatic parting of the ash, no sudden clearing of a path. There is only ground to cover, which is also what makes the mission such a deadly risk: We have no way of knowing if the spells are working.

So we'd better move fast.

Thirteen

WE BEGIN TENTATIVELY, TESTING THE GROUND AND LEARNING THE contours of the dunes that spill around us. But then we become bolder, striding forth like a roiling thundercloud, kicking up ash that burns our eyes and makes us cough. Yet beneath the discomfort lies an undercurrent of satisfaction. We are among the first humans to cross this landscape in years, and in this instant I think we all believe we will save Avinea.

The feeling doesn't last long.

Elin hears it first. She stops, head twisted toward the darkness behind us. "What is that?"

"It's the ash," Terik says, waggling his eyebrows. "It whispers, if you listen long enough."

"Just don't listen too long," Gideon chimes, elbowing Elin as he passes her, "or it'll bury you ten feet deep."

The others laugh nervously, but Chadwick silences them with a scowl. "It's the sea hitting the cliffs," he says. "The sound carries."

Jarrett holds out an unlit lantern. "Do we need a light?"

"Absolutely not," Chadwick says. "The whole purpose of traveling at night is to remain unnoticed."

But then something cries in the night, a hair-raising screech that stops us all dead in our tracks, and we tip our faces to the dark sky, searching for the source.

"What was that?" Jarrett demands, bracing his legs as he reaches for one of his two swords.

Gideon simply rolls his eyes. "Does it matter? It's the Burn."

"The shadowbred," North says tightly, resuming the pace. Then, more loudly, "We knew to expect opposition."

Rialdo twitches as the others fall in line behind North. Like me, he was raised to believe in only one villain in Avinea—the plague. The more nuanced legends are surprises. "And what are the shadowbred?"

"A myth," Chadwick says irritably, "intended to keep idiot fortune hunters from entering the Burn and getting eaten alive."

"They say the earth wasn't the only thing Merlock poisoned," North argues. "The shadows themselves began to feed on the poison, to breathe, and they began to grow hungry. And now they hunt. *Supposedly*," he adds drily, on seeing Chadwick's withering look.

"That is ridiculous," Elin says, but without any conviction.

"Is it?" Gideon arches an eyebrow, walking backward to better see our expressions. "The hellborne have given in to their darkest vices. They're all cowards, deep down, and the dark is just another fear they don't want to face."

"You are completely full of shit," Cohl says, not unkindly.

Gideon laughs, bright and startling in the darkness. "Why do you think so many of the hellborne wander out of the Burn at night?"

"Because they're hungry," I say. "They want slaves and clean blood—"

"Because they're afraid of the dark," he interrupts. "And if we're the best Avinea has to offer, maybe you should listen to Prince Corbin before we become the last Avinea has to offer."

"Enough," Chadwick warns.

The others continue to joke in hushed whispers, to stave off our growing unease. I envy them their shared camaraderie. My fingers close around the shell in my pocket to remind me that I'm not alone either, even if my sister is hundreds of miles away.

But jokes only last so long. Within the hour, we've returned to somber silence. Every unaccounted sound becomes a threat that we turn toward in unison; we strain to see into the darkness around us. When Chadwick calls for a rest two hours later, we drink from our canteens in a tight circle, as if to shut out the growing shadows.

"How much farther is this watchtower?" Elin asks, mopping sweat off her face. Despite the wintry air, the Burn is warm beneath our feet, and our packs feel heavier because of the ash we have to kick through—as thick and unyielding as snow. While Chadwick has attempted to lead us through the narrow gulches of thinner ash, dunes of it still rise around us, blotting out the sky in some instances, carved into monstrous shapes by the wind.

"We would save time if we just . . . magicked ourselves there," Jarrett says. His glasses are pushed up to his forehead, filmed with grime. The skin around his eyes is lighter than the rest of his face, giving him an owlish look. "That'll cut time off our need for these protection spells. It'll even out."

"There's not nearly enough magic for that kind of spell," Sofreya says quickly, stricken. "Not to mention—"

"It's beyond your ability," North finishes for her. Sofreya flinches at the assessment, but he doesn't seem to notice. Rialdo does, however, eyebrow inching higher with interest.

"Then just send Locke ahead," Jarrett presses. "Whatever that spell was, it got her to Dorrent in seconds."

"Right. And then what? Locke holds Merlock hostage for us until we all arrive? Or better yet, she kills him single-handedly?" Chadwick snorts and shakes his head, dismissing the thought as ludicrous, despite having suggested the very same idea only two nights ago. It stings when the others laugh at my inexperience, and whether Chadwick meant it as such or not, his comment feels like an accusation. I turn and take a step away from the circle, sufficiently wounded.

"Locke," Chadwick warns. "Stay close."

I ignore his reproach. I'm not used to relying on planning by committee, and it's frustrating, to be standing still when all I want is to move.

"Locke!"

"I'm *right here*," I snap, spinning back toward him, only to freeze. A hellborne woman stands in front of me, grinning widely, showcasing a mouth of poison and rotted teeth. Even more have circled the others, an entire tribe. Some carry torches, the flickering light casting deep shadows across their pitted, cracking faces. Others carry weapons built from scraps found in the ruins of the Burn: twisted metal and petrified wood fashioned into pole arms and axes.

I don't even hear Chadwick give the command; his soldiers react without prompting. As one, swords are unsheathed and the defense begins. I scramble for one of my daggers as the woman advances, her axe weighted in both hands. She leans back for the swing just as I free the dagger, only to drop it into the ash at my feet. I bend for the blade, and her strike narrowly misses me.

To hell with the dagger, I think. I tackle the woman at the knees, and we sink into the ash, choking on it as I pin her to the scorching ground. In her surprise, she drops her axe and begins to grapple with me, yellowed fingernails clawing uselessly against my iron breastplate. I reach for my second dagger as a man grabs me by my shortened hair and yanks me back. My feet fumble for traction but find none, and I end up on my knees with my back to him as he twists my hair around his forearm, exposing my throat. Ash settles in my eyes, blurring my vision.

"Where is it?" he demands. "I smell it on you."

The protection spell. Cast on my forearms, it is not muted by the iron armor I wear. Even beneath our uniforms, the magic calls to the hellbornes' addiction.

By now the woman has regained her feet—and her axe. After unsheathing my second dagger, I slam it behind me, feeling the blade sink into something soft, possibly fleshy. Heat pours across my hand, but I know the value of a weapon and refuse to relinquish it, wrenching it free as the man releases my hair with a curse. Ignoring the pain in my scalp, I lunge forward, swinging for the woman's throat. She backs out of the way and I stumble, plunging back into ash.

"Faris!"

A bright, crackling light illuminates everything in perfect clarity . . . and then the hellborne begin screaming in agony. I back away as fast as I can. I know this spell, and I know how it ends. As expected, the hellborne clutch at their cracking chests, where poison steams into the colder air before their hearts evaporate and they fall back, dead.

An eerie silence follows the spell. North still stands, hand outstretched, shoulders heaving with the force of what he has done. His eyes meet mine, and my lips part to—what? Thank him for saving me? Chastise him for using magic? There's no need for either. Horror fills his face, remorse as he realizes the repercussions of his choice. Beside him Chadwick stands back, stunned.

The ground around us begins to shiver, and then buckles with a bone-knocking *boom*. I struggle to my feet, only to stagger to keep balance.

Cohl is the nearest to me, arms thrown out. "What—" she begins, just as the dunes of ash that surround us collapse in an avalanche, swallowing everyone in its path.

Fourteen

AVALANCHES WERE COMMON IN BRINDAIGEL, BUT OFTEN HARMLESS. Shelves of snow would collapse into the gorge that surrounded the kingdom, rarely reaching us on the other side. At most, the farming terraces would need to be shoveled clear—an opportunity for people like me, when jobs were scarcer to come by in the cold.

This is so much worse.

As a wall of ash hits me, I somersault head over heels and backward again, flattening against the earth, before being swept back up toward the sky. Without my mother's spell to help me, ash clogs my nose and my ears and begins seeping through my flattened lips, filling my lungs. But then my feet find ground, and a body collides against mine. I reach out, clutching for purchase, finding an arm and grabbing it tightly. The two of us emerge from the first undulating wave of ash, coughing and sputtering, too blinded to see each other until we've wiped our faces clear. Jarrett has lost his glasses, and he squints at me, eyes red-rimmed and watery. "Locke?"

A second wave hits, smaller than the first, strong enough to knock us off our feet. We lose hold of each other, but moments later, I'm able to brace my weight against a third, smaller wave, then slog my way toward Jarrett.

Straight ahead, North and Chadwick stand back-to-back, guarded from the ash by a spell. North's hands glow silver as he launches himself forward and grabs at a flash of skin. Cohl is yanked to her feet and handed off to Chadwick, who pushes her onto a shelf of rock that's been exposed, where Rialdo and Elin already stand. Rialdo silently watches North, but Elin screams the others' names, shielding her eyes to search around her.

"North!" I yell.

His eyes meet mine. Relief wars with something else, but before he can do anything, the ground shifts once more, and Jarrett plummets from view. I dive for him and grab a fistful of his uniform tunic, holding so tightly, I feel the fabric start to tear.

Another flash of light. Ash swells out of our way, forming towering walls on either side of us. North stands at the opposite end, straining to contain the ash—fighting against his father's corrupted magic with more of his own. His body shakes as his hands glow silver in the dark, casting erratic shadows around him. Chadwick finds Sofreya and Terik, and I haul Jarrett after them, bypassing North as he closes his hand into a fist. The ash drops like wet sand around all of us. A moment later the moon reappears, no more than a wink of welcome overhead.

"Gideon," Elin says. "Where's Gideon?"

We all stare at the ash behind us, as still as the harbor on a windless day. Elin takes a step forward, to the edge of the rock, but Chadwick holds her back, expression grim. "It's too deep," he says. "We'll lose you, too—*your majesty!*"

North launches himself off the rock, lands chest-deep in ash, and begins fighting his way through. Chadwick calls him back, but North ignores him until, several feet out, he nearly slips. Only then does he return, avoiding our eyes. He accepts Jarrett's offer of an arm up and scrambles back atop the rock, looking haunted.

"I'm so sorry," he says, spreading his hands and staring at them in dismay. "I didn't consider how hungry the Burn would be."

Like the rotting manor home I saw Merlock in, collapsing with the weight of whatever spell he used to summon North's childhood image. After so long with nothing new to feed on, North's spells were like firewood to the acres of ash around us. Even now, the ground hums.

"We have to keep moving," Chadwick says grimly. "Magic like that will be felt for miles."

Elin shakes her head, still searching the ash. "Gideon—"

"Knew the risks," Chadwick says, rubbing his mouth, his voice hoarse. "We all did."

The shock of it leaves us all silent, before Cohl voices the question on everyone's faces: "Why did you use magic against them? Those hellborne had no spells to protect them. I thought we were here to fight for you, not the other way around."

The accusation makes North flinch, his eyes straying toward me in silent confession. "I reacted the way I know how," he says, voice hollow. "I've spent too long on my own."

"You panicked," Rialdo says flatly. "You saw Locke go down and risked the rest of us to save her."

Chadwick shoots North a warning look not to answer, a hand pressed to North's arm. "What's done is done," he says. "We move on. Gideon will be greatly missed, but he would not want us to sacrifice ourselves or this mission on his behalf."

Nobody argues, but something changes as we resume our journey; a shiver of resentment against North begins to emerge, as narrow as a thread, linking Chadwick's soldiers.

We don't stop all night, and in the light from the first edge of pink in the sky, a watchtower rises on the horizon. North beckons us to stop, and the soldiers crouch low to hide their positions, surveying the scene. There is no smoke, no footsteps, nothing to indicate that anyone is here, nor do we see any rising ash in the distance to hint at someone nearby.

"We'll send a scout ahead while the rest of us fan out and approach from all sides," Chadwick starts, surveying his soldiers.

"Or we throw the plan out the window and charge in with swords raised," Elin mutters, as North ignores Chadwick and launches himself to his feet, striding toward the tower.

Chadwick sighs, shoulders slumping in defeat as he pushes himself after North. The rest of us exchange glances and follow. Jarrett and Cohl maintain some sense of the original plan, splitting off to approach the tower from opposite sides, but the rest of us keep straight, jogging to catch up.

An eerie silence clings to the tower; the nearby settlement is still haloed with smoke. Not the hazy, diluted veil of the Burn but the curling tendrils of a campfire recently extinguished. Bones, dirty syringes, and heavy footprints mar the ground, and there's an epithet scrawled in the dirt: *Long live the withered king.*

Baedan. She hurled those same words at North less than a month ago, after nearly breaking him in her effort to obtain his blood.

North ducks into the tower, only to emerge moments later, expression as dark as thunder. He approaches the smoldering fire, kicking at its embers with a barrage of profanity that shocks the rest of us to silence.

"Run the perimeter," Chadwick orders after a moment. "Spread out and ensure no one is still here."

Terik, Jarrett, and Elin dutifully break apart as Chadwick approaches North, directing him into the tower. I follow discreetly, keeping to the shadows.

"How did she know?" North asks, pacing the tiled floor of the tower. "How could she possibly get here before us? What source does she have that's better than ours?"

"Perhaps it was coincidence." Chadwick notices me. "Wait outside, Locke."

"She's *mocking* me," North says. "She knew we'd be here."

"He can't be far," I say, ignoring Chadwick, fumbling the latches at my waist. "It was his campfire I saw from the beach, and that was barely eight hours ago. Get me out of this armor, and I can pinpoint his location again—"

Crossing the floor, I stumble over a clutch of stones, and they scatter beneath my feet. We stare at them in silence as North crouches, hand hovering over one of them with an unreadable expression.

"He was here," he says, and his voice sends chills down my back.

A shout outside draws our attention, and we hurry toward the noise. Cohl stands, one gloved hand hooked around the throat of a man struggling to stay on his feet. His clothes hang off him in tatters; his hair is matted and thick with grime, skin blistered and cracked. Poison seeps from open wounds, spreading along his collar, in his hair. His face is familiar, thinner than before but still filled with unwarranted arrogance. Kellig. Baedan's more talented spellcaster and a man who tried—and failed—to kill me several times.

"I found him skulking through the buildings there," Cohl explains.

North sees Kellig and tenses, but Kellig only grins, exposing the missing tooth taken from him by the opium dealer a month ago.

"Your majesty," he says, in a voice worn thin from the ash-cloaked air of the Burn. "An honor to be in your presence again." He tries to bow, but Cohl only tightens her stranglehold, and he chokes, shooting her a furious scowl.

North exhales, annoyed. "Kill him," he says, and turns away.

"Wait! You did this to me!"

North pauses but doesn't turn. "No," he says, "I killed you. *You* chose to become hellborne."

Kellig's features twist into a sardonic expression. "Oops," he says.

Cohl applies pressure, and he buckles to his knees as Elin selects a blade from several strapped to her thigh. At Elin's nod, Cohl tips Kellig back against her propped knee to expose his chest. "Wait!" Kellig cries out again. "North, you stupid bastard, listen to me. I can help you out there. I know the Burn and all its tricks. And I know you're running out of time."

North doesn't stop walking. Kellig becomes frantic, his voice inching higher. "North! Baedan's two steps ahead of you. You'll never catch up to her, not without me!"

That, at last, elicits a response. Chadwick raises a hand to stop North, but North returns in a flash. He grabs Kellig by the chin, holding his face steady. "I'm not chasing her. I know where I'm going."

Kellig grins, savoring the temporary foothold he's gained. "You're going to follow *her*, aren't you?" He nods at me, hazel eyes flashing once as they meet mine. Like Tobek, Kellig blames me for a great deal of what happened a month ago. "Bad idea, old friend. How do you think *I* found you?"

Chadwick edges closer. "What are you talking about?"

"I saw her back in Pilch, doing her little magic show," Kellig says, waving his hands in a mocking gesture. "And so did any other hellborne who happened to smell that spell in the air and then looked up to see it unraveling across the sky. And that includes our dearly beloved Baedan."

Chadwick straightens as my stomach sinks. I hadn't even considered that using the spell would leave a trail of magic, and in a wasteland like the Burn, clean magic is a beacon.

Did Baedan get here first because of me?

"Not an hour after you magicked yourself home," Kellig says, "that place was overrun with hungry hellborne. Anywhere you search will be the same. And next time, maybe one of them will actually wise up and start waiting."

Suddenly the sound of his rattling, damp breathing clicks into place. "That was you in the trees that night," I say, incredulous. "What were you doing there?"

His smile is slick and oily. "Reconnoitering."

But North is frowning. "Pilch? Don't you mean Oksgar?"

A low burr of warning sticks in my throat as I look to Chadwick for help. North still doesn't know about my unauthorized confrontation with Merlock.

"They're barely a day apart," Chadwick cuts in smoothly. "It's an easy mistake to make."

"Pilch doesn't have a church," North says.

"What difference does it make?!" Jarrett angles himself into the conversation. "Our entire strategy was based on Locke's spell leading us to Merlock. We can't use it now unless we want every hellborne in the Burn on our asses."

So often I resented my mother for making me a weapon. Now that my one usefulness has been stripped from me, I realize just how valuable a gift it was.

"Ah," Kellig says. "But I know how to find him without using magic."

North shakes his head. "You're lying. If you knew where Merlock was, you'd be riding Baedan's back to glory."

"There's no glory in the Burn," Kellig says ruefully. "I'm a lone wolf these days, my friend."

"Cut out his heart," North says. "We don't have time for this."

"I know about the rocks," Kellig calls. "The little trail of bread-crumbs Daddy dearest leaves behind."

North freezes. "What?"

"The stones only tell us where he's been," Chadwick says

tightly. "We have no idea where he's going."

"You would if you were able to catch the spell he leaves behind before the Burn consumes it," Kellig says.

Stunned silence follows his comment. "What spell?" North asks, even as Elin says, "Why would he leave a trail?"

"Maybe he wants to be found," I say, thinking back to that night I saw him in Pilch. Why else would he leave clean magic like a calling card in his cairns?

"Then why are we chasing him?!" Elin explodes.

But it's obvious. If he knows North is coming, he also knows Baedan has bloodbound herself to North and forged a blade able to destroy Merlock. He can't afford to stand still.

"Daddy wants to talk," Kellig says, "and I know where he'll be waiting."

"And so will Baedan," Chadwick says.

North's jaw clenches. "What are you asking in return?"

Kellig's smile vanishes. Poison seeps down his throat where Cohl's gloves have broken through the thin, damaged skin. "I get you there first, you kill the king, inherit the earth, and reward your obedient servant with a long and happy life."

"You think I'll save you after the Burn is destroyed."

"You saved your boy. The apprentice."

North's silence stretches into awkwardness. "Tobek was infected, not hellborne," he says at last. "I can't excise death. You're asking the impossible."

Hope. Kellig is asking for hope, despite it all. It unsettles all of us, I think. The hellborne are meant to be monsters. Regret is all too human.

"You need every advantage you can get," Kellig presses. "This is war, my good prince, and you're in enemy territory. There's not a hellborne out here who's going to take your side, but there are hundreds who know that Baedan's got a pretty new knife and a real chance at Burning the world down. So you can kill me or you can beat Baedan to your father's next destination." He swallows hard, eyes briefly dropping from North to the arm Cohl has wrapped around his throat—the arm bearing a protection spell. A flicker of hunger crosses his face, a shadow of greed.

Scowling, Chadwick clamps a hand on North's shoulder and wrenches him away to discuss the matter in hushed voices. Elin begins to draw lines across Kellig's chest, as if plotting where to cut to reach his heart, but the others are gravely silent, watching. Waiting.

I can't be silent. Barreling my way into the conversation, I plant my feet between North and Chadwick, giving them both pointed looks. "Why are you even entertaining this idea?"

"Your opinion was not requested, Locke," Chadwick says.

"He tried to kill me, more than once," I remind North. "His loyalties change on a whim. You can't possibly trust him! Or Baedan. For all we know, she left him behind on purpose to lead you astray. We know how to find Merlock!"

"And by the time we reach him, he'll have left again," North says flatly. "We can't afford to run your spell dry by allowing it to go uninterrupted. It was a bad idea to begin with. I never considered the ramifications of utilizing it here in the Burn. It was selfish of me to ask you to come."

"I wanted to come."

"It was a mistake," Chadwick says.

North sighs, rubbing his eyes. "If we can overtake Baedan, we can take back the blade she forged with my blood," he says. "At worst, it removes our competition. At best, she's on the right trail and we're that much closer to Merlock. We kill two birds with one stone."

"And what if that stone is poisoned, your majesty?" I ask darkly, before stalking back toward the others. Sofreya offers me a sympathetic look, but I shrug it off, straightening my back and staring across the horizon. I am more than my mother's spell, I tell myself. I am Cadence's sister, and our success is her freedom. The others have their own reasons for being here, but mine is my sister. Having abandoned her twice already, the least I can do is ensure that leaving her behind a third time is worth it. She can hate me all she wants, so long as she's free of Bryn's influence at the end.

"So what's it like, turning hellborne?" Rialdo's voice startles us all. He stands apart from the others, cigarette case in one hand. He clicks it open and closed with his thumb.

Kellig gives Rialdo a long, pointed once-over. "You'd never last out here," he says. "You'd be eaten by sunset."

Rialdo clicks the case closed and slides it into his coat, looking away. "This whole thing is ridiculous," he mutters.

"Says the boy who's here to play hero," Terik says.

"I'm here because my father believes in this kingdom," Rialdo snaps. "He wants nothing but success for this expedition, and yet he has doubts as to its leadership." His eyes cut toward Chadwick with a sneer. "A young man who's never fought in battle, at the side of an infant prince who has no support from his own people."

"And I suppose you're the leader we need," Cohl says.

"Of course he's not," says Elin. "He's not an heir. Just a spare."

Rialdo's face darkens as the others laugh, and despite myself I feel a glimmer of sympathy, but it quickly fades. Bryn told me that the entire Dossel family knew Avinea still existed, and every one of them chose to remain in Brindaigel, supporting their father's lies because it benefited them. As far as I'm concerned, Rialdo deserves whatever fate the gods have planned. Yet his retort unsettles me. Is that why he's really here? He can't kill North literally, but he could figuratively, by sowing seeds of discontent amongst his own men.

"It's not that far back to the *Mainstay*," I say, gesturing the direction. "Davik will keep you safe and sound if you want to turn back and wait with her."

Rialdo shoots me a dark look, but before he can speak, North and Chadwick finally return. Kellig tries to straighten his shoulders, only to wince as Cohl knees him hard in the back.

North's lips thin as he surveys all of us. "We're losing time," he says. "We keep moving."

"And this one?" Cohl yanks Kellig back to his feet.

North stares at Kellig in silent challenge, but Kellig only smiles, knowing he's won. "Bring him," says North.

Fifteen

IT ISN'T LONG BEFORE BAEDAN'S FOOTPRINTS ARE WIPED AWAY BY THE wind and we're truly reliant on Kellig to lead the way. He avoids all questions regarding where we're going, but I see Chadwick and Jarrett passing the map between them, attempting to guess. North is too preoccupied to notice, keeping a blistering pace with Kellig. North speaks to no one, and I watch him with mounting concern. There's a recklessness in his behavior, a frantic desire that has bypassed duty and become obsession.

The Burn is killing him faster than expected, I realize. Instead of worrying about how long my mother's spell could protect me, I should have worried about how long North has until the infection reaches his heart. Seven days was optimistic. He'll never last that long.

It's not just North I worry about. Rialdo's speech earlier, his assertion that Perrote could salvage this kingdom when North fails, seems to have sparked a sense of mutiny amongst the soldiers. They follow orders as directed, but they speak low amongst themselves, their sense of loyalty starting to cave to a more primal instinct for survival of the fittest.

The Burn is eroding all of our defenses, and no one else seems to notice.

North would have us walk all day, but Chadwick pulls rank and cites our exhaustion as he orders us to make camp that afternoon in a village called Tortin, on the second floor of a hollowed-out townhome. He separates the others into watches and patrols. Even Sofreya is placed on guard, but he passes over me without a glance.

Any guilt I felt earlier hardens into resolve. I am not worthless, I want to say; you do not know me, or how I can fight. You do not decide my value.

While the others prepare their bedrolls in a close circle, I stick toward the back of the room, where shadows darken the floor and hide my shaking fingers as I fumble with my things. There, safely tucked at the foot of my bedroll, is Chadwick's dagger. I weigh it in my hands, tasting fear on my tongue. What I couldn't do in New Prevast now feels like a challenge. I *can* do this, and I will. Trusting Kellig is a mistake; hunting Baedan is too. We don't have the time or the resources to waste on frivolous vendettas, and if Chadwick can't make North see how imbalanced this plan is, I need to rewrite the equation.

"Locke."

I startle, shoving the dagger into my boot and spinning to see Chadwick. "Yes?" I say carefully, aware that the others are now watching.

"A moment, if you please," he says, already striding away, assuming I'll follow.

I do, into the ash-covered street outside.

"Where are we going?" I ask.

"He actually listens to you," he says darkly as he leads me down a small side street of broken cobbles and sagging walls to North, sitting on a stone with his hands cradling his face. He looks up on our approach with a guarded expression, and my stomach sinks at the bruise-colored shadows spreading through his fingers. Sofreya's protection spells aren't working on him.

"How bad is it?" I ask.

When North feigns confusion, I give him a withering look, and he shrugs somewhat helplessly. "I don't know," he says. "Does it matter?"

"When your team is upstairs ready to plot mutiny, then yes," I say, "it matters."

"I'm the Prince of Avinea," North says weakly. "You are not allowed to chastise me."

Chadwick drops his folded arms and looks up toward the darkening sky. "This is what I was talking about. Your obstinacy will kill all of us."

"Shut up," North says, not unkindly.

"You shut up," I say, and they both look at me, startled. There are shadows twisting across North's face that have never been there before. "You're losing the right of an opinion, your majesty. If you don't get a handle on this, you're going to lose them, and if you lose them, you lose the city. *And* the kingdom. That"—I level a finger at the spell nestled by his throat—"is useless." Stepping forward, I hover my hand above his heart. "This has to be strong on its own, and right now it's killing you."

North stares at me with an unreadable expression. "The skill is in cheating," he says. "If you could use your spell to clear the earth, just a patch, I could—"

"Ask Sofreya for that," I interrupt. "If I take off this armor, I go sailing across the Burn and Baedan knows we're on her tail. Not to mention it's an open invitation to anyone else who might be looking for dinner tonight."

"I don't trust Sofreya."

"Why not?"

His eyes cut toward Chadwick, who latches his hands behind his neck and paces away from us. Lowering his voice, he says, "She's stealing my magic."

I straighten with a flash of nerves. "What are you talking about?"

"I think she might be leading the hellborne after us," North continues. "She's leaving clues for them to follow. Marks in the ash. Arrows pointing the way."

We tracked the footsteps of an entire tribe of hellborne for less than a quarter of a mile before the wind swept the rest of the tracks away. If we were being followed, they'd have to be close enough to see us. Arrows drawn in the ash would be worthless. And yet, from the panic in his eyes, I see he truly believes that Sofreya has betrayed him.

I frown, glancing behind me to see Chadwick still pacing restlessly. "We need her immediately," I call to him. "North needs to be excised right now, or he'll never last through the night."

Chadwick swears under his breath but dutifully turns back for the town house. I kneel in front of North, gripping his arms, careful to only touch the sleeves of his coat, none of his exposed skin. Despite myself, I can't help but mourn the bones I feel through the fabric, the hard edges that imply too many sleepless nights and too many uneaten dinners. He was already thin to begin with; now he's bordering on skeletal.

His eyes lock onto me with a wanting that feels naked. It's a too-long look, a moment of weakness, a spark that ignites in my belly and begins to smolder. Even with Sofreya's spell protecting me, I can't ignore the stirrings of my blood, the desire awakened by his proximity, his face, even *this*—this half-mad suicide mission to kill his father and save the kingdom.

Cadence, I remind myself, but her name isn't the rope I need to pull myself to safety that it once was. Her accusations have thinned our connection to more of a thread, easy to snap, easy to lose. For weeks—months, even—Cadence was my only light, my triumph at the end of all my perils. In this moment she feels forever away, my greatest loss. Would she come with me if I left Avinea? Would I leave if she didn't? Or would I sacrifice my freedom and stay a servant to Bryn forever, if only for the chance to stay close to a sister who hates me?

North touches the curving shoulder of my breastplate, fingers skimming the iron, leaving tracks in the accumulated dirt. "Your mother gave you such a gift," he says, as if in a dream.

"No," I say, pulling the armor on more securely. "She forced me to take something I never wanted. Something that"—my thoughts stray to Frell—"I was never intended to carry."

"She had a higher purpose—"

"I was six years old," I snap, "and Cadence was barely two. My mother had no right to seek a higher purpose. She had no right to take *my* future away from me without so much as a map to guide me in the right direction!"

I swallow hard, surprised by my own hostility. I thought I was beginning to forgive her, to see her in a different light—not as a mother who abandoned her daughters but as a woman fighting for their freedom.

"Avinea would be lost without her," North says. "Without you. Had I not met you—"

"You had a plan before you met me. Now that my spell is useless? Fall back on that plan and forget this one ever existed."

"No. Faris, I needed you. I still do. Why do you refuse to believe that?"

I want to be strong but I'd rather be weak; I can't encourage his attention even as I crave more. My emotions waver, battered by the infection in my blood. "Stop it," I finally say. "This is cruel, North. And it's not fair."

I realize my mistake the moment it leaves my mouth, my feigned indifference to him shattered in an instant. He latches on with an intensity that terrifies me. "Did you lie to me?"

Adrenaline spikes down my back. How could I be so stupid? North isn't the only one being eaten alive by the Burn; it's weakening my defenses as well. "No."

"Did you lie to me?" he repeats, bending forward, fingers closing tightly around my upper arms. "Because I think you need me too, but you refuse to admit it."

"My decision is not open for interpretation." I stare at him, concerned. I've seen this once before, his anger and the way it erupted so suddenly when I brought an infected girl into his wagon, cornering him into excising the poison from her blood. His frustration with me was palpable, a flaw he was fighting to control.

I see it here now, and he's losing this battle. He'll never make it to Merlock. Or even back home. Not unless Sofreya excises the poison and we turn around immediately.

Horrified, I turn to call for Chadwick, but North tightens his grip on my arms. "All right," he says, matching my furtive tone, "maybe you don't need me, but you *want* me, Faris."

My mistake is in not pulling away. North cradles my face in his hands and kisses me, hot and searching and filled with greed and desperation combined.

And then he's yanked back by a furious Chadwick, and North stumbles off the stone he was sitting on, expression wild. I cover my mouth, and Chadwick holds a hand toward me, the other still clenched in the collar of North's coat. Behind him, Sofreya watches with wide eyes and a jar of clean rocks clutched in one hand.

"Are you all right?" he asks.

I drop my hand. "Yes," I say in a voice not entirely my own.

North pulls out of Chadwick's grip and rakes a hand through his hair. His wedding ring flashes in the sunlight.

"Go back to the others," Chadwick says to me.

"We have to turn around," I say, pleading. "Chadwick, he'll never make it—"

"Locke! For once, will you do as I say and not argue with me?!"

Anger rises up in response to his tone. He's not listening to me—

and he never will. Frustrated, I fall back a step and then turn, nearly bolting for the safety of the town house. North's kiss still hums on my lips, and it makes me want to cry with frustration. Not because it was wrong.

But because I wanted even more.

It's the Burn, I tell myself; this isn't me. I know what I want most, and despite everything it is still in New Prevast, watched over by an executioner and a princess with a stolen crown. But I reason that Cadence can survive without me. She can't, however, survive without North. Nobody can, except the monsters of Avinea.

And I will not let them win.

Deep down, I always understood that I was never coming back from that night in the dungeon when Alistair injected me with magic and Bryn told me I had no choice but to be her redundancy. She will never release me from this binding spell if North succeeds; she can't risk it. Even if she agrees to leave Avinea forever, I would be right there with her, ensuring North never retaliates. All I can hope is that Cadence walks away from Bryn's guise of friendship unharmed.

With a sharp turn, I steer away from the town house and cut clumsily through the abandoned streets of the village. With several blocks between me and the others, I finally sink to my knees, palms flattened to the ground. Wind snaps between the buildings, bitter cold despite the heat trapped in the barren earth.

Silence settles over me. Ash drifts across my shoulders, soft as snow. I feel like a broken shadow in a broken world, and the only clarity left is the weight of Chadwick's dagger pressed against my ankle. Withdrawing it from my boot, I stare at the cracked leather scabbard against my knees until my vision blurs.

Numbly I unlatch the breastplate from my shoulder and let it fall to my side. My mother's spell swells into action, but I pin it back a moment longer as I savor the slow burning buildup of pressure in my chest—pain that I can control to combat the pain in my heart that can't be touched.

And then I release the spell.

The Burn dims around me as the horizon rolls closer. I can see the phantom smear of old Prevast in the far-flung distance, no more than a charcoal smudge, but the spell keeps me above the abandoned Burn, where shadowed animals roam in packs, and tribes of hellborne addicts crane their heads toward the magic brightening the sky.

The spell dips me dangerously low to the ground, but there's nothing—no one—around me. I land on my knees, the dagger still tight in my hand. After gaining my feet, I spin in a circle. The hairs on my neck stand on end; I feel as though I'm being watched, but there is nothing but an empty landscape and a mournful wind. No landmarks, no hiding places. No Merlock.

Fear rolls down my back. Is the spell beginning to fade? Will I be able to make it back? Should I *go* back now, and let us take our chances through the Burn as planned? It's a coward's choice, and I refuse to entertain it again, even as I feel the temptation eating through my veins—the easy way out.

I make another circle, heart aching in my chest. A gust of wind blows ash into my face, and I put a hand up to block the worst of it. Something moves on the horizon, a blur of motion, and I squint for a better look. Merlock?

Shadows. As the sun dips lower in the sky, behind a haze of clouds above the horizon, the shadows begin pooling together across the dunes, knitting into place like some monstrous puzzle. They rear on bent legs, forming a hybrid monster of a man.

It takes a step toward me and splinters apart, only to reassemble in a new configuration of misshapen pieces, less a man now and more a beast, hulking and curved low to the ground. Smaller shadows crawl over larger ones, forming claws. A forked tail emerges, flicking toward the sky, kicking up plumes of debris. The only light is its slitted eyes as they turn to me and narrow with a razor focus.

The shadowbred.

My stomach plummets. I know how to fight the hellborne; in theory I even know how to fight Merlock.

How do I fight shadows?

My mother's spell pulls me directly toward the monster, but instinct tells me to run. The shadowbred takes a lumbering step toward me, rattling the very earth beneath my feet, and I stagger to stay balanced, fingers flexing on the dagger. Anxious, I unsheathe it and brace my weight. The sun briefly reappears in between the clouds, glinting off the blade, directing a flash of light that hits the flank of the monster. The shadows recoil, exposing a narrow slit that quickly seals back together again.

It's a minor infliction, and yet it's proof enough: Even shadows can be defeated.

Chadwick's voice fills my head, directing my posture, my position, my stance. *Knees bent, arms loose, don't lock those elbows, Locke.*

But then another conversation fills my head, Chadwick explaining what a dagger forged with royal blood can do—including cutting through the king's spells to his heart underneath. The shadowbred beast is monstrous and ugly and terrifying, *but . . .*

It's still only made of magic. Merlock's magic. And if my mother's spell is leading me to this monster, maybe Merlock is hidden within it.

I raise the dagger as the shadow beast lumbers closer. The blade may cut through spells, but that doesn't mean the spells won't retaliate, so I keep an eye on my surroundings, marking the easiest path to run.

"Merlock!" I scream. "You want to talk? So come out and talk, you coward!"

The beast launches itself off its back quarters, blotting the sky behind it as it sails toward me. I barely have time to think, to swing before it envelops me. I slam the dagger up, and it skims down the middle of the beast, breaking the shadowbred apart into two smaller forms that hit the ground behind me and kick up a tidal wave of ash. Gold shimmers where the blade scorched the edges of whatever spell is fueling the monster and cut the threads of magic that bound it together; smoke dilutes into the air like blood.

While I've managed to wound it, I've also managed to piss it off, and now two beasts prepare for a second attack, claws digging into the earth for traction, scraping down to the barren stone beneath the Burn.

Wiping ash off my lips, I brace my weight and hold my stance, forcing a smile. An act of false courage, intended to intimidate a wavering opponent at the Stone and Fern Tavern. I don't have to be stronger to win; I just have to last longer.

The beasts launch forward with a roar of rushing wind, knocking me to my back. I swing wild, reckless, and shadows pull apart and begin to worm into my hair, across my scalp, threading around my legs like dark ribbons, pulling tight. Gone is my forced confidence, replaced with rising panic. *Stop it,* I tell myself, *slow down, breathe.*

Blood thunders in my ears as I turn the blade to my palm, prepared to cut myself out of this nightmare. Instead, the sun emerges from behind the clouds one last time, setting the Burn ablaze in light. The shadows thin, turn translucent, disappear.

But for how long? The days are too short; already the sun is half-sunken behind the horizon.

Panting, I remain on my back, eyes runny with ash, pulse erratic with adrenaline. I laugh once, hoarse and frantic. It is not a victory . . . but it's not a defeat. Rolling onto my knees, I sit up and adjust the dagger, opening my palm before cradling the edge of the blade against the skin. It hovers, uncertain, as I sense I'm not alone. Twisting, I see a figure standing on a dune behind me, brooding and dark and familiar.

Merlock.

The hairs on my arms stand on end as I rise to my feet, staring him down. No more running, I tell myself; no more fear. Whether I wanted it or not, this is my fate. Given to me by my mother, met for my sister.

But Merlock turns his back to me and walks away.

Fury floods my veins. To turn your back on an opponent like that is nothing short of arrogance, a dismissal. I am not a threat, he seems to say.

Then why doesn't he face me?

Growling, I start running for him, legs pumping, thighs exhausted from two days of pushing through the Burn. I lower my head against a rising wind, tracking the thread of my mother's spell as it carries me over the rise of ash—only to stop abruptly when I reach the top.

Baedan and her hellborne tribe are spread across the bottom of the rise, astride horses twisted into something monstrous by the dead magic they've been bred upon. Clotted fur hangs off their bony frames; they have muzzles pitted and slick with poison, and eyes that glow silver. A campfire burns in the distance behind them, abandoned now, as they chased the scent of magic toward me.

Merlock strides past them without a second glance, coat snapping at his legs. My mother's spell hovers in his wake, and the hellborne stare at it greedily. Some try to catch it between their hands, balancing precariously on their horses.

Baedan dismounts, pulling a blade from a sheath at her hip, the iron flashing dully. A dagger forged with North's blood, the same as the one I hold, able to kill a king. She wears an eye patch now, a square of black against her skin, to hide the socket that used to hold the eye North destroyed with magic. As Merlock continues past her, she takes a step after him, blade raised for a killing blow.

No. I will not come this close only to watch her win.

My hubris is quickly punished when Merlock jerks one hand up toward the sky without breaking his stride. At once the ground begins to rumble, bouncing loose debris, sending drifts of ash spilling downhill behind him.

Baedan freezes, but Merlock does not. He flicks his hand, and half a dozen hellborne are flung off their beasts, several yards in either direction; Baedan falls to her knees. Behind me, storm clouds roll across the sky and blot out the sun completely. With mounting dread I turn to see a new shadowbred beast pulling itself from the earth, ready to fight. Smaller, writhing shadows twist and dissipate around it, blurring the edges of the monster into a smoky haze. It tips a pointed head to the sky and opens a gaping mouth full of serrated shadow teeth.

Sainted mothers and their virgin daughters.

I move to cut my palm, but the blade is gone. The shadow-bred is already barreling forward; I have no time to lose. Swearing beneath my breath, I start running downhill, directly toward Baedan as several narrow fingers of shadow stretch past me and begin to close into a fist—

"What are you doing?!"

I blink, disoriented. North is now bent over me, holding Chadwick's dagger in one hand. He must have taken it from my body here, thereby leaving me unarmed out *there*. A small cut on my forearm explains my sudden return. Already he's pressing a bandage against the wound to keep the Burn from infecting my blood.

I sit up, still tasting panic in my throat, ash in my mouth. Ignoring his question, I clutch my armor to my chest and stagger to my feet, scanning the street around me. More shadows and half-buried ruins. No sign of Baedan, monsters, or Merlock.

"You used the spell without telling anyone." He focuses on the bandage, tying it off with tight, jerky movements. "You could have been lost out there!"

"But I wasn't," I say, shouldering my armor back on, buckling it shut. Now that I'm safe, I'm flooded with frustration at the lost opportunity to fight Merlock, to end this once and for all. "He was *right there*, North! I saw him! I could have—"

Done what? a voice whispers in my head, full of recrimination. You could have fought off the hellborne, a shadowbred monster, *and* survived long enough to face Merlock? He flicked his wrist, and the hellborne went flying. You need courage in the fighting ring, but delusion never wins anything.

"You could have what? Faris, what were you doing . . . ?" With my arm safely covered, North finally examines—and recognizes— the dagger in his hand. His face drains of color. I can't meet his eyes as I snatch it back.

Chadwick rounds the corner behind us. "Corbin! What is going on?"

The captain has half a second before North launches into him, tackling him to the ground. "You son of a *bitch*! When were you going to tell me you sent her to her slaughter?!"

Chadwick holds off North's attack, looking to me in surprise, and then alarm. "I didn't—it was her choice—"

"I told you weeks ago that it was not an option!"

"You have no more options left," Chadwick says, teeth clenched. "You are my only concern, your majesty. Locke understands that."

"He's right!" I grab North's coat and drag him back as the others arrive, drawn by the shouts. "It was my decision."

North barks a bitter laugh, bent over his knees to catch his breath. "Oh, give it a rest, Ben. We're not children playing swords anymore. Your only concern is your own ambition. I've known it from the day we met." Disgust twists his features as he looks to each one of us in turn. "You're all out here for the same reason: a land grant and a title. You swear your fealty to me, but when the time comes, you'll take your fistful of gold and run. Well, then go." He waves his hand dismissively. "I don't need you."

Chadwick accepts Elin's hand up to his feet. "Corbin—"

North takes a swing, but Chadwick easily steps out of range and North loses his footing, staggering forward as rage flashes across his face. "Do not address me as your *equal*! I am not your friend! I am your prince, and all of you"—a trembling finger wavers at each of them in turn—"are wasting my time!"

"He's completely mad," Elin murmurs.

"It's the Burn," I say desperately, reaching for him, then stopping short. Poison threads across his fingers, knotting into larger blooms at his knuckles. More creeps up his throat, toward his face. "It's eating past his protection spells. Did you not excise him?"

Sofreya presses her hands to her hair. "Yes, but—"

But his learning that I was willing to sacrifice myself has brought everything rushing back.

"What is going on?" Cohl holds both hands out as if to keep us from attacking one another, though no one has moved.

"Our intrepid princeling seems to be keeping secrets," Rialdo says, not even bothering to hide his smirk. "Looks like he's not strong enough to resist his daddy's magic."

"Are we really going to talk about kowtowing to fathers?" I ask.

A dark expression crosses his face. "What does that mean?"

"You're a coward like your father," I say.

"And you're a whore like your mother," Rialdo says. "She got what she deserved, and you'll be the same."

I lunge for him, but Elin and Chadwick intervene, hauling me back.

"Don't," Elin warns—the kindest thing she's ever said to me.

"Stop it, both of you!" Chadwick releases me and rakes a hand through his hair, pulling most of it loose of the ponytail. "This— this is what the Burn feeds on. This anger and pettiness. If you cannot control your emotions, we cannot continue forward."

"Maybe that's for the best," Terik mutters.

"You've got bigger problems than moving forward," Kellig says, wetting his lips. That desperate, greedy look is back in his eyes— the hunger. His eyes are all pupil, his voice hoarse. "You threw a lot of magic out there."

"Baedan is miles from here," I say darkly, adjusting my armor.

"Baedan is not the only threat in the Burn," Kellig says, eyes cut- ting toward me, "and if the right tribe finds us, you'll never make it back to your ship."

"Maybe we should leave some bait," Rialdo suggests.

Sofreya grabs my hand and pulls me away before I can punch him. "Don't listen," she murmurs. "Poison on the tongue comes from poison in the heart. Not all monsters are bred in the Burn."

I force back a cutting reply, still itching to fight, to hit, to scream. But I notice a subtle shift in dynamics as the soldiers exchange looks of matching shades of exhaustion and suspicion. Their faces are closing down and they seem to edge closer together. Us versus them.

"We'll return to New Prevast," Chadwick says, rubbing his mouth. His long hair hangs loose against his face, and it's strange to see him so rumpled, with his tunic hanging out from beneath his uniform jacket. "We've made too many mistakes already; we can't risk more. We'll return with the queen and an army and proxies—"

"No!" North grabs Chadwick by the front of his coat. "We do not turn back! We're too close."

"These are my soldiers," Chadwick says, voice dangerously low. "Their lives are my responsibility. They will not die because we were too stupid to admit defeat."

"Baedan saw Merlock," I jump in. "She was right there with me! We don't have time to go back!"

Chadwick clenches his teeth and shoots me a look as sharp as daggers.

"This is ridiculous," Rialdo says. "You've already sacrificed one man for this madness. How many more before you're satisfied?"

"Gideon was not sacrificed!" I round on him, furious at how easily he manipulates his words into weapons. "You all saw what happened. It was the Burn! It could have taken any of us! And this is the Burn too. This is not who North really is! The poison is destroying all of us, not just North!"

It's a useless argument. They know so little of North beyond whatever Chadwick may have told them and a few short weeks of shared preparation. Their prince was too long away from the palace, his absence too long seen as cowardice. Their faith is entirely in Chadwick, and it appears to be to fraying.

"*You* have a choice," North says. "But *I* do not. I move forward."

Chadwick's shoulders slump. "Corbin, I beg you."

"I'll go," I say suddenly. "I can find Merlock again. I can fight him—I have the weapon. And as long as I have strength, I have a chance."

"That's suicide," Cohl says.

"I knew that when we left New Prevast," I say. To Chadwick I say, "You know that if we go back now, we'll never return. Don't do this to him, Ben. Don't give his crown away so freely. At least make them fight for it."

"Ben," Rialdo repeats. "Am I the only one she doesn't have her claws in?"

North rounds on Rialdo and slams him into the wall. "Give me one good reason why I should spare your father the effort of killing you himself."

"You have witnesses," Rialdo says with a pointed nod to the others. Chadwick tries to pry North back, but it's too late—a ribbon of poison bleeds into Rialdo's skin, a ghostly smear of damp charcoal that begins to bloom down his throat.

Horror crosses North's face; guilt. He backs away, hands curling into balls that he shoves under his arms. "Where are my gloves?"

"He poisoned him!" Elin grabs Terik by the sleeve. "Did you see that?!"

"It—it was an accident," North says shakily.

"Here." Sofreya darts forward, a stone webbed with magic in one hand. "It hasn't gone far; we can extract it."

"You are unfit to be king," Rialdo snarls, leveling a finger at North. "You're an animal, Corbin. Do you hear me?! A bullet to the head would be a mercy for a man like you."

"Stop," Sofreya begs. "You'll only spread the infection faster like this, and I can't excise all of you! Ben? Cohl? *Please.*"

They both step forward and hold Rialdo down as Sofreya draws the poison out. It was an accident, and barely more than a trace, yet Rialdo's panic is contagious, spreading through the others. Once Sofreya finishes, Rialdo sinks to his knees, flattening his palm to his throat and checking his fingers as if expecting to see poison come away. "This is what my father was afraid of," he says. "Poor planning, terrible execution. We are stumbling blindly in the trail of a madman, and it will kill all of us. We go back to New Prevast and we return with an army. A *strategy* beyond the spell of a girl like her. *Guns.*"

I punch him as hard as I can, satisfied by the double crunch of his bones beneath my fist and his head as it recoils back against the wall. "Guns will not kill shadows," I say.

Chadwick hauls me back as the others close around Rialdo like a shield. The crack between us has widened into a ravine. If we don't jump now and join sides again, we'll be separated irrevocably.

"It's over," Chadwick says. "That's it. We're going home. All of us," he adds.

North turns away, hands folded over his head. He's shaking, struggling to fight back the infection burning through his blood. "One more day," he pleads, and I see myself in this moment, begging Thaelan for another night. But where I wanted one more day to plan, North needs one more day to execute.

Wait.

"Pack your things," Chadwick orders. He releases my arm. "We head back immediately."

Kellig straightens. "You're not leaving me out here."

"I'm not leaving," I say, mind spinning.

Chadwick covers his face with his hand and growls. "Locke, for the love of gods and sainted virtues—"

"Perrote knows about this spell," I say. "He'll take it for himself if I go back. Then he won't need North; he won't need any of us. We get one shot, Ben, and this is it. And so long as my sister is still breathing—while she still has a chance to be saved—I am not giving up."

"I'm coming with you," North says in the silence that follows.

"Shut up," Chadwick snaps.

"You're demoted," North says.

"I resigned hours ago," Chadwick says. "I'm here as your friend now, which means I don't have to listen to you." He turns to me. "You have no idea what's out here, Locke. Dagger or not, without magic, neither one of you is in any condition to fight! We're better suited to taking you back to the *Mainstay* where it's safer to try this again."

"Look, Merlock was only a few miles away," I say, gesturing the direction with an open palm. "He was walking north, toward Prevast. If I can get to the outskirts of the city, I won't need magic to protect me."

Elin snorts. "Of course you won't."

"The sewers," I say, ignoring her. I saw them labeled in the maps spread through the library in New Prevast, but dismissed them as useless. But now. My breath hitches. "The hellborne thrive in the Burn. They have no reason to go underground. The tunnels will be made of stone; the Burn won't have bled through them."

Chadwick stares at me with a touch of respect and, dimly, a spark of hope. "Those tunnels haven't been used for twenty years," he says. "They could collapse, or be flooded, or . . ."

I don't flinch away from his gaze. "Or they could be empty."

"I've been down there," Kellig says suddenly. "I could navigate the entire city if I needed to."

"Which means Baedan can too," Chadwick says.

But Kellig shakes his head, grin spreading. He has the upper hand again, a guarantee. "Like the girl said, Baedan thrives on the Burn. Pride keeps her out of the sewers."

His words settle over us, intoxicating in their feasibility.

"Then that's the plan," North says at last. "We keep going."

"And now we're following the most inexperienced member of this entire expedition," Elin says savagely.

The others chorus their own protests, but North meets my eyes and offers a bare, honest smile that hints at the first night we met, when he asked me for nothing but my name. So much has changed since then, and yet right now we're both still the same: ready and willing to fight, no matter the cost.

I smile back, albeit weakly.

Chadwick rubs his mouth as he surveys the landscape and the wintry skies overhead. "One more day," he says, as if bargaining with a petulant child. "If we don't catch up to Merlock by tomorrow evening, we turn around. No arguments. Agreed?"

"Captain, is that wise?" Jarrett exchanges troubled looks with Cohl.

"Do you trust me?" Chadwick asks, challenge in his voice.

Nobody answers immediately, and it's apparent that when they finally force a mumbled agreement, it's out of habit and respect, not conviction.

Chadwick beckons Sofreya forward. "Keep an eye on North," he says. "I'll pin him down if I have to, but do not let that poison get past those protection spells again."

"Ben." North's eyebrows are furrowed and his expression is bleak. "Thank you."

Chadwick grabs North by the collar of his jacket and briefly dips his own head to North's in a gesture of familiarity. Of friendship. "You're going to be a villain at the end of this story no matter what we do now," he says softly. "Make it count."

Releasing North, he straightens, pulling his hair back into a tidy ponytail. "Gather your things," he says. "We find a new camp before the hellborne arrive."

Sofreya stays behind to excise North once more, as I follow the others back to the town house to gather our packs. I'm too far away to hear most of the whispers, but I feel the weight of them, the sharp edges that warn of rising animosity.

"He's as mad as his father," I hear Elin say.

"He's not your only choice," Rialdo replies. "My father has magic enough to clear the Burn for an entire army, not just a handful of sacrifices. Nor does he have tainted blood to contend with."

"Then why isn't he out here now?" Jarrett asks. "Why send us unarmed into the Burn?"

Rialdo doesn't answer, but I understand now. Perrote wants to be the hero to save Avinea after its rightful leader fails—so no one will argue when he assumes control and North is completely demolished.

Sixteen

By the time we gain enough distance from the town house and any hellborne I might have attracted there, we're all exhausted, too tired to even complain when Chadwick orders our stop in the middle of a wasteland of ash with no protection from the bitter wind. Jarrett starts a fire, and we huddle around it, pensive and silent, daring glances at each other, trying to guess how deep the Burn has taken hold, who will be the next to snap, and how. North's greatest vice is his temper, but what would Elin's be? Or Terik's?

North separates himself from the fire—and the recrimination of the others. He sits alone, a slumped figure with a tattered map, staring across the Burn toward the shadowed form of Prevast on the horizon. Once again I'm reminded of cold nights on the farming terrace, plotting impossible escapes that turned ludicrous the later the hour and the more barleywine I drank. Seeing North now

awakens that same aching longing, a desire to succeed, marred by
the bittersweet sorrow of knowing the much higher probability
of failure. I resist the temptation to join him, aware of the way
the others keep me tagged from the corners of their eyes. Instead
I stay close to the fire—and to my dagger. No one has spoken a
word of dissent all afternoon, following Chadwick's commands
with a dutiful compliance I don't fully trust.

After dividing us into shifts, Chadwick approaches North, offering him a canteen as he takes a seat beside him. Together they
study the map, no doubt debating Merlock's likely target—and
why, if he wants to talk, he keeps moving forward rather than doubling back. I envy them their friendship, strong enough to survive
a day like this.

Kellig watches me from across the fire. He's been begging for
scraps of magic from Sofreya all evening, to no avail, and the hunger I saw earlier has returned, manifested with the addition of a
nervous shudder that wracks his entire body. He hasn't injected
any magic into his blood since joining us, and the withdrawal looks
torturous.

He deserves it.

The light dances over the slick cracks of poison on his face and
the dark bruises on his throat where Cohl's fingers sank through
the skin. He opens his mouth as if to speak to me, but I quickly
turn away, focusing on the sky overhead, gauzy with clouds. On
instinct, I raise my hands to frame the dimly lit stars. *Almost there*,
I think, and the words are a satisfying weight, like the shell in my
pocket I picked up for Cadence. Another promise, but this one
for me.

When I fall asleep, my dreams are strange beasts, glimpses of Merlock in between stretches of darkness and flashes of a silver light. A cairn of stones is built upon my lungs, pressing me down, cutting off my air. I wake with a gasp, to find Kellig bent over me, hands flattened against my chest.

My immediate reaction is one of panic. He's a transferent, and has tried to steal magic from me before. I grab his wrist and twist it, knocking him back, only to feel my mother's spell unleash itself.

"Stop," he says, rocking onto his knees and slamming his hands back onto my chest. Something hard scrapes against my coat, and I realize—my armor is gone and he's holding a small knife to my chest, the iron blade muting the spell.

Surprised, I look at him again. "What happened?" I ask, taking the knife from him and pressing it harder against my chest.

He releases me with an audible sigh of relief, pulling back several steps. His hands tear through his hair and then lock behind his neck. Once again he's shaking. "You sleep like the goddamn dead," he growls.

Ignoring his rebuke, I sit up sharply, scanning the camp. The fire went out hours ago and is covered with a layer of ash. Both my armor and my pack are gone. The only relief is Chadwick's dagger, still hidden in my boot, but the relief is soon replaced with sour panic. No food, no water, no weapons, miles from the edge of the Burn.

And then I see North's body sprawled several yards from me. I lower the knife in my haste, only to slam it back into position, swearing under my breath.

"When did they leave?!" I demand, dropping to my knees beside

North. Chadwick is only a few feet from him. Both have been stripped of their weapons.

"Hours ago," Kellig says darkly.

I shake North, lightly at first, then more fiercely. His eyes flutter open, only to close again as he swallows hard, eyebrows furrowing in pain. "Faris?"

Relieved, I curl my fingers into the fabric of his coat, briefly dipping my forehead to his chest before leaving him in order to wake Chadwick. Chadwick lashes out like I did, nearly kicking me off my feet only to stop short as he winces with pain. He rolls onto his side and coughs.

"What the hell, Locke?" he rasps.

I straighten, scanning the horizon. Nothing, *no one*, in sight. "Your canteen," I say flatly. "They must have put something in the canteen." One of the palace doctor's pills, no doubt, intended to stop our hearts before they turned hellborne. A small dose of that would knock anyone out.

Catching my tone, Chadwick frowns and pushes to his feet. He cringes as he surveys the abandoned camp. Fury melts into resignation.

"Even Sofreya?" he asks softly, wounded.

"It doesn't matter," North says. "We didn't need them anyway."

"Yes, we did," Chadwick growls. "Locke has no training, you're falling apart, and now we have no weapons or supplies. Not to mention they have a head start! If they reach the *Mainstay* before us—"

"Davik will not sail without us," North cuts in, eyes sliding toward me. He finally realizes my armor is gone and frowns. "Faris?"

"I'm fine," I say, and then, begrudgingly, "Kellig—"

"Saved all of you instead of eating you, which is what they suggested I do when they let me loose," Kellig says, pointing at each of us in turn. "*And* I kept any hellborne from tracking *her* down. So just remember that."

None of us speak.

"You're welcome," he mutters.

Chadwick pats his pockets, assessing what they've left him with. Very little. A small knife, his clothes, and his canteen. He sniffs the contents before taking a small sip.

North quickly does the same. Relief floods his face as he produces a small leather bag from an inner pocket. It rattles with the familiar click-clacking of stones no doubt threaded with magic. I wonder if he stole them from Sofreya, believing she had stolen them from him. "We're all right," he says. "We move forward."

Chadwick kicks through the ash, searching for anything left behind. "No."

"Nothing has changed," North says. "We've just lost unnecessary weight."

"No!" Chadwick hurls his canteen down. "I'm done, Corbin. I'm *done*! We have no food, no water, no weapons, very little magic, no men, and no way home even if—*if*—we get out of the Burn alive."

"We kill my father," says North, "and we won't need a ship home."

Chadwick's fury is nearly palpable. "We've failed, Corbin! Do you understand?! This is it! This"—he extends his arms and turns in a circle—"is how we die. In the Burn, like the idiots we are."

"You gave me one more day," North reminds him. "Davik agreed to one week. She will not sail until then."

Chadwick's arms drop to his sides as he stares at North. "I'm done."

"I'm not," North says. "You do what you have to do, Ben, as will I. Either way, we part as friends." He turns to me, eyebrows raised in silent question.

A part of me wants to admit defeat. Palms on the floor and a possibility of going home. Bound to Bryn, yes, but alive, with the chance to see Cadence again. But *almost there*, I remind myself. Neither decision is easy; only one is right.

I take my place beside North, knife still clutched to my chest. Chadwick slumps, deflating. Briefly closing his eyes, he shakes his head.

"Come on," he says as he straightens, already pushing past us.

"Ben," North starts, but Chadwick holds a hand out, stemming any further conversation. He unbuckles his empty scabbard and wordlessly hands it back to me. Quickly shrugging out of my coat and tunic, I fight the pull of my mother's spell for several precious seconds in order to tighten the scabbard across my chest, the iron buckle pressed into the soft linen of my undershirt—as close to skin as I can manage without stripping naked in front of them.

The day passes in morose silence, punctuated by glimpses of the capital city looming ever closer. We reach the outskirts by mid-afternoon, and in unspoken agreement, we all draw to a stop. I've seen Prevast before, both from the sea and from my first meeting with Merlock. And yet it's entirely different to see it from here, spread so wide that it encompasses the entire horizon with its petrified remains. It's enormous. Overwhelming. So many lives lost, so many homes destroyed, all in the name of magic.

A broken heart broke this beautiful city, and I look to North, whose expression is unreadable. Does he see the risk of history repeating itself in these ruins? Even clean magic is an addiction. And while North intends to wean Avinea from its magic codependency when he is king, will the demands of his people and his need to prove his ability to rule subvert that intention?

Will expectation destroy him the way it destroyed his father?

Moving forward, we pass a camp, the embers of its fire still warm, a hopeful sign that we're not far behind Baedan. Less hopeful is the body of a young boy left half-buried in ash. A slave, Kellig tells us, bought for his clean blood and left to rot once he became too infected to be worth anything but food for the wolves who live in the city, bred on the poisoned flesh of the hellborne. They howl as the sun begins its early winter descent behind the toothy skyline, sending chills down my back. But there's no time for a burial, and it hurts to leave him with nothing but North's hasty prayer.

As we approach the outskirts of the city, North begins testing sewer grates, to find that most have rotted shut. As we wind deeper into the streets, however, we find a narrow alley with tilting buildings that have kept the cobbles from filling with debris. North crouches, twisting a grate open with a screech that echoes. Wincing, he waves away a cloud of displaced ash and peers below.

"Not flooded," he surmises, looking to Kellig. "Which way are we headed?"

Kellig wets his lips. "I'll take the lead."

"Of course you will," Chadwick mutters.

"Wait." North silences us as voices carry from the main street, too low to be recognizable but too deep into the Burn to be anything but hellborne. His hand strays to his pocket and the pouch of stones, but I shake my head.

"Don't waste them," I whisper.

"We might not have a choice." Chadwick falls back a step, bracing his weight in defense. At the mouth of the side street, Baedan and several of her tribesmen stare at us, surprise giving way to fury.

So we're headed the right way after all.

"Go," Chadwick orders, grabbing me by the shoulder and shoving me toward the grate. *"Go!"*

I jump and land hard on my feet, stumbling down a slope of ash before reaching solid stone. The heat of the Burn above has been trapped in the tunnels, and it's almost too much for me in my heavy coat, but there's no time to yank it off. North and Kellig are on my heels, Chadwick right behind. From above, Baedan orders several men to kill us, while barking at the rest to continue on.

It's a race to Merlock.

Whether he actually knows the tunnels or not, Kellig moves at breakneck speed, trying to lose the hellborne on our heels. Dimly I'm aware that we're moving downhill—toward the ocean and the castle. Water leaks through cracks in the walls; the stone turns rough, scaled with barnacles, the air filled with silt and the smell of brine. The warmth is lost to more frigid temperatures; ice coats many of the tunnel's surfaces, making for treacherous footing, forcing us to slow. We follow a series of switchback tunnels that rise higher, turn narrow, and eventually intersect with an underground bridge hidden beneath the real bridge that spans the inlet separating the castle from the city itself. The way forward is closed off by a heavy iron gate, locked against unwanted entry. Beyond is another world entirely: marble slab floors, gilded arches, and weather-damaged tapestries threaded with veins of silver and gold—starlight and fire, gifts from the gods. This must be the king's tunnel, his escape route during an attack. A six-foot span of the floor has broken loose, exposing the crashing ocean thirty feet below.

Chadwick kicks at the lock, but it's been rusted in place and doesn't budge. Behind us voices swell in the tunnels as Baedan's men draw nearer. Swearing under his breath, North grabs the lock and casts a simple spell that briefly illuminates his features. The lock falls loose, and he tosses it aside before he drags the gate open. We hurry through, just as a girl with dark braided hair rounds the corner behind us. She shouts her victory, three men right behind, all of them armed with heavy weaponry.

Fading light spills in from the broken floor, but shadows cling to the corners and drip from the walls, awakened from their slumber by our arrival and North's spell. Several begin to gather, slinking along the edges where the light doesn't quite reach. There are unlit torches braced against the wall, but there's no time to grab one.

We run.

The bridge groans beneath our weight; the entire structure seems to sway in the brutal wind snapping through the inlet. Kellig launches himself over the hole in the floor, landing on his shoulder and sliding several feet on the opposite side. He scrambles back, out of the way as Chadwick lands on hands and feet. North grabs my arm, and we jump together, splintering apart on the landing. The force of it knocks me to my knees with a bone-rattling crush that steals my breath and brings stars to my eyes. My mother's spell swells and nearly overpowers me, and I waste precious seconds adjusting the scabbard over my shoulder to mute the spell again.

North pulls me to my feet toward the opposite end of the bridge, to another locked gate. Shadows dart toward us, wrapping like rope around our ankles. North raises a hand, a spell already igniting in his fingertips as behind us Baedan's men make the leap.

North's spell blasts the gate open, and we dive through to the other side. He slams it shut, teeth bared with effort as he holds the bars between his gnarled hands. When the girl with the braid catches up to us and slams into the gate, North backs away, revealing twisted iron woven together, unbreakable. It was an expensive effort, and I see the pain it cost carved into his face. One less hour to survive the Burn, I think.

"Open it!" The girl rattles the gate as three men join her.

"Kellig, you bastard," one of them growls.

Kellig tips his chin and bows in a mocking curtsy. "No shame in jumping a sinking ship." Then, with an eyebrow cocked, he says, "Mind the shadows."

The four of them spin to see the shadows gathering into a monstrous, hulking form, hunched shoulders, rigid claws, and an open mouth full of teeth.

"Don't look," North says softly, turning me away. But I can't avoid the screams as they rip through the tunnels around us. Kellig hangs back, as if to savor the sounds of the dying, his fingers flexing at his side. When Chadwick prompts him for directions, he jolts. His eyes are all pupil again, and his tongue slides across his lips in an incessant circle, maybe trying to taste the remnants of magic—or the sound of screaming—still in the air.

North holds my arm, firmly but gently, leaning away from Kellig when he passes us to resume the lead. Chadwick frowns at Kellig's mannerisms, exchanging a strained look with North. Out in the Burn, everything was already dead, and our spells were diluted by the open air around us. But in here, penned in by stone walls and close quarters, with North's skin still humming from using magic, Kellig's behavior is harder to ignore. Kellig may want a second chance, but until then he's still hellborne.

On this side of the bridge, the tunnels were built for luxurious, unhurried evacuation, and there are fewer branches to choose between. Yellowed candles flicker to life as we approach, only to die out as we pass. North spares a precious moment to examine one, dipping his hand around the flame and watching it brighten and dim as it dances around his fingers. A haunted look crosses his face, and when I nudge him, inquisitive, he retracts his hand, dragging it through his hair with a shaky smile.

"It's spelled to react to my blood," he says. "My father's blood. The monks at Saint Ergoet's used something similar to verify my legitimacy."

"We have to keep moving." I touch his arm, surreptitiously checking his hands for any sign of spreading poison. His skin has taken on a darker hue, but it could just be the shadows spooling around us, trailing our every move. They keep their distance, and I have to wonder if that's because of Merlock's blood too. North will be inheriting not just a broken kingdom but the monsters it bred as well.

Our footsteps echo against the vaulted ceilings; our shadows dip in between pillared columns. It seems ridiculous, the excess used to make an underground escape look pretty.

Yet I can't help but stop and stare when we reach a domed rotunda framed in colored tiles, with a heavy iron chandelier hanging from the ceiling. Water drips from the walls; the edges of the room are covered with frost and slick algae. I almost smell sulfur.

There are remnants of another life buried here: furniture arranged in a facsimile of a home. Couches and thick carpets have been pulled to one side; on the other side are heavy bookshelves loaded with glass and stone ornaments that have grown cloudy and green with age. An enormous dining room table with room for twenty, but set for one. Bone china, wine goblet, silverware laid out in neat precision on a cloth napkin. There's even a bed, tucked behind a swag of drapery, the coverlet smoothed perfectly, its lace edge rotting apart.

"What is this?" I ask, incredulous.

"A place to hide," North says quietly. "If the castle was under attack, or the tunnels were blocked, Merlock could be protected down here."

"Protected or trapped?" I ask, picking up a pipe from a stack of dusty books, before dropping it again and wiping off my hand with a shiver.

"Look." Chadwick nods toward the dining table, where several stones have been neatly stacked in a round cairn. All black, full of poison.

"Is this—" North begins, but Kellig shakes his head, eyes squeezed shut. He's rocking back and forth on his heels.

"No," he rasps. "Baedan's going to the ballroom. I don't know what *this* is."

Bemused, I look down, only now noticing the way the floor is worn along the center, much like the wallpaper in Dimitr Frell's stairwell, where somebody dragged something along the same path for years. There's even a small detour to the table, where Merlock stacked his stones.

North's expression has shifted, turned strange. "I know this place."

"That's impossible," Chadwick says. "You've never been this deep in the Burn before."

"No. Not physically." North turns in a circle, head thrown back to scan the painted ceiling overhead. "The monks told us about this room during our lessons. Do you remember, Ben? Merlock would meet with Corthen down here, where no one would see them."

"Does it matter?" I ask, strained. "Baedan isn't admiring the history of the palace as she storms it!"

North shakes himself, swallowing hard. "You're right," he says. "It's nothing. Let's go."

He brushes past Kellig, their shoulders colliding. With a moan of frustration, Kellig lashes out, grabbing North by the arm. His other hand yanks back North's sleeve, exposing the protection spell on his wrist. North tries to twist out of the way, but Kellig holds firm, sinking his fingers into the spell, igniting it a bright silver as he begins transferring the magic from North to himself.

Chadwick reacts half a heartbeat before I do. Between us, we separate them, Chadwick slamming Kellig against the wall as I tug North's sleeve down, pulling him closer to me. Kellig begins thrashing, trying to reach Chadwick's spell instead. What little he managed to steal from North has already been consumed by the poison in his hands, and he begins screaming, scrabbling at Chadwick's face. "Give it to me! I've earned it!"

With a move I've seen practiced a hundred times, Chadwick's arm cuts across Kellig's throat. Kellig crumples to the ground unconcious. Panting, Chadwick steps back, wiping his mouth with the back of his hand, before his eyes meet North's. "I have no way to restrain him," he says.

From somewhere above us a heavy boom sends a drift of colored plaster raining down around us.

"That sounded like a door," I say.

North nods in agreement. His fingertips glow silver with magic, his entire body crackling with a nervous energy that charges the air around us. "Leave him," he says, voice husky. "The shadows will be more merciful than I could hope to be."

"The ballroom," Chadwick repeats.

"I can find my way from here," says North, still seemingly lost in another world as he gives the rotunda one last lingering look.

We leave Kellig behind us as North breaks into a run, consumed with an iron resolution that would terrify me if I didn't feel the same building pressure behind my skin. We chase the dark through several tunnels, stopping only when we reach a heavy wooden door, warped with moisture and webbed with cracks. We spare a moment to catch our breath and steel our nerve. But then, while no one gives the word, I hear it above my racing heartbeat all the same:

Now.

Seventeen

CHADWICK KICKS THE DOOR OPEN INTO A COCOON OF HEAVY VELVET drapery. We edge through a servants' hall and into the ballroom, the slick marble floor reflecting the stormy twilight outside. The ocean glitters in its endless horizon beyond a wall of glass doors that overlook a veranda jutting over the water—the one we saw in passing from the *Mainstay*. Bitter wind gutters through the broken glass, twisting my hair out of its bun. I shove my hair out of my eyes as we make a quick circle.

The room is empty. No stones, no Merlock, nothing to indicate we're on the right track.

Frustrated, I move toward the veranda, nearly slipping on the broken ice-coated tiles when I step outside. Hellborne birds jostle for space along the crumbling balustrade, charcoal feathers streaking embers into the wind.

Nothing.

I swear into the wind, clutching my hair back with both hands. Chadwick joins me, giving the balcony and the sea beyond a cursory glance before his eyes meet mine. I nod at the unspoken question, already shouldering out of my coat as I storm back inside. Dropping my coat to the ground, I ignore any sense of propriety and yank my tunic off next, then work the latch of Chadwick's scabbard. Goose bumps riddle my bare arms, and my fingers shake from both the cold and the fury that we trusted Kellig, that we may have lost our final chance of finding Merlock.

On the far side of the ballroom, two sets of double doors slam open with a thud, knocking several crystals loose from one of the four chandeliers overhead. The sulfuric taste of magic fills the ballroom just as North is knocked back, and he skids across the floor. Baedan stands at the top of the grand staircase leading to the dance floor, grinning, flanked by two dozen men and women dressed in furs and leather, armed with iron and metal.

Did Kellig set us up? Is this a massacre?

North scrambles to his feet but hesitates. Baedan's guarded with a spell written above her heart. Only magic can disarm it, and we have none to spare on her.

"There you are," she says. "But where are the armies risen from the ashes, called in celebration of the prince and his new bride?" She cocks her head with a smile. "Don't tell me you came all this way alone?"

"Disappointed?" asks North.

"Not in the slightest," she says, and attacks.

Magic scorches the walls and the marble floors like lightning. North casts a counterspell and dives out of the way. I slam behind a column, knocking the scabbard off. My mother's spell unfurls almost lazily, so unlike all the times I've used it before. I watch, transfixed, as it drifts higher, toward the ceiling. Is Merlock on another floor?

And then I see it. An orchestral balcony, with a tiny curved stairwell leading up to it. Most of its treads have rotted out, but the matching rail is still in place, elegantly carved to mimic the floral motif of the hanging tapestries. My mother's spell snakes its way up.

He's here. Still hiding.

North is embattled against Baedan, wasting precious magic, while Chadwick focuses on the hellborne, most of whom don't have the luxury of protection spells. Even armed with a simple knife, Chadwick strikes with a furious grace.

"North," I call, and he risks a look over. I point the way, and his expression tightens, turns iron. He nods, but is immediately drawn back into the fight. I can't wait for him, for either of them.

Almost there, I tell myself. I dart toward the balcony, my dagger clutched in one hand. Years of scaling the rooftops of Brindaigel make the decimated stairwell an easy climb, and I follow my mother's spell with mounting fear. The infection in my blood feeds on it, and I force myself to slow down, to breathe. Rushing headlong into anything never garnered me a win in the fighting ring, and being reckless now will cost more than a handful of silver tretkas.

Blood pounds in my ears as I reach the balcony, sidestepping a small circle of stones—the topmost one still pale with silver magic, newly placed. Merlock has taken a stand at the balustrade, his back to me as he surveys the ballroom below, seemingly ignorant of my approach—and of the fight unfolding. Instead he watches flickers of memories that have appeared and are now waltzing below us: women in ball gowns and men with black waistcoats.

From this angle it's easy to see North in the way Merlock carries himself, tall but stilted, proud yet bent beneath the weight of his abandoned responsibilities. His skin is as thin as vellum, the veins beneath as black as ink. He's not in his tattered uniform but all in black, his circlet a tarnished gold, battered and bent out of shape.

That he still wears it surprises me. Does he consider himself a king, even after all that he's done? And why wear it here but not out in the Burn? It's almost as if he dressed for the venue.

I can tell his attention is not on his son, and it annoys me in a way that feels personal. Merlock knew North existed. Was North not worthy of some small act of contrition? How could Merlock turn his back on him, dismissing him the way he dismissed all of Avinea? A part of me begs to know, the part of me that still mourns the mystery of my mother and longs to believe that she regretted her decision to leave us behind.

My blood is too warm, the infection too hungry. Sweat rolls down my back; the dagger jostles in my hand. A single blow to the back will cut through all his defenses. From there, rip out his heart and bind it in twine.

I take a step forward.

All at once the world slows to a shuddering crawl. Beyond Merlock's shoulder I see North's eyes widening as he twists away from an oncoming spell. Chadwick is midswing with his blade, teeth bared and his sandy hair flying loose. Baedan stands on the bottom tread of the ballroom stairs, braced against the recoil of magic.

Even the smoke of their battle hangs suspended around the columns and chandeliers, like colored clouds dripping from the sky, or twining between the legs of Merlock's ghostly memories. Threads of magic unfurl across the room like twisted braids, forming complicated patterns mimicking those hanging from Dimitr Frell's ceiling, exposing the complexity of the magic that North and Baedan use. When I look down, I see my mother's spell with the same clarity. What I called a thread is really a series of knots and lines, the work of a skilled seamstress.

But I can also see the edges of the threads beginning to fray from too much handling. The spell won't last much longer.

"I warned you once not to follow me," Merlock says, his voice like thunder in the muted silence around us. "Yet here you are. Again. I did not suffer your mother's stupidity, and I will not indulge yours."

My heart seems to slow in time with the world around us as he turns to face me. "To your credit, you stand with far more conviction than she did the night she came to my rooms, with a blade hidden beneath her robes. I could smell her nerves even through her silks and perfumes." He smiles, cold and cruel. "She paid for her inexperience in more ways than one that night. I like to believe I inspired her to do better next time. And there was a next time. Only, she knew better than to bring a dagger then. She brought a needle and a piece of thread."

I stare at him, stunned into silence. My mother was a—a *courtesan*? North once said Merlock would give magic to his favored mistresses. Is that how she first learned magic? It would certainly have granted her access to Merlock.

I don't even realize how close Merlock is until he's right in front of me, his fetid breath warm across my face. "A single prick of a needle," he says softly. "A single drop of blood, bound tightly in thread. With the right spell, that's all she needed to unravel my Burn. How long did it take her to cast this? And now look at it. My blood hums in your skin, wasted."

The vessel, I realize with a lurch. My mother must have intended to transfer her spell to a vessel—a *weapon*—to be used not just to hunt Merlock . . . but to destroy the Burn. How else could the spell bare the earth beneath my feet? It was Merlock's blood, protecting me from his own magic.

And then, with a wrench of guilt, I wonder, if I had allowed North to remove the spell like he wanted to, would he have been able to recognize it for what it was and utilize it in the way my mother intended? Could I have spared North the poison that tore his expedition apart, that even now is killing him?

I'm tired of questions and guesses. With a strangled growl I lunge forward, as Merlock opens his hand, spreading his fingers wide. Against my will, my own hand mimics the motion, and the dagger falls to my feet. As I bend to retrieve it, Merlock grabs me by the same shoulder he previously wounded.

"This does not belong to you," he says as his fingers sink through the skin above my heart. He twists his wrist, and I feel something fundamental snapping loose inside me. Knots of magic—my mother's spell—shimmer and crackle around his fingers like a ball of unspooled thread, temporarily connecting us. Agony shears down the side of my body, and I scream as he pins me to the wall, tightening the magic in his fist, pulling at the edges still anchored in my skin.

North stumbles into view, hands on either side of the stairwell, straining against the spell that has slowed the rest of the room to a crawl. He accidentally kicks the pile of stones, scattering them. "Faris!"

He stops. Merlock turns. They stare each other down, father and son united for the first time as frayed edges of magic stretch back toward me, eager to find a heartbeat to hold on to. I resist, flattening myself against the wall. Magic this battered will start to rot immediately.

"Corthen," Merlock whispers raggedly. That same look he had in Pilch returns, haunted and yearning. "You finally came."

North gapes at him. "What did you call me?"

"North!" I kick the dagger toward him. It teeters on the top of the stairwell and then overbalances, sliding down one tread.

He retrieves the knife slowly, eyes still locked on his father. "I am not your brother. You murdered him twenty years ago."

Merlock seems to startle out of his trance; his flickering memories vanish. "Of course," he says, more brusquely. "The unsung bastard, home at last, here for his inheritance." He rips the remaining magic loose from my chest and shoves me aside. I trip over the scattered stones and slide across the balcony, hitting against the weak balustrade. A section gives way and clatters to the floor below, and I totter, half over the edge.

North takes a step toward me but falters, eyeing his father warily.

Laughing, Merlock balances the shimmering ball of magic on his palm, then extends it toward North. "Is this what you want?" he asks, and the ballroom transforms around us, dust and age polished away to the gold and glittering marble of its former glory.

The chandeliers brighten with hundreds of flickering candles; music begins to play, and the ghosts of dancers reappear in coat-tails and ball gowns pulled straight from a story I might have told Cadence to help her sleep.

"No," North says hoarsely. "I don't want any of this."

Merlock spreads his arms wide, an open target. "No? Then why are you here? Because you know this kingdom deserved to die."

"North," I plead, pulling myself farther back onto the balcony. "Kill him!"

North is startled by the reminder that I'm still here, and he briefly focuses on me, concern written across his face.

Merlock drops his arms with a sigh. "You stupid boy," he says. "You can't save any of them. And until you realize that, you'll never inherit your full potential."

With a grunt, he spins on his heel, hurling the ball of magic across the ballroom. North lunges forward, dagger raised, but Merlock throws him back with a flick of his hand, slamming him against the wall. The dagger falls, spinning wildly across the balcony floor as Merlock vanishes down the stairs.

No. Growling, I struggle to my feet as behind me the ballroom explodes, knocking me onto my back again, only this time, there's no balustrade to break my fall.

But North is there, hands locked around my wrists, hauling me to safety as around us the walls begin to fall, chandeliers crashing to the floor below, crystal scattering.

"Are you all right?" he asks, touching my face—skin against skin that burns with our shared infection. Shoving him aside with an incoherent admonishment, I grab the dagger and bolt for the stairwell, nearly pitching face-forward as the ballroom continues to shake itself apart around us. By the time I reach the ground, it's too late.

Merlock is gone. And so is our only means of tracking him.

North joins me, grabbing at my arm as a thundercrack splits the air. The floor buckles beneath us, and we crash into a tilting column. I hug it for balance as an eerie silence fills my head, save for a bright, sharp ringing that echoes in my teeth. The floor cracks down the length of the room and we're standing on the wrong side. While the hellborne scramble to the far wall, still firmly attached to the castle and the cliffs supporting its weight, the floor where we stand drops several feet, tipping precariously. North and I haul ourselves onto the now-horizontal side of the column to keep from falling backward, toward the ocean below us. Loose debris is already breaking through the veranda doors and sinking into the freezing water.

Sounds explode around me, crashing and ebbing in undulating waves. Voices spark, but nothing makes sense as the entire castle seems to scream in agony. North leans in, his voice muted despite his proximity. "We have to jump!"

I shake my head at the enormous crack. "We'll never make it!"

"Faris."

"He was right there!" I can't even look at him, I'm so furious. Terrified. Guilty. The floor sags lower, and I tip my head back, fighting tears. Like mother, like daughter: We both plan big but fail to execute. What hurts the most is knowing that, like my mother, I'm leaving Cadence nothing but questions about my intentions, my feelings. Let her hate me as long as she lives, if she could just know I loved her absolutely.

Is that what my mother asked of me?

"Corbin!" Chadwick emerges from the rubble and dust on the opposite side of the crack, blood oozing from a wide cut in his thigh. He tosses a braided curtain pull our way, and North catches it. He winds it around his arm before he hooks me around the waist and pushes me to go first. I start to climb, staggering against the sharp pitch of the floor as Chadwick braces against a sturdy column, knotting the pull off before hauling up the slack. When I reach the broken edge of the floor, he has to hoist me past the gap. As soon as I'm on solid ground again, he tosses the pull back to North, who scales up far more quickly than I did.

"The tunnels!" North shouts as he draws closer, and Chadwick nods grimly in reply.

Behind us, the hellborne seem to recover their bearings, still led by Baedan. Her eye patch is gone, half her face darkened with freshly spilled blood. Our eyes meet through the veil of haze, and her lips curl back in a snarl of fury.

"North," I warn as he pulls himself over the edge of the crack. His eyes widen before Chadwick hauls him up and out of the way of her spell. It hits Chadwick instead, and he stumbles from the blow. I cry out, grabbing for his coat—he's too close to the edge of the broken floor—but I miss and he loses his balance, free-falling before hitting the doors of the veranda far below. The weak glass begins to splinter as debris falls around him. He gains his feet, fear bright across his face when he looks up at us.

He knows. We all do. Even if we had rope to reach him, Baedan's spell is already at work, smearing his skin as though it were snow-melt on a warm day.

North begins swearing, one word after another in a string of profanity as he coaxes magic into his swollen fingers, but Baedan is almost upon us and he has to make a choice. Neither one is easy; only one is right. Chadwick can't be saved.

With a cry that splinters my heart, North blasts Baedan back into the rubble. Spider-thin lines of poison appear on his face, following the curve of his throat and the line of his jaw. He sags back, breathless, as the remaining glass in the veranda doors cracks beneath the weight of too much pressure. The floor shudders once in warning and then breaks loose of the cliff side completely, rattling the entire castle around us. With a groan, the back half of the ballroom plummets a hundred feet to the ocean below, and Chadwick disappears.

Eighteen

No.

No. My denial stutters on repeat, rising in pitch until it becomes a scream.

On hands and knees, North stares numbly at the water churning below us, choked with debris that bobs and eddies in the waves. The floor shifts dangerously again, and he loses his balance, tipping precariously close to the edge. He makes no move to save himself, and I grab his sleeve, and, when that doesn't work, I grab his face, skin on skin, forcing his eyes to focus on me.

We have to run.

North nods in understanding, and we head back for the tunnels, but he's a ghost, a wraith who floats behind me. It feels like defeat to leave Chadwick behind, but it's the only way to ensure survival. We can't fight Baedan face-to-face again.

Adrenaline takes over as we stumble through the candlelit

tunnels, under cracked plaster ceilings and delicate marble arches, untouched by the carnage above. Anger pulses through my veins with every step I take—*fury*. Merlock was right there and I hesitated, and now Chadwick—

No.

He knows how to swim, I reason. Maybe he'll find something to hold on to, and when the *Mainstay* sails past—

NO.

I am not a child and I do not believe in fairy tales. Chadwick is dead. I repeat it to myself, a cruel mantra that cuts through the haze of my pain and brings a much needed clarity. Chadwick is dead, Merlock is not, and I now have a hole above my heart where my mother's spell used to be.

We have failed in every possible way.

North and I run side by side in silence, but when we reach the rotunda with his father's stones laid out on display, North skids to a stop. There's a new one on top, still shining with fresh magic.

I stare at him, blood echoing in my ears. "What are you doing? We have to get back to the sewers before Baedan finds us!"

But North doesn't hear me. Trembling, he approaches the cairn and picks up the stone, turning it between his poison-soaked fingers, which quickly stain the glowing magic black. In an instant he screams, hurling the stone at the wall, overturning the dining chairs. His hands curl into his hair before he straightens, eyes flashing with fire. The poison in his face is spreading, casting shadows beneath his cheekbones.

"I will kill you," he says, and it's eerie, the calmness with which he speaks his vengeance. It still somehow fills the entire room with hate. "Do you hear me, you coward? I will cut your goddamn heart out and I will destroy you."

Footsteps pounding down the hall. Baedan.

"North," I plead, beckoning him to follow me.

North stares through me. He notices that his hand is bleeding and gives it a vague look of surprise before a glimmer of remorse overshadows his fury. "No," he says. "This ends now." Turning, he starts backtracking the way he came, leaving me to stare after him.

No.

"North!" Choking on his name, I crash after him, chasing the flickering path of torches that ignite and extinguish in his wake. But he outpaces me, and the farther I go, the more wild my guesses become as to which way to turn, which way to follow. All at once I'm thrown back to the night beneath Brindaigel, and panic seizes me, bright and overwhelming, pulling me one way even as my head screams to go the opposite direction. *Stop,* I tell myself. *Breathe.* Do not make this mistake again; do not get lost.

I hug myself and close my eyes, stilling my nerves. Slow, steady; one breath, then another.

Someone grabs me around the waist, and I scream, throwing a wild punch that skids past a bristled jaw and tangles of matted hair. I grab a handful and pull as Kellig swears at me, releasing his hold around my waist. I back up warily as he prowls around me, massaging his scalp with one hand.

"You're not leaving without me," he says. He's managed to fashion himself a weapon from broken glass, and he levels it at me in warning. I swallow hard; we've danced this waltz once already, but there's a terrifying desperation in his eyes that suggests this will be our last. His addiction has overcome him. He's shuddering uncontrollably now, teeth bared and his free hand flicking open and shut in a ceaseless pattern. My own trembling fingers inch for Chadwick's dagger in my boot as voices curve around the walls behind Kellig. Baedan would have split her men up to cover more ground. I can handle a single hellborne on my own. Maybe two.

But right now my heart races, my mind blurs as I struggle to remember the most basic of facts. There are no draperies on these walls, no gilded furniture or painted ceilings or ornate arches overhead. Instead they are rudimentary, practical: servants' halls. So going up will take me back to the castle. Going down will eventually lead back to the sewers and the city and possible escape—

The bridge, I remember with a jolt. How am I going to cross the bridge without North to unlock the gate?

One thing at a time, most pressing concerns first. The bridge doesn't matter if I can't make it there.

Kellig lurches forward, ready to fight.

I turn around and run.

Swearing, he gives chase as I wind more deeply into the servants' halls, where the darkness creeps closer, more absolute, our footsteps rousing shadows from their sleep. Without North's blood to light the torches on the wall, I rely on my own failing vision and flashes of light breaking through the ceiling where the castle floors have rotted out. Seeing a door ahead, I veer toward it, fighting with the rusted hinges. Kellig catches up to me, and I swing the dagger wildly—a warning—catching on cloth, on skin, on muscle.

Kellig sags back, eyes wide with disbelief as viscous blood begins to ooze out of his stomach, coating the hand he presses to the wound. "Wasted move," he growls. "You have to aim for the heart."

Bracing my weight against the wall, I kick him in the knee, and he falls back with a curse that rings to the rounded ceiling. Turning back to the door, I wrench it open and haul myself inside—and hit a solid wall.

No. No, no, no. This should be a servants' hall—

But it's a service lift. Damp, fraying ropes hang from out of the darkness, connected to some ancient pulley system above, where weak light shines through another broken door somewhere within the castle itself. Kellig is already on his feet again as I scan the slick stone walls for a foothold. The walls are worn smooth with use; there's no way I can climb them.

My stomach tightens with a cramp as I grab the rope, giving it a test pull, only to swallow back a scream of pain as my entire upper body ignites from where Merlock tore into my flesh. Sliding the unsheathed dagger into the back waist of my trousers, I bite down on the leather scabbard and ignore the pain, hauling the lift up the shaft, inch by grating, squealing inch.

Kellig grabs my foot, using my weight for leverage as he leans into the bottom of the lift, forcing it back down. The rope burns through my hands and I fight back sobs, kicking at him with a slurry of prayers and profanity. Torchlight brightens behind him just as he hauls himself in, cramming to fit beside me. He swings the door shut, and for a moment we stare at each other in the muddied darkness. But his hunger returns, his desperation, and I slowly reach for my dagger as voices bloom into focus in the hall, two, both male. Not Baedan.

Fingers locked around the dagger, I close my eyes and hold my breath; maybe Kellig does the same. A moment later the torchlight dims and disappears through the chinks in the doorway, and I sag against the wall, my legs too weak to support my relief.

But there's still Kellig to consider.

"North can't save you," I say, and it's a broken whisper of a plea. It's a weakness, and I hate it, the way I hate how my hands shake as I clutch the dagger behind my back, laying out the floor, marking my moves. Weighted step forward, swing from the hip, straight through the heart and mind the ribs.

A choked sob escapes me at the thought of it, but Kellig stands between me and freedom, and I am not dying in the dark all alone. If nothing else, I will die beneath the stars, and nobody, especially not an ugly, cowardly man like Kellig, will stop me.

"He *won't* save me," Kellig agrees, stepping forward. He curls a hand behind my head, but I hold: steady, wait, *breathe*. Useless words, a pointless mantra. I'm shaking so hard, my teeth rattle, and I can feel the poison in his skin leaching into mine. "But he'll save you, which means you're my ticket out of here, sweetheart."

His fingers dig into my hair as I move, burying the dagger into his chest and twisting it hard to the right, the way Chadwick taught me. Kellig howls, slamming back against the door of the lift. It shudders open, and he tumbles out in a tangle of arms and legs and unearthly shrieking that will draw whatever shadowbred monsters we've already awoken in these tunnels. I feel them gathering, the air tightening in warning.

At first, I doubt. Was I too low, too high? Is he still alive?

Then, remorse. *Is* he still alive, or is it too late to try to save him?

Why should I? a bitter voice whispers, and I hate the way the thought spreads so easily through my veins. Kellig made his choice; the consequences are his to face. In the hall the murky light flickers and dims, then disappears.

The shadows are coming.

Bloody fingertips tent along the edge of the doorframe as Kellig tries to pull himself to his feet, but fear eclipses all else. I lean over his body and pull the door shut, crushing several of his fingers in the process. Trembling, I back against the opposite wall as Kellig continues to scream at me. He pounds on the door, but his efforts are weak and getting weaker; above his cries I hear the hiss of shadow, loud and getting louder.

Kellig renews his efforts, fear edging his voice. "You—selfish— *bitch*," he slurs, gasping between each word. "Open—the—"

He begins to scream.

I cover my ears, sliding down until my knees are pressed to my chest and I can feel my heartbeat ratcheting against my spine.

And then silence.

It presses down on me from every angle, eerie in its absoluteness. I swallow hard and lower my hands, watching the door with my breath trapped in my throat. The dagger can cut through the shadowbred, but the dagger is buried in Kellig's chest, and I'm not ready to risk getting it.

The seconds add up to minutes, and nothing comes sliding through the door in search of me. Slowly I unfurl, and my heartbeat evens out to a dull throb in my shoulder. I tip my head back, to the glimmer of light somewhere above. The light catches on flecks of ash floating lazily in the air, illuminating them like starlight.

But the light goes out above me, too immediate to be sunset.

Goose bumps race down my back as I hear the phantom scrabble of shadowed claws clicking down the wall. I jump up and open the door, scan the hall, step over Kellig's body, ready to *run*.

But the dagger.

I hesitate, torn, before I look back. When will I ever have the chance to face Merlock again?

I don't want my ability to murder a man efficiently to be the lesson I remember Chadwick by. He taught me far more—and far better—than that. A blade forged with North's blood, with enough blood to conduct a bloodbound ceremony hidden in its handle, would be deadly if left in the wrong hands. Not to mention, the dagger is my only defense. It would be stupid to abandon it, and I have made too many mistakes already.

Reluctantly I return to Kellig's body, corroded now, and stripped of skin. I have to brace a palm against his chest to wrench the blade free, and when it releases, I stagger back as fast as I can, turning my head to vomit. Dimly I'm aware that the blood spilling from my shoulder feels cold; my fingers feel numb. I'll freeze down here if I don't start moving.

After an agonizing moment of debate, I take his coat, too.

Nineteen

SLOWLY I LURCH BACK TOWARD THE MAIN TUNNELS, LIMPING slightly, stopping constantly, listening, forever listening. When I reach the rotunda, I survey North's destruction with a sense of detachment.

Someone's coming.

Every inch of me wants to collapse in frustration and exhaustion. Will the gods never grant me mercy? But my heart still beats, and so, gritting my teeth, I pick up speed.

"Faris!"

North. I turn as he enters the rotunda, relief carved across his face. The poison is gone, I realize, but so is most of his color. "Faris," he repeats, more softly, jogging toward me.

I meet him halfway, and strike him as hard as I can, again and again and again until it breaks everything left inside me and I sag against him, choking on dry sobs.

North holds me up by the elbows while leaning back to avoid my weakening blows. "Faris, please don't—"

"Don't you ever do that to me again! You never leave someone behind!"

North steadies me, eyes wide. Wounded. Confusion slowly gives way to remorse, and he seems to wilt where he stands, too old and too young at the same time. "I'm sorry. . . . I—I was coming back; the poison needed to be excised, and—"

"I didn't know that!" I fight out of his arms, then stagger several steps back. "I didn't know if I would ever see you again!" Frustrated, I take another swing, hitting him in the shoulder, my own shoulder howling in reply. "Damn it, North!"

That same soft scuttling I heard in the lift has followed me here. I look past North, to the tunnels behind him. The shadows seem to swell, and despite his proximity, the candles along the wall go out, one by one in an unwavering line moving toward us.

"We have to go," I say. "Baedan's already in the tunnels; she might even be ahead of us."

"Faris."

I give him a look that cuts off whatever apology he was preparing to give. It wouldn't be good enough. Not in a million years.

"You're bleeding," he says desperately as I begin yanking candles from their holders. We'll need the light out in the Burn. "We can't risk going anywhere until we cover the wound."

"We can risk the sewers," I say darkly, and start moving.

North stays a step or two behind me, stopping when I stop, following where I lead. I don't look at him, but I feel him watching me. When we reach the bridge, he sacrifices more of our precious magic to open the gate, and we bypass the bodies of Baedan's men, only to stop at the six-foot span of missing floor. Vertigo strikes when I see the water below; panic flutters. I squeeze my eyes shut and blot out Chadwick's face, replacing it with Cadence's. I have to get home now, for her. No matter how much it hurts.

I barely make the jump, my feet sliding out from under me on the landing, spilling me hard onto my shoulder. I don't move, even after North lands beside me. Instead I rest my cheek on the icy marble, seeking relief from the burning in my skin. North touches my back, but I shake him off, finally dragging myself to my feet.

I don't feel safe until we're deep within the belly of the city. Only then do I stop at a wide junction, with half a dozen tunnels branching off in all directions at all different heights. After positioning a candle for light, I sink onto the raised lip of stone framing a central drain. North carefully sits beside me, still watching me warily.

"I'm not going to break," I say.

"It's all right if you do," he replies.

I shake my head tightly, refusing to yield to my tears.

North doesn't say a word about my newfound coat as he helps me out of it, leaving me shivering in my blood-soaked chemise—my tunic carelessly discarded in the ballroom. A glance to my mangled chest makes my stomach turn, and I look away, swallowing back too much saliva. It'll take more than eleven stitches to sew me closed again.

We don't mention the deeper scar it leaves: Without the spell, there's no second chance at finding Merlock. If Baedan picks up his trail again, she'll find him long before we have a chance to return with more supplies.

After pulling on his gloves to avoid our infected skin colliding, North cleans my wound with water pooled at our feet, then bandages it with a strip of his own tunic. His touch is gentle but proficient; he works with a methodical grace, but there's a careful guard between us he doesn't dare broach. Overhead, shadows flicker and dim in the candlelight as I roll my guilt across my tongue, softening the edges like a rock worn smooth by the river.

"You were right," I finally say, my hands squeezing my knees so tightly, my knuckles turn white. "My mother wove her spell with Merlock's blood; it could have been a powerful weapon. Had I let you take it from me in New Prevast, you would have known what to do with it; it wouldn't have been wasted. Chadwick was right: I never should have come."

"Faris."

"He asked me to kill Merlock before we left," I continue. "I couldn't do it. I put you in danger—all of Avinea in danger—because I thought I would *succeed*." A bitter laugh escapes me as I shake my head. "My arrogance is going to kill everyone. Except Merlock. You were right: It is selfish to sacrifice the many to save the few."

"Faris." A hard edge enters his voice, forcing my eyes to his. He shifts his weight, our knees striking against each other. Eyebrows knitted, he brushes hair away from my temple, the leather of his glove clammy against my cheek as his thumb follows the curve of my face. "Saving Avinea was never your responsibility. Nor your mother's."

I stare at him, flooded with remorse. "Cadence is my responsibility," I say. "And I've just condemned her."

Without waiting for his reply, I retrieve our candle, grateful for the pain in my shoulder to keep me focused on what matters now: surviving.

Wordlessly we continue through the tunnels, pushing as far as possible before taking shelter in a half-collapsed tunnel far from the castle, still slightly warm from the Burn overhead. North watches as I stack a series of stones at different intervals, a security system I picked up in the Brim. If anyone tries to enter the tunnel while we sleep, they'll knock the stones loose and we'll have a brief window of warning.

Neither one of us mentions that if something finds us, we're already dead.

Despite the warmth of the tunnels, there's a warning chill to the air that burrows under my coat, into my blood. North and I avoid each other's eyes, but we cannot avoid the inevitable: We need each other to stay warm.

"We can sleep back-to-back," I finally say. "That should be safe enough. We'll have to take shifts to keep the candles lit."

North nods agreement. "I'll take the first one," he says, ever the gentleman. "You need some sleep."

I'm too exhausted to argue, so I lie down on the ground, closing my eyes as he positions himself beside me. Even through our coats I feel his bones, and my stomach somersaults. Is he also thinking about that night we spent in his wagon, pressed this close together?

The tunnel echoes with eerie noises; small somethings scuttle in the dark. I'm almost asleep when North asks, "Who got left behind?"

I tense, eyes flying open. "What?"

"Back there, beneath the palace. I've never seen you so angry. I deserved it, but . . ." He shifts his weight, his hip angling into my back. "Who got left behind?"

Just the memory of his leaving makes me angry again, and my hands curl into loose fists beneath my cheek. "I did."

Months have dulled the edges of Thaelan's memory into an ache, like a fading spell buried in my skin, but as I unravel our history, the memory brightens again. North listens to our story and never interrupts, and my voice is raw by the end of it, my heart hollow. But I'm oddly comforted, too. Alistair knew pieces of me through Thaelan, but to confess to North every truth and every lie we told somehow validates that Thaelan once lived, that he was loved.

And that letting him go is the right thing to do.

"When he left for the barracks that night, I didn't know he wasn't coming back," I finish. "I never said good-bye."

Shadows inch closer, waltzing with the guttering flames of the candle positioned by our heads. Even more shadows pool down the walls around us, dripping like ink.

"I was coming back for you, Faris." North says.

"I didn't know that."

"I will always come back."

"Don't say that. You cannot promise the impossible."

He turns, propping his weight on one arm as he looks over my shoulder at my profile. "I wanted to kill someone," he says. "I wanted someone to suffer for what happened to Ben. I stupidly thought if I could find Baedan . . ." He bows his head, guilty. "But I didn't. I only came back because of you."

"No," I say, emphatic, rolling onto my back to see his face. "You came back because it was the right thing to do. Don't make me the reason for your actions; I cannot be the reason you fail."

"I would have walked away in that instant, abandoned it all," he says. "Ben was right. We needed more men. More magic. We needed to come back with a better plan—"

"It's not your fault that he died."

"Don't absolve me," he says tightly. "Hold me accountable for my sins. Ben trusted me with his life, and I betrayed that trust. I ignored his advice, his orders, his actions—I let my vices win. And tonight . . ." He breaks off, shaking his head, turning his face away. "I was no better than my father."

"Don't do that." I sit up with a flash of concern. "That is poison in your blood, do you understand me? Guilt runs stronger than any magic, and if you let it, it will kill you. You are our king, North, but Chadwick—any of us—would have died for you, not for that but because you are our friend."

North dips his head. "Merlock knew I couldn't kill him. Even before I did." He looks at me from beneath his knitted brows. "I'm terrified that my heart is too weak for this world."

"Why would you say that?"

"Your mother died to protect you," he says. "You would die for Cadence. But even now, after all that he's done, I can't help but wonder why my father would choose *this* as his legacy, over me. I actually thought he wanted to speak to me, to make amends . . ." Snorting, he shakes his head and sucks in a deep breath. "It's ridiculous, I know, because I will kill him. I just wanted the chance to forgive him first."

I resist the urge to embrace him, desperate to feel his weight, his heat, his *being*, this sad, lonely boy with the odds perpetually stacked against him. Nobody would bet on him in the fighting ring, and yet I'm all in. I've seen the iron underneath the fear, the determination and sincerity with which he speaks of saving Avinea, no matter how indifferent its people are to his sacrifice. Instead I hover my hand above his heart. "This has never been your weakness," I say.

"What if I'm really just like him?" North asks. "What if this is just the beginning? I feel it in my blood, Faris; it's all there, waiting. The anger. The selfishness. It's getting easier and easier to lose control. Sometimes I almost wish I would. If I had magic in my blood the way he does—"

"But you won't give in to it."

"How do you know that?"

"Because you were born the only heir to the throne. You had the privilege to do anything you wanted, and you decided to be North. Hero of Tobek the apprentice; caretaker of Darjin the magic tiger; friend to Captain Benjamin Chadwick"—my voice hitches, and I pause—"saving grace to Faris Locke; and above all else, the rightful King of Avinea. You could have hidden away, safe in the palace, like they think you did, but instead you gave up everything. You love this kingdom more than it will ever love you, and that is why you will never be your father. We lost Chadwick today, and yet here you are, still standing, where your father would have broken. Because you will always be North. Steady as a star."

His fingers unfurl, just enough that his fingertips brush the edge of my knee. Not an accident, an acknowledgment.

"My need to leave Brindaigel was only an idea," I add. "There was never really a plan for what came next, and that's why it failed. If you want to save Avinea, you need to know what happens next, because I guarantee that Bryn and her father already have their next five moves planned."

He speaks to his chest, head still bowed. "Tell me what to do."

"Survive."

"You make it sound easy."

"We're in the sewers of Prevast, trapped in the Burn with no guaranteed way home," I say. "There's nothing easy about it."

North nods as his eyes meet mine again. I recognize the look, the wanting. "Faris," he begins.

But surviving starts here. Now. "Good night, North." I turn around again, resettling myself. A moment later he turns away as well.

Twenty

AFTER A FEW SHORT HOURS OF SLEEP APIECE, WE CONTINUE FORWARD, eventually emerging from the sewers on the outskirts of the city. Dawn has broken, but the sky is storm-gray and ominous, warning of a change in the weather.

After double-checking that all our wounds are covered tightly, North fumbles in his pocket for any remaining spell stones that might still have magic in them. Our eyes meet above the span of his palm with mutual alarm. One stone, two people.

It's not nearly enough.

"I can repurpose some of my own spells," he says with a forced smile to hide the fear in his eyes. "We'll be fine. It's not that far."

It took us two full days and one endless night to reach the city, and that was with Sofreya's protection spells still holding strong. Mine might last another day or two if I can keep my vices tempered, but North's are long gone by now, with the amount of poison he's pulled in and pushed back out of his body.

Yet at his insistence I expose my forearm so he can cast a renewed protection spell to replace Sofreya's faded one. When his bare fingertips brush my skin, a warm rush of desire floods through me, and my heart quickens in reply. I close my eyes, grateful that he's not an intuit and cannot tell what secrets my blood hides.

Once free of the city, we stand on the edge of a vast expanse of horizon that is broken only by the occasional tree or crumbling building, with the ocean spread to our right. There are miles of ash and shadow, full of poisoned wolves and deadly magic. We can risk heading east, a longer journey toward the edge of the Burn, or backtrack south in the hopes that the *Mainstay* has not yet set sail. In the end, we choose the slim hope that Davik will still be anchored.

Decided, our eyes meet with mutual misery at the daunting task ahead.

We start walking.

Even with the protection spell, the Burn scorches through the soles of my boots; the ash that settles against my skin burrows deep. With no canteens and no water, the sea becomes cruelly mocking, so close and so useless. I'm staring at it with a dry throat and parched tongue when North stops to check if the infection has made any progress beneath my skin.

"What about you?" I ask, my voice harsh, cracked. My clothes stick to me, damp with sweat. The entire left half of my body buzzes.

North displays his hands: swollen and shaking but clean of any poison. He smiles, but it's a shadow across his face, barely there and gone. The mountains that have emerged on the horizon don't move any closer, but the city has fallen too far behind. We're caught somewhere in the middle of nowhere, and exhaustion settles over me, mental and physical. The ash becomes a tempting pillow, and I resist the urge to pitch myself into a dune and let the Burn sing me lullabies like my mother used to do.

My mother. So few questions answered; so many new ones to ask. I'm starting to realize that no matter how much I want it, I will never know the full image of her. The best I can do is piece together an impression. The basics are there, but only if you squint and overlook the blurry edges. "Merlock said my mother was a courtesan. Like yours."

North gives me a guarded look. "It's possible. If he knew how powerful she was, he would have wanted her close."

"Then how did she get to Brindaigel? The Burn had already begun; she knew she had to stop it. Stop *him*. She even had a weapon waiting. A real vessel, not—not *me*."

"If she was loyal to Corthen during the war, she would have known about Brindaigel."

"And it was a good place to hide until she knew how to cast her spell." I sigh, pitying my father. Did he ever love her, or did he only use her the way she seemed to have used him, learning what she needed until the time came to leave him behind? "Either way, I guess she wasn't exactly a hero, was she?" Snorting, I rub at an ache in my neck. "I don't suppose Perrote factored into her plans."

He studies my profile. "She wanted to save Avinea."

"Only so that people like her could have access to its magic," I say darkly. "If this is the damage one man can do, imagine what would happen if an entire kingdom became corrupted. Perrote's stories would actually be true: Avinea would be consumed with a plague."

"You said there was a weapon waiting for the spell. If it was cast with Merlock's blood, and your mother intended to forge a weapon with it . . ."

"You think she planned to inherit the magic herself?" The idea leaves me breathless. My mother may not have been a hero, but to be a villain no better than Bryn or Perrote?

"Or she intended to destroy magic completely," he says cautiously, as if afraid of my reaction.

"Is that even possible?"

"If she was able to find Merlock and cut through his spells, she could also theoretically cut out his heart and leave it to die. Without a proxy or an heir to bind it, it wouldn't survive."

"And neither would the Burn." I shake my head at the sheer nerve it would take to believe herself capable of executing such a plan. But then again, didn't I believe I had a chance to kill Merlock? Beneath the wonder is renewed guilt at using the spell so superficially, losing it so pathetically.

Shaking my head, I force a rueful smile. "I suppose I should stop being so quick to assume the worst of her and maybe, finally, give her some credit."

North is silent, squinting toward the horizon. Then a tiny, playful smile crosses his lips as his dark eyes slide toward me. "Do you think our mothers knew each other?"

"Do I think they plotted anarchy together in the halls of the castle?" I ask, and North laughs, a bright and startling sound that elicits a grin from me in response before North touches my arm, directing me back into motion.

"I hope they did," he says.

So do I.

We make good time—or so I tell myself. But as the sky begins to darken and the shadows start to stretch, we have no choice but to take shelter for another night in a farming silo that stands alone in a sea of nothing. The roof is gone and the stone walls have turned black from dead magic, but they still keep out the worst of the wind.

North gathers scraps of old farming supplies, the wood withered and gray but flammable. Once a fire is started, he orders me out of my coat to check my bandages. Blood has seeped through in several wide patches, but rather than risk undressing them, he simply layers more scraps of his tunic over top.

Despite myself, I lean into his touch. It's the Burn, it's his proximity, it's the way I feel tired inside and out. North hesitates, uncertain. He clears his throat and avoids my eyes, and I close mine, humiliated that I cannot control my own desires even though they would kill us.

When he hands me back my coat, I catch him eyeing the blood dried along the front.

"I killed him," I say, and my stomach cramps with the memory of it. This wasn't Bryn ordering me to pull a trigger; it was me pinning a knife through a man's chest to save myself.

"You put Kellig out of his misery," says North. "When I'm king, the Burn will be eradicated and the hellborne hunted. There's no future for them in Avinea. It's only a matter of time."

"When you're king," I repeat. "You've never said that before." For North to acknowledge his future—to speak of it as a certainty and not as a lingering question—it makes my heart race, as if he's scraped off a layer of ash to reveal the grass still growing underneath.

North grins, embarrassed, pushing himself to his feet. "I will be king," he says, "but not tonight. I'll take first watch again."

Wolves howl in the distance, and ours is not the only fire we see, yet I still feel safe here, with North standing guard, a tall figure framed in the silo doorway, black against a stormy sky.

But I'm far from safe, as evidenced by the words that slip out before I can stop them: "I'm cold."

North startles, then turns, expression guarded. "We can't build a bigger fire."

"I know," I say.

My head aches. I can feel my blood thickening in my veins, and yet when North wordlessly lies beside me, it's a blissful heat that spreads like starlight. As previously, he positions his back against mine, but I stop him. "No," I say. "Like this."

At my prodding, he rolls onto his opposite side, facing toward me, and I edge into him, my back to his stomach. His arm hovers, uncertain, before resting lightly against mine, and then, when I don't protest, with more settled weight.

"Cadence and I would always sleep like this," I say, an attempt to excuse my weakness under the guise of innocent necessity.

North exhales softly, pressing his chin against my shoulder. "Go to sleep," he murmurs.

...

The next morning is misery. We are both groggy and sore, exhausted. The way ahead is interminable; the way back, impossible. We don't speak; we don't tease; we don't point out the rising ash cloud behind us or speculate on who—or what—might be causing it. It doesn't matter who's following us now—we have no real defense anyway, except to move forward as quickly as we can.

At first I ignore the blob of shadow on the water that appears early in the afternoon, dismissing it as a mirage. But when North sees it too, our eyes meet with almost delirious thrill. The *Mainstay*. Davik held true to her word. Even without North, she stayed anchored.

There's still a chance to make it home.

We try to pick up our pace with renewed energy toward a tangible goal. Yet our steps have become slowed, labored; every breath hurts. North loses his footing, and when I bend to help him to his feet, his coat sleeve falls back, revealing dark lines of poison inching toward his wrists.

He sees me looking and forces a bitter laugh that's half-manic, before yanking the sleeve back down. "You see everything about me so easily, Miss Locke," he says, still kneeling in the ash. He closes his eyes, forehead furrowed.

Numbly I pull back the collar of his coat. All his spells are gone, and the shirt underneath is soaked in sweat, sticking to his bony frame. Poison crawls across his shoulder, creeping toward his heart.

Fear rolls down my back and pools in my stomach. We're still hours from the cliffs and any possible assistance. A glance behind confirms that we're still being hunted. "Can't you excise it?"

A tired smile. He lifts a hand to demonstrate the small stone he drained of magic hours ago, now black as ink. "Not big enough."

"If we dig under the ash—" I start scraping it back with my hands, searching for earth.

"Faris."

"Or take it from me," I say, pulling back my own sleeve, exposing the spell he cast yesterday.

North's smile wavers at my surprise to find it gone; his eyes turn hazy, red-rimmed and watery from too much smoke. "It was a weak spell to begin with."

I drop my sleeve, staring at him. Terror threatens to hold me down, and my blood sings its agreement: *Stay.* Embrace your vices, embrace North. Death is not the only option.

"Get up," I say at last, sliding an arm beneath his shoulders, hefting him to his feet.

"Faris."

"Get up!" Growling, I shoulder his weight against my own, biting through the pain as I stagger for balance.

"I'm sorry," North says. He swallows hard, as pain creases his face. "I've held off as long as I can."

"What are you talking about?! We're almost there—I can see the boat from here—"

"It's the only chance I have of facing my father again," he says weakly, immune to my panic.

God Above, he's talking about turning hellborne.

I release him, stricken. "No," I say, and then, more furiously, "No. That is not an option!"

But it is an option, and from the way he forces a guilty smile, I realize that he saw it as an option long before he set foot in the Burn.

"Everyone needs a fail-safe," he says. His smile vanishes as his fingertips graze my cheek. "Go back to Cadence. Perrote will be forced into the Burn to find Merlock, but Bryndalin will stay behind to guard her throne. Since you don't have your mother's spell anymore, you'll be safe."

"Safe from what?! You—"

"Will find my father and inherit his legacy," North cuts in, fingertips sliding down to my lips. "And you will survive."

"And what about you?" But it's in his face, the eerie calm of acceptance. He'll inherit Avinea's magic and then do what his father never could.

Destroy himself to save the world.

"No," I say. "Alistair will figure out how to get this poison out of you, North, but you have to get home first. You are not giving up."

Clenching my teeth, I drag his arm back over my shoulder and start lurching forward again. "Burning this kingdom to the ground is your father's legacy, not yours. You believe there's something worth saving in this world, and I'll fight for it, North. Because I believe in *this*. You cannot lose your heart." I flatten my palm against his chest. His heartbeat thrashes, erratic and uneven. "Avinea needs you just the way you are. So keep moving."

Yet, as the afternoon drags its heels in the ash, the *Mainstay* is no longer a beacon of hope, but rather a mocking reminder of how far we have yet to go. North is barely on his feet and I'm losing strength fast. Even now, the skies darken overhead, stretching violet fingers of shadow across the Burn. Once the light disappears for good, the air will turn frosty again and our bodies will become more cumbersome with the cold. The clouds overhead are the warning color of dull slate.

The color of snow.

North struggles to match my pace, emotions warring across his face. "Don't let go of me," he croaks.

I adjust my stance, bowing beneath his weight. "I'll hold on as long as you do."

We fight inch by inch toward the *Mainstay* and the cliffs that mark our camp on the beach below. *Almost there*, I tell myself, even as the sky turns black at its edges and the cold locks my muscles and our footsteps start dragging. *Almost there*, I repeat when the pale sails of the *Mainstay* finally sharpen into focus.

North stumbles, pitching forward, pulling me down with him. Choking, I sit up, but North remains sprawled on his back, eyes closed. Poison has begun spreading up his throat, past his jawline, darkening the already dark stubble on his chin.

"North." I weakly jostle him, to no avail. I try pulling him into a sitting position, but he's dead weight and my strength is fading. "North!" Frantic, I press my ear to his chest, searching for the whisper-crash beat of his heart. There, but only barely.

I stare toward the cliffs, debating the distance. Should I leave him to get help? Would I be able to find him again, in this growing darkness? From here the *Mainstay* doesn't look so far—I could be there and back again in an hour, maybe.

If I have an hour left in me. And if I can trust anyone on board to actually help. Davik would, but that would leave her ship without its captain. An easy target for mutiny.

You never leave anyone behind.

Biting back tears of frustration, of grief, I start pulling him toward the cliff, stopping every few feet to catch my breath and summon my strength. My bandages pull loose with the movement, ripping away, but I can't be bothered with them now. The hell-borne tribe that has trailed us all day seems to hang back, watching me. Waiting for me to die—or to join their ranks. With no magic left between us, all we'd be good for now is food.

Baring my teeth, I show them my palms, still in the air—a ridiculous act of defiance, but proof that I am not yet defeated.

With my sleeves pulled over my palms for protection, I cradle North's face in my hands, ignoring the way my blood heats with interest when my exposed fingertips skim his jawline. Already the ash is beginning to claim us; if we don't move, we'll be buried by dawn.

"Don't do this," I say fiercely. "I'm still here. And I will always be here because I can't—I *won't* leave you behind."

It's a slow-spreading admission through my blood. This is what prompts people to abandon their children, to steal from kings, to sacrifice themselves so that others might live.

Love.

"I lied to you," I whisper as tears flood my eyes. Lowering my head, my lips hover by his ear. "I need you, North."

No response. My words are not made of magic, and they have no power to heal. Disappointed, I drop my head to his chest. Is this it, then? My only chance to say good-bye, stolen from me once again?

Shouts draw my attention; dancing lights are coming closer. With a shot of adrenaline I rise to my feet, unsheathing Chadwick's dagger and positioning myself above North, just in case. It's a mockery of bravery. Exhaustion pulls my arms down beneath the slim weight of the blade; the muscles in my back scream in protest with every move I make.

I can't fight anymore.

Captain Davik's brothers plow past me without a second glance, bending for North. Sofreya and Cohl are close behind, ready to offer assistance. Silver spells shimmer on their skin, glowing in the darkness. I stare at them, flabbergasted by their arrival after they abandoned us both to this fate.

My legs start to buckle just as Cohl grabs my arm, holding me steady. "Where's Captain Chadwick?" she asks, scanning the dark horizon behind us.

I stare at her, unable to speak. It didn't occur to me that nobody else would know—that I would have to be the one to tell them. I open my mouth, unprepared. But Cohl hears the words anyway. She nods once, expression grim, guiding me forward. One foot, then the other.

It begins to snow.

Twenty-One

RETURNING TO THE *MAINSTAY* IS A SERIES OF STACCATO IMAGES THAT bleed together into one barely understandable blur. Somebody carries me at one point—Tieg, probably—and I'm sick more than once on the choppy waters between the beach and the *Mainstay* itself. Once on board, someone forces a glass of water into my hands, and I'm sick again, on the floor of the galley.

North is carried into Davik's quarters, and we weigh anchor, aiming for home. Sofreya disappears inside for hours before she tends to me, excising what she can, buying us time to return to New Prevast.

The harried explanation I receive for the others' betrayal is likewise fragmented. Upon returning to the *Mainstay*, free of the Burn's insidious influence, Cohl and Terik realized the error of their ways and insisted on a search-and-rescue mission—which Captain Davik demanded of everyone if anyone wanted to make it home on her ship. The only real innocent was Sofreya, coerced into going to protect the others on their way back. Like me, she's had a little basic training. Unlike me, she lacks the confidence to use it, and she complied out of fear.

There's guilt enough to confirm the story in the faces that peek in on me as I sleep away most of the following day. Even so, that evening I lie awake as light from the galley cuts across my face. I listen as everyone toasts Chadwick with drinks and stories of a beloved captain . . . conveniently forgetting their role in abandoning him in the Burn. But they are nothing but loyal tonight, and it infuriates me. The Burn intensifies weaknesses. It doesn't create traitors from loyalists.

When I can no longer bear the hypocrisy, I force myself out of bed on shaky legs and stumble down the short hall to the deck above. As much as it hurts, it's a relief to stretch my muscles and confirm that my body still works, despite how mangled it feels.

Bront stands at the helm, and he lifts a hand in acknowledgment. I wave back, moving to the railing to watch the coastline cut sharp edges in the water behind us. There's nothing out there but darkness and the occasional blister of light from one of the few villages still clinging to life on the edge of the world, and I press closer to the icy railing, squinting my eyes against the salt of the ocean. Stars glitter overhead, but the moon is a barely-there wink in the sky.

"I knew I'd see you out here eventually," a voice says, and I glance back to see North standing against one of the masts behind me. He straightens and walks toward me, slow but steady. When he reaches the railing, he leans against it as though he needs the support.

I try to smile but give it up as useless. "I needed some air."

"And some starlight."

"Always," I say. Then, "Why aren't you with the others?"

"They knew Ben as a captain," North says. "I'll honor him in my own way, as a friend. Not to mention," he adds drily, "I'd be tempted to throw every one of them overboard."

We share a smile before he plunges his hands into his coat pockets. "I have a new plan."

A hollowness sharpens inside me, as if he's already taken the first step away. "Which is?"

"I'm going to run."

When I stare at him, incredulous, he lifts his shoulders in an elegant shrug. "Dossel won't finance a second trip into the Burn. He'll go himself, with enough supplies to last for weeks. It'll be proof of how strong he is. How weak I am."

And to the people of Avinea, desperate for a return of magic by any means possible, it won't even matter that Perrote isn't their king. They'll worship him anyway if he succeeds.

"He's going to come after you," North says quietly. "He'll want your spell to find Merlock. But Bryndalin has every reason to keep you alive. Especially while I'm gone, because that means there's a chance that I might succeed before her father does. And she will always ensure she has an ability to negotiate."

"And if you don't come back?" I ask. "You barely made it out alive this time; you need time to recover, time to plan—"

"You'll survive," he says simply. "Like always. You'll find a new way to keep Cadence safe."

"North—"

"Baedan is still out there; I can't waste time."

"And how are you going to compete with her? Kellig is dead, my spell is gone, you're wandering blindly and alone into the Burn—"

"I won't be alone," he interrupts. "Cohl has agreed to come. And Sofreya, as well as both of Davik's brothers."

"Cohl left you out in the Burn once already."

"And she's made amends," North says. "Pickings are slim in the middle of the ocean, and I can't do this alone."

"Do what, exactly?"

A spark of light fills his eyes. "I know where he's going."

I stare at him. "The spell stone under the castle? But by the time you get back into the Burn, he'll have moved on—"

"I can't stop thinking about what I could have done differently to save Ben," says North, overriding my argument. "I see it playing out again and again, every moment leading up to that instant. If I had been faster, if I had seen Baedan first—"

"You saw what Baedan's spell did to him. You know he was already dead."

He shakes away my sympathy, forcing a smile. "The point is guilt. For years my mother told me that it's what destroyed my father. That killing his brother broke his heart and sparked the Burn. For a moment beneath the castle, I understood how easily it could happen."

He pulls a small black book from his pocket and opens it to a crude map he's drawn of the northwestern edge of Avinea. Then he hands the book to me. "The night I met you, I had a lead that last placed Merlock in Pilch." He taps a dot low on the map, near the mountains where he discovered Bryn and me in a hellborne marketplace. "A week later your mother's spell took you outside the palace in Prevast. Now a *month* later, you tracked him from Pilch to Prevast again over the course of a week."

"I don't understand," I say.

"Pilch," he says, "is where Merlock and Corthen were born and raised. Oksgar is where Merlock killed his father when he was twenty-two, and was subsequently crowned king. The watchtower in Dorrent—it marked the outer edge of the spell that protected Prevast while Merlock went to war in the Wintirlands, and it was where the first battle between him and his brother took place when he returned."

Goose bumps pebble my skin, and I hug myself as he continues. "The ballroom in Prevast." He jabs his finger emphatically. He's breathless, and there's a hint of excitement in his voice. "That's where Merlock executed more than a dozen traitor provosts from the orchestra balcony in the middle of a party celebrating his victory in battle. His chambers underground, where Corthen allegedly offered a truce, at the cost of Merlock's abdication. And then the stone he left two days ago, instructing his brother to find him in Islar—where Corthen had a secret military compound that Merlock burnt, killing more than a hundred of Corthen's men. He's not running, Faris. You were right." His dark eyes meet mine, and there's a light in them that's been dimmed for weeks. "He's atoning. But not to me. His guilt has consumed him so entirely that he's addicted to the punishment of retracing the same steps over and over, trying to find the one decision that could have changed the past."

So it wasn't North that Merlock was remembering in Pilch. It was Corthen.

It seems absurd that Merlock would waste twenty years running in circles, and yet—how often have I relived that night beneath Brindaigel, cruelly wondering *What if?* Holding tight to Cadence instead of letting her run; turning back to join Thaelan instead of hiding from Alistair? How much could I have changed with one different decision? It's an easy spiral to slip into, difficult to pull yourself free of.

North exhales softly. "I have to go back. If I can't kill him after all that he's done, I don't deserve this kingdom."

The wind snaps between us, and I drag the hair out of my face. "But where is he going after Islar?"

He returns to his map. "By following his logical process, I can guess he'll continue southwest. He met his brother in their final battle here, on the fields outside Arak. Three months later Corthen's body was interred here, in Kerch. If I'm right, he'll follow his path, and when he realizes he can't change the past and Corthen isn't coming back to absolve him . . ."

"He goes back to the beginning to try again," I say with a shiver.

North lifts his eyebrows in agreement. The wind rifles pages of his book, flashing glimpses of pencil drawings, and, curious, I turn the page forward. And then again and again. The pages are filled with dozens of drawings of flowers, detailed as if copied from a book.

"What are these?" I ask, transfixed.

Sweet, awkward North emerges as he searches for an answer, reminding me of the shy first kiss we shared, when afterward he asked if he had done it right. "I wanted you to see the best of Avinea," he says at last. "I know right now it leaves a lot to be desired, but I swear to you, if you look hard enough, this kingdom can be beautiful. It's worth saving."

I study him, but his expression is guarded, prepared for the inevitable worst when I remind him—once again—that we can't be together. Did he hear anything last night in the Burn, when I finally confessed that I'd lied? The way he waits, so nervously, denies the idea.

Only then do I realize it's not anger that drives me to hit him for wanting to leave, for wanting to do it alone. It's fear.

I can't bear to lose him, too.

"Come with me," he whispers.

"You know I can't. As soon as Bryn realizes I've run off with you, she'll retaliate."

"I can mute the binding spell's effects," he says. "Long enough for us to find Merlock."

"With what magic? You didn't even make it five days in the Burn with Sofreya's protection spells—"

"Darjin," he says, but it clearly hurts to say it.

"Absolutely not. You can't risk going back to the castle."

"I don't have any other choice. I can take what magic Sofreya has left on board, but otherwise, Darjin is my only option."

"Then save what little you have," I say. "Don't waste it on me when I can't do anything for you. Besides, it's not me I'm worried about. Like you said, Bryn won't kill me while there's a chance you might succeed. But if I leave Cadence behind again, Bryn would destroy her." And not through death; she would be more clever—more cruel—than that. She would rob my sister of what innocence she has left, twisting her into a mirror image of herself.

"We'll take Cadence to Revnik. Lord Inichi is well protected within the city. She would be safe."

Panic begins to resurface, called by the familiarity of the scene and the ease with which he deflects my protests, just like Thaelan. I've been here before, and I know how this ends. A choice made in haste and a consequence that will never stop screaming.

But, I think, and it is intoxicating in its possibilities. *What if?*

"No," I say at last. "We both know you have a better chance running now. Without me."

North swallows hard and slides his book back into his pocket. "I had to ask."

"I'm sorry—"

"Don't." Sighing, he reaches out, hesitant, knuckles almost skimming my cheek before his fingers curl through my hair. "I know you made your choice," he says, "and I will honor your request and never mention this again after this moment, but I love you, Faris. And this"—he lowers his forehead toward mine, but doesn't touch me as his voice drops to a husky whisper—"is our good-bye."

I stare at his throat, stricken. What do I say to that? Do I feign indifference again, for—for *what*? For North's protection? My coldness has done nothing to diminish his own warmth; for all the damage I assumed I would cause, he has not wavered from his path to kill Merlock, and I am tempted—*so* tempted—to simply give in.

Twice now I have rebuked his heart and damaged my own in the process. It isn't loving him that will destroy us; it's the pretending otherwise. Even virtue turns to vice when taken to an extreme.

Am I the ironhearted daughter my mother tried to make me, or am I nine perfect stitches and no questions asked, forever hiding like my father?

I embrace North in a rush, fisting the back of his coat in one hand. North startles, caught off guard. He returns the hug, tentative at first, but then with more resolve. My chin fits so perfectly against his neck, but he's already weak from his recovery. I know he can't risk awakening the poison in his blood to the poison in mine. But I hold on, battered with grief as I close my eyes against my tears, committing him to memory.

"Don't ever let go of me," he murmurs.

"I'll hold on as long as you do," I reply.

Someone clears their throat, and we break apart, avoiding each other's eyes. Cohl stands a respectful distance away, backlit by the lights belowdecks. "Davik needs you, your majesty," she says.

"Of course." North lifts a hand in acknowledgment as his eyes meet mine. He opens his mouth but hesitates, searching for the right words to say. "Lord Inichi," he finally repeats. "Just in case."

I nod in understanding but can't bring myself to speak.

After one final lingering glance, North turns away and strides belowdecks without looking back.

Twenty-Two

NORTH IS GONE BY MORNING.

I knew to expect it, and yet I feel oddly displaced, as though I were left behind by mistake and will be remembered any minute. Rialdo says nothing, but Elin is livid, storming around the galley spitting profanities and personal vows of mutiny. But underneath her anger I recognize the shimmer of fear that she chose the wrong side, and that when North returns, it will be as a king.

Davik also says little to anyone, but her expression remains grim as she navigates the remaining coastline toward New Prevast. With no prince in the palace, Bryn will fall into the highest position of power—and through her, her father. And Perrote will not show mercy to someone who smuggled a prince off her ship.

It's only once we've passed beneath the Bridge of Ander that we notice the crowd pressed onto the docks a dozen thick, held back by soldiers in Brindaigelian colors—many of them armed with old pistols. The sight unnerves me. While Corthen had ordered a shipment of guns from the Northern Continents during the war twenty years before, it was said that most had been destroyed. With Perrote controlling Brindaigel through loyalty spells and executions, he'd had no need for them beyond the occasional show of power by his officials.

But, like the magic, he clearly kept them for himself. That he expected to welcome North home with armed soldiers only confirms that North was right to run. Neither Bryn nor her father had any intention of wasting time in stealing this kingdom from him.

Perrote waits ahead of the crowd, Bryn at his side. He rocks back on his heels, hands clasped behind his back, expression inscrutable as Davik jumps to the dock to tie off the ship, sleeves rolled up despite the cold, exposing her tattoos. Two fishermen weigh the gangplank, and Davik returns on board as Perrote escorts Bryn on deck, pausing to run his hand along the weathered railing. He tips his face back to the patched canvas sails before his eyes settle on all of us, eyebrow arched in silent question.

"He's gone," Rialdo says, scowling as Bryn kisses his cheek in greeting. His bag is slung over a shoulder, his own uniform coat unbuttoned to the rumpled tunic underneath. Just over a week away from the amenities of the palace doesn't sit well on him; he looks shaggy and unkempt, half-wild. Ash still streaks his hair. "He launched this morning."

Bryn startles, eyes sliding to me as though expecting an explanation, but Perrote's expression doesn't change. "I see," he says. "And where might he be going, I wonder?"

"One can only assume he's continuing this madness," Rialdo says darkly.

"He has no magic. No supplies. And"—Perrote glances over the others on deck, taking silent tally—"even fewer men than when he started."

"And yet he left her." Rialdo jerks his thumb in my direction.

"Of course he did," Bryn says, eyes narrowed. "He can't save her from her responsibilities." Her fingernails dig into her forearm, but I barely flinch in response. I've survived a week in the Burn. Bryn will have to do more than pinch to hurt me.

"Then he must know where Merlock is." Perrote watches me down his nose, eyes narrowing in thought.

"Which means we have no time to lose." Bryn steps forward, sliding her arm through mine, pulling me close to her side. "We'll leave at dawn."

Her eagerness surprises me, since she knows her father will kill her the moment she inherits Merlock's magic. But it also concerns me. Bryn does not play nice, and if she's supporting her father's plans, it's because she has plans of her own.

"Perhaps Captain Davik could shed some light on our missing prince," Perrote says, and two soldiers dutifully step forward, pushing past me to approach Davik at the helm. She doesn't resist, but as they march her toward the gangplank, she catches my eye and winks. I'm too stunned to react, envying her show of bravery when her fate is all but sealed.

Perrote turns back to the crowd, resting his hands on the ship's railing. "Your prince has abandoned you," he calls, his voice strong, unrattled. "He has chosen his father's fate: to hide from his sins like a coward."

I feel my entire body tense with unspoken defense, but who would listen to me? And the crowd doesn't want to hear it. They want soldiers with stolen weapons and a man in a silver circlet with magic to spare, a ready-made king to replace their own missing royalty. Despite twenty years of the Burn, they're still prisoners of their own vices and complacency.

For one furious moment, I think like Merlock, *They don't deserve to be saved.*

"Brindaigel will not be so cruel," Perrote continues. "We will adhere to our alliance and support this kingdom, with or without its prince's help. And if that means finding Merlock and ending his cowardly bloodline once and for all . . . so be it."

Cheers. Actual cheers of gratitude for a man who just revealed his intention of stealing the kingdom from its rightful heir. My skin crawls with disgust, and it takes every ounce of self-control not to claw Perrote's lies out of his mouth with my bare hands.

"Those pistols are loaded," Bryn says tightly, as if reading my mind. "And I need you just a little bit longer."

Perrote leads the way back to the docks as the crowd parts in reverence. He openly basks in their adulation with an arrogance that boggles, and when we reach a waiting carriage, he turns back to the crowd and raises his hand in final acknowledgment.

Bryn rolls her eyes and pushes me into the carriage, then slides in beside me. Rialdo follows, sinking into the seat opposite, before Perrote finally ducks inside. His smile immediately vanishes as the

footman shuts the door, and he looks at me with a terrifying loathing, as if a mask has been slipped off and a shadowbred monster
were lurking beneath.

"You know you look like her," he says. "Let's hope you're not
stupid enough to die like her."

"I don't intend to," I say, face hot with adrenaline. "Not until I
finish what she started."

Perrote snorts, shifting his focus to Rialdo. "Did you find
Merlock?"

"*He* didn't," I say, before Rialdo can answer. "He ran back to
the boat long before North found anything. If you want to inherit
Avinea, you'll have to find Merlock yourself instead of sending a
coward proxy to do it for you."

Rialdo shoots me a furious look, but I ignore him—and the
ensuing pinch from Bryn—staring out the window to resist the
temptation of shoving my dagger, still hidden in my boot, through
Perrote's neck. It's more satisfying in thought than it would be in
practice: His protection spells would spare his life, and I'd be killed
immediately by his guards.

I don't even wait for the footman to open the door when we
arrive at the palace, jumping instead onto the gravel as Bryn leans
out the door behind me.

"You have not been dismissed," she snaps.

"And neither have you," Perrote says to her. "I want you in the
council room immediately. And *she*"—he directs this to a guard—
"is now a prisoner and does not leave her room under any circumstance. Somebody find my provost. I want to know if Corbin
placed any spells on her before he skins her."

"This is still *my* kingdom," Bryn says icily.

"Let's see how long you manage to keep it," Perrote replies, brushing past her.

She glowers at his back and then turns to me as if to speak. Before she can, the guard roughly grabs my arm, escorting me into the palace. I don't fight—now is not the time—but when we reach my bedroom and I'm unceremoniously shoved inside, I'm ready to explode. I survey my small bed, the bureau, the simple dresses and the matching shoes that hang in the wardrobe. I lift up a candlestick, prepared to hurl it against the wall, when a shriek of laughter stays my hand.

Crossing to my window, I nudge it open and peer outside to the inner courtyard and the hedge maze garden, still green despite the approaching winter. A flash of color darts in between two rows of the maze, chased by a slower, limping shadow and a ball of orange fur.

I lower the candlestick, watching Cadence hide behind a hedge, only to jump out as Tobek rounds the corner toward her. She laughs when he startles, and she starts to run, skirts kicking up at her heels. This is not the girl I left behind over a week ago, so meekly desperate to earn Bryn's approval. This is Cadence. My sister, whom I thought I had lost in the Brim.

What have I missed while I was gone?

I tip my forehead against the window frame, swallowing past the lump in my throat. They find a seat, and Tobek bends down, grabbing a handful of stones that they examine between them. They toss out the worst, keep the best. Cadence leans closer, her blond curls against his dark waves as Darjin grooms himself at their feet. Both seem completely ignorant of our return, immune to the threats swelling within the walls.

She's not even wearing gloves.

For so long I've treated Cadence like a touchstone, a talisman against my weaknesses, a reward for my sacrifices. In the process I've reduced her to an idea and forgotten that she's a Locke. Of course she knows how to survive; it was bred into our blood. Instead of trying to protect her, I should be asking for her help.

Dropping the candlestick to the floor, I sink onto my bed, burying my face in my hands. Bryn needs me alive, but her father doesn't. Once he finds out I no longer have my mother's spell and the means to find Merlock, he has no further use for me. Bryn is already losing her tenuous grip on her crown; if he wants me dead, no amount of protesting from her will stay his hand. But how do I get Cadence out of here without being noticed? A glance outside confirms that she and Tobek have left the gardens, but where would she go within the palace, if Bryn were trapped behind council room doors?

Standing, I grab the candlestick and crack open my door, verifying that Perrote's guard is still in the hall, alone. He stands with one shoulder slumped to the wall, inspecting his reflection on the blade of his short sword. By the time he catches a flash of movement behind him, it's too late. The candlestick strikes him flat in the chest, and he crumples. After shoving the hair out of my face, I grab him by the arms and drag him into my room, out of sight. At best, I've given myself ten minutes before somebody comes looking for him—and me.

With trembling fingers I strap the guard's sword around my hips. In the distance the bell tower of Saint Ergoet's Monastery tolls the hour and calms my racing heart. One foot, then the other, I tell myself.

Only then can we start running.

Twenty-Three

"YOU LOOK LIKE HELL," ALISTAIR SAYS WHEN I EDGE INTO HIS STUDY, carefully closing the door behind me. I haven't even changed out of my clothes from earlier, or Kellig's bloody coat.

"Likewise," I say, scanning the room and then looking at him. There are dark shadows beneath his eyes that weren't there when I left, new lines carved by his mouth. "Where's Cadence?"

"Haven't seen her." He pushes himself to his feet and approaches, an empty glass in one hand. The smell of alcohol precedes him. "You came back alone."

"North's still alive," I say, and Alistair sags in visible relief. Approaching his window, I look out at the harbor and the lights coming to life along the Bridge of Ander. Guards move between the waterfront and the palace, ferrying supplies toward the dock. An enormous merchant ship stands at attention, far more impressive than Davik's dogger.

When I turn, Alistair is staring at me. "You're leaving again," he says, voice flat.

"We have to. They'll kill Cadence—"

"We," he repeats. "*I* have sacrificed sleep and meals for almost two weeks, but *we* are going to run."

"Alistair—"

"I help you, and you help me," he says, voice rising. "That was our agreement! And now you're just leaving me behind?!"

"I got you out of Brindaigel," I reply, just as hotly.

"I got *you* out of Brindaigel," he growls. "All you did was move me from one dungeon to the next, and for what? Six weeks of reprieve was always a best-case scenario, Faris. We both knew we were facing war, and when that first strike happens"—he snaps his fingers, bright and startling—"I'm gone. Perrote's spell turns on and I turn off, and there's nothing I can do about it, but what do you care?"

"That's not fair. When North finds his father—"

"You could have asked Corbin for anything. So why didn't you ask for my freedom? If his blood was so important to you, why didn't you give me more time?!" Angrily he tosses his empty glass aside. It thuds against the carpet and rolls under his settee.

I back up, into the edge of his desk. "Your freedom is not his to give."

"Neither was your sister's."

I close my eyes, count to ten, remind myself to stay calm. His anger stems from fear. "Perrote has an entire army of soldiers but only one executioner. You're far more valuable as you are."

He sweeps an arm across his desk, causing a landslide of papers and instruments to tumble to the floor at our feet. "You think Perrote doesn't know what I'm doing down here? You know better than to believe I'll be pardoned for serving the interests of another man. I can't go back to Brindaigel!" He grabs a slender vial of my poisoned blood from its velvet case and hurls it across the room. It hits the wall and shatters, blood dripping down the pale stone walls. "I *won't* go back," he says, shaking, running a hand through the side of his hair. "I can't, Faris."

I brace my weight against his desk, blood pounding in my ears. North once told me the reason he saved my life was because I never asked him to. My strength was his weakness, and in contrast, Alistair's desperation feels like an infection, its own deadly plague—made more vile because of how familiar it feels.

"I've kept your sister from being eaten alive by the great family Dossel," he says darkly, plucking a cigarette from his case and sliding it between his lips. He immediately swipes it back out again, leveling it toward me. "That was our agreement! And I'm close. So close. Another week, maybe two." He tries to light the cigarette, but his hand wavers and he shakes his head in miserable defeat, flicking the cigarette aside. "Why couldn't you have just waited a little longer? Why couldn't you have given me an actual chance?"

"It wasn't my decision," I say softly. "You know that."

Sighing, he sinks onto the settee, dragging his hands over his eyes. "I've executed thirty-three people on his orders, and I know—I *know*—that when it's my turn, no one will offer me a merciful death."

The fragility in his voice hurts because it hints at a hopelessness I don't know how to fight. I always had Cadence, or even North—

some spark to ignite the fire inside me to get up and keep going. But there's a weariness in Alistair's tone, a lost quality that scares me. A boy who cuts himself to find control might be tempted to find his freedom in much the same way, if he truly believed he had no other choice.

Crossing the room, I kneel in front of him, clutching his hands on his knees. I see potential in him, not just because his experiments could save North's life, but because of the life still burning inside, despite being smothered beneath so many scars.

It is not an easy thing, to survive.

"North knows where his father is going," I say, voice low. I don't have time for this, and yet I need to make him understand that there is still hope. "He has a head start."

"Get out."

I blink. "What?"

He stands, knocking me aside, and opens his door. "We had an agreement, Faris: You help me; I help you. But *this*. This is not helping me."

"Alistair—"

"I have work to do," he says, eyes menacing as he shoves me into the hall. "Your sister is no longer my concern. Consider our agreement rescinded."

He slams the door behind me, and I stare at it, wounded. Yet a part of me relishes his annoyance because it justifies my own anger in return, the simmering resentment I haven't truly relinquished since that night in the tunnels. Spinning, I take several steps down the hall only to falter.

Inwardly cursing my decision—I *need* to find Cadence—I return to his door, pressing my palm to the wood. "I forgive you for all the things you've had to do," I say. "You are not a monster, Alistair Pembrough, and they will never make you one. You will survive this because that's what we do, you and I. No matter the cost."

I wait a beat, heart aching. But if he heard me, he makes no reply.

From somewhere outside, a shouted command cuts through the silence of the hall. I tense, cocking my head, straining to hear. More commands soon follow, as the spell around my wrist ignites, summoning me to Bryn.

They know I'm not in my room.

Cradling my wrist to my chest, I look down the hall, adrenaline soaking my every nerve.

Sofreya's rooms. Maybe if Cadence is still with Tobek—

Alistair's door slams open, and I startle. "Alistair," I begin, but wilt upon seeing his expression. Slack, empty: his worst fear realized.

No. There's no reason for Perrote to need Alistair to fight. Yet when I clumsily pull aside his shirt to the branded mark above his chest, it glows silver-white, as if recently cast. It burns beneath my hand, a scorching warning: Nobody leaves Brindaigel. Like Dimitr Frell, Alistair was only here on borrowed time. He's a golem now, a slave like Cadence was, because of me. If they know I'm gone, they'll hunt down any possible allies until they find me.

Cadence.

Perrote removed her spell as a stipulation of the wedding treaty, but is she still free of his control? Did Perrote have his own failsafe? She's denied me any chance of asking.

I have to find her, now. I take a step back but hesitate, losing precious seconds as I search Alistair's face for some flicker of life buried beneath the magic. Cadence was fully conscious under the king's spell, which means he is too. Trapped, unable to scream for help.

"North will find his father," I say. "And we will come back for you, Alistair. I promise."

Alistair grabs my wrist, crushing the blisters of magic swelling beneath Bryn's summons. He begins to turn my arm, twisting it out of position. Swearing, I knee him in the upper thigh, and he staggers back, releasing me. But he was trained, the same as every other Brindaigelian soldier, and an instant later I'm ducking a strong left hook, stumbling back into his study. When he lunges, I sidestep him, only to get caught by his desk. He crushes me over the blotter, wrenching an arm behind my back, straining the bandages at my shoulder. My free hand canvasses the desk, past scattered papers and books and chunks of pumice, finally landing on a key. I wait a beat, breathe. But it's now or never.

I push back and turn, kicking his legs out from under him. He hits the floor, and I bolt from the room, locking the door behind me. A heartbeat later Alistair rattles the knob, and I back away until I collide with the opposite wall, breathless from the fight.

More shouted commands and returning cries of resistance; someone within the palace has apparently raised a defense, and I dimly wonder who would risk it when they're so clearly outnumbered. And yet, it's a spark of hope I hadn't expected: North still has allies.

The wall behind me groans in warning, and I startle as Cadence emerges from a hidden panel. She's still dressed as before but now has a canvas satchel slung over one shoulder. I breathe her name in relief and take a step toward her, but stop when she leans away, eyeing me warily.

"You came back," she says, before urgency reclaims her attention. "Where's Pem?" Her eyes slide to the door—and the key still in the lock. "They're coming to take Pem. We have to warn him!"

"Cade, don't—"

Ignoring me, she unlocks his door, and it flies open, ricocheting against the wall. Alistair staggers toward me, swinging a fire poker. It hits me across the hip and breaks skin, before he rips it loose and readies for another blow.

"Stop!" I hold my hand out in useless plea, but Alistair can only be commanded by Perrote now. He swings again. I dart out of the way, but not before he lands a second blow across the tops of my thighs.

Cadence gapes at him with big blue eyes. "I know it's not you," she says, face crumpling. "You promised you would never hurt us!"

Did he? I don't have the chance to ask; Alistair raises the poker once more, but I tackle him to the ground, wrestling it out of his hands. I toss it aside, and Cadence hurries toward us.

"Don't hurt him," she begs of me. "Please don't. He can't help it. They're making him do it!"

"I won't," I say, struggling to keep Alistair pinned. He's not a brawny man, but I've spent a week in the Burn and have little strength left. "But he'll hurt me if I let him go."

A new sound enters the fray, deadly familiar. Gunfire. It's close enough to echo, coming from an adjacent hall. Cadence flinches back. "Are they coming for me, too?"

I want to burn down the world for putting that fear into her voice. "No. They're coming for me." The spell on my wrist is now scorching the skin around it. Bryn won't kill me herself, but how long can I ignore her spell before it burns me from the inside out?

Doors are kicked open in the next hall; soldiers bark orders demanding that servants stop their duties and show their hands.

"We have to go," I say.

"Pem's coming with us."

"Cade, they can track him with that spell. They'll be able to find us. He's safer here, and we're safer far away." Alistair begins to struggle beneath me, grunting with the effort. I lean my weight into him. "It's the same reason I could never risk taking you out of the workhouse. Perrote would have found us both and killed us."

She stares at me, flyaway hairs springing loose of her curls. Grabbing the fire poker from the floor, she clutches it to her chest and swallows hard. For half a heartbeat I see the defiant little girl who fought my governance tooth and nail but still curled next to me every night because it made her feel safe.

"Pem comes with us," she repeats.

I swallow my frustration at being forced to have this conversation here, right now, when there's no time. Alistair finally knocks me back, and my head slams against the wall, hard enough that I see stars. I stare at him helplessly, and he stares back, expression as flat as the shallows in the farming terraces in the Brim. But inside he must be screaming, raging against the spell, hearing every word—and every hesitation—between us.

Growling, I roll out of the way to avoid a kick to the stomach, and lurch to my feet, grabbing Cadence by the sleeve of her coat.

Ignoring her protests, I drag her toward the open panel in the wall as two soldiers turn the corner of the hall. One of them raises a pistol and shouts for us to stop.

Alistair lunges; the soldier shoots. The bullet hits the wall and carves a divot in the paper as Cadence swings the panel shut behind us. It clicks home, and we hesitate a moment, pinned in tightly together. The soldiers begin pounding at the wall, searching for the catch.

"You can only open it from the inside," Cadence says numbly, features outlined by the sliver of light that bleeds through where the panel hinges. She's still holding the fire poker in both hands, knuckles strained white.

"Where does it go?" I ask, twisting to see behind me. When she doesn't answer, I bend down to see her face-to-face. "Look, Alistair is tough, Cade. Just like you."

"He's a prisoner like me," she says.

"You're not a prisoner anymore." Tentatively I smooth her curls away from her face, and when she doesn't resist, I clutch her hand in mine. "He's safer here at the palace. Perrote could hurt him if he tries to leave. But we'll come back for him, Cadence, just like I came back for you, all right? I promise."

"You didn't come back for me."

"I was going to," I say, trying to hide how much her words hurt. "Why do you think I did any of this?" Wetting my lips, I clutch her shoulders, feeling every fragile bone beneath her coat and the silk dress. "Listen to me," I say, "sometimes saving somebody means you have to leave them behind for just a little longer to make things safe for them. But that doesn't mean you're never coming back.

And we're coming back for him. All right? I promise."

Her expression flickers, uncertain, but before she can respond, footsteps sound in the dark tunnel stretching ahead of us. I swear under my breath, tensing for another confrontation, but Cadence shoves past me. "Tobek?" she calls.

He emerges from the shadows, his own bag and crossbow slung over his shoulder. When he sees me, his smile disappears. "Oh," he says. "So you're coming too?"

"Where are we going?" I ask.

"The monastery," says Cadence. "Prince Corbin keeps horses there."

I stare after her as she starts down the narrow passage. "And where were you going to go?! And when were you going to tell me you were leaving?"

"You were already gone," she says flatly from over her shoulder.

Tobek scowls at me. One more thing to blame me for: ruining his heroic escape plan. I meet his look with a scowl of my own, only to cringe as Bryn's spell tightens like a shackle around my wrist. If North could mute the spell's effects, maybe someone else can do the same.

"I don't suppose the monks know any magic," I say through gritted teeth.

"Lord Inichi does," Tobek replies, turning after Cadence.

Of course North would give his apprentice the same instructions he gave me. But Lord Inichi is in Revnik, on the other side of the Kettich Mountains. It's a day's journey, at best. I don't know that I'll last that long.

Cadence walks with confidence, turning here and there without pausing. "Tobek taught me all the secret passages," she says, and despite everything, there's a hint of pride in the admission. She knows something that I do not. I wonder if this was just a game she played with Tobek, or if she's like me now and maps the tunnels of the world so that she'll never get lost again.

We exit near the gardens at the edge of the front veranda. Snow is falling, dusting the ground and freezing our breath as we huddle in the shadows, out of sight of the line of soldiers standing on the drive. Out here in the cold, Bryn's spell feels like more of a dull ache, and I welcome the temporary relief.

The palace gate is a hundred yards away, guarded by a lone soldier—for now. But there are dozens of soldiers marching back from the dock, their movements eerily synchronized. More golems.

"One isn't so bad," Tobek says, peering around a hedgerow.

"But a locked gate is," Cadence points out drily.

"Give me the poker, and stay close," I say, holding a hand out.

"No," she says, hugging it closer to her. "You already have a sword. Use that. This is mine."

Inwardly growling, I say, "Don't watch. And when you reach the gate, start climbing."

I don't give her a chance to argue, already breaking into a run, unsheathing the sword in a cumbersome move that mocks my lack of training. The soldier seems to look right through me as I approach, but when I'm only a few feet away, he draws a pistol from a holster and aims it, completely expressionless.

I call his bluff. Perrote won't kill me, not until he knows my mother's spell is gone.

"I'm so sorry," I say as I swing.

The flat blade of the sword hits him in the ribs, and he goes down; from there, a simple choke hold the way Chadwick taught me until his body goes slack. Throwing a glance behind me, I abandon the useless sword and shove his pistol into my coat pocket instead. I launch myself toward the gate, but stop when I see Cadence lingering over the soldier's body.

She nudges him. "Is he dead?"

"Cadence! Come *on*," Tobek says, already halfway over the gate.

"No," I say. "Only unconscious. Here, I'll give you a boost—"

"Why didn't you kill him?"

"Why would I kill him?" I frown at her, troubled by the ferocity in her expression as she glares at the soldier in his bloodred uniform—the color of the guards who carried her out of the dungeons that night five months ago, the ones who patrolled the workhouse and never stopped the men who came to prowl. "It's not him we're fighting," I say, grabbing her shoulder, forcing her to look at me. "He's a prisoner, just like us. Just like Alistair."

A shout from the veranda is followed by a gunshot that hits the gravel ahead of us. I flinch, pulling Cadence into my arms. A figure stands, outlined by the torchlight behind him, demanding that we stop, ordering men to give chase.

Rialdo.

Wordlessly I take Cadence's poker and shove it through the bars of the gate. Then I brace my hands and Cadence steps into them, hoisting herself up as I scramble to follow. Several more shots are fired, but they go wild. It's a small relief. Perrote may have hoarded weapons for twenty years, but his men are ill-trained with them.

Not that I would test that theory in close proximity.

I land on all fours in the gravel on the other side of the gate. Cadence grabs her poker and we break into a run, angling for the lights of the city. We don't slow until we reach Saint Ergoet's and the vine-laden archway that frames the courtyard. Tobek dashes forward to claim the horses from the stable, only to stop. Two horses are already saddled and waiting, guarded over by a familiar figure. Silver beaded skirts, long red hair, and a pocket watch dangling from one slender hand.

"Thirty-four minutes and nine seconds," Bryn says, snapping the watch closed. "Faris, that is appalling."

Twenty-Four

MY SHOCK TURNS TO DEFENSE, AND I BRACE MY WEIGHT AS I EDGE between Bryn and my sister. "Let them go," I say.

"Where?" asks Bryn, looking around the courtyard sardonically. "Back to the palace, maybe? To my father? Is that really what you want? I have not kept Cadence protected all this time so that you could sacrifice her now."

I stare at Bryn. "What are you talking about?"

"Where is he?" she asks, moving closer. Soft prayers come from the monks' rooms on the second floor of the monastery, where doors are propped open to the courtyard. Voices rise and fall in a symphony of gratitude and blessing.

When I don't answer, Bryn exhales loudly, hands on her hips. "Of course. Why would he tell *you*?" She shakes her head, disgusted. "Noble Corbin has thrown us both to the wolves."

Snow begins to collect in the collar of my coat and melts against my neck. My voice is hollow. "You are the wolf, your majesty."

Bryn's face tightens; I have half a heartbeat to brace myself before she slaps me. "What trespass have I ever committed against your beloved North but the audacity of holding a man to his word? He swore an alliance with me and would have rescinded on that agreement, but no. *I'm* the villain."

She paces away from me, only to turn back on her heel, her anger renewed. "I am not your enemy and I never have been. Yet despite my every offer of friendship, you vilify me again and again. And now his arrogance—his *selfishness*—has just destroyed everything!"

I refuse to raise my hand to my cheek, to give her the satisfaction. "What are you talking about?"

She half-laughs, breathless and harried. "Do you really think I want to share my crown with a *man*?!" When I open my mouth to respond, she rolls her eyes and begins pacing again. "I don't want *magic*," she says. "I don't want this godforsaken kingdom with its disgusting people and its filthy plague. Corbin can have it. All of it!"

"You want Brindaigel," I say, stunned.

She raises her chin, narrows her eyes. "Did I not make that clear to you the first day we met?"

"And you think North would agree to that?"

"I think I have exactly what he wants in return," she says, with a pointed look at me.

My stomach somersaults. My freedom in exchange for Brindaigel? Would he do that?

Of course he would.

"Then why didn't you come with us?!" I explode. "We needed

magic out there! We needed an amplifier! We could have defeated Merlock with you!" If she had come, Chadwick might still be alive, and North wouldn't be facing the Burn all over again.

"My father can't inherit without my link to Merlock," she says, "and if I had gone traipsing into the Burn to support my wayward husband, my father would have followed with an army. I don't care how magical Corbin would become. He can't fight a bullet through his head, and neither can I. It was far safer to stay separated, even if it meant allowing my father to play the concerned ally who would safeguard this kingdom on my behalf should my husband fail. But there's nothing stopping my father now that Corbin appears to have given up. Avinea will cheer when he kills my husband. But before he can do that, he needs *my* blood and *your* spell, and if we don't leave now, we'll both be dead by the end of this. As much as it might break your little heart, we need each other now."

"The alarm at the palace," I say slowly. "He's looking for *you*."

"He's looking for both of us," Bryn says darkly. "Don't act so surprised. My father has already tried to kill me once. His opinion has not changed now that I'm an heir to Avinea." Turning, she mounts one of the horses in a smooth, graceful motion. When none of us moves, she rolls her eyes. "By all means, stay and think it over. Wait all night if you want. My father will never think to look for us at the monastery my husband grew up in."

Her sarcasm is a cruel reminder that this is the only place in New Prevast where North ever felt at home. And lingering here is a guarantee that Perrote will retaliate against the monks still caught in evening prayer, implicating them in treason for no other fault than being in the same place at the same time as us.

"What's your plan?" I ask.

"You tell me."

I look to Tobek, who stares at the ground, and then to my sister, clutching his arm. The safe choice would be to run, to seek out Lord Inichi, and to wait for North to return, triumphant.

But with Bryn's amplification abilities, North would be better prepared to face his father.

"Ticktock," Bryn says.

The sound of the soldiers carries in the cold night air, drawing closer. There's only one way out of the monastery, and if we wait too long, we'll be trapped.

Tobek growls, mounting the second horse. He holds the reins and stares ahead, expression tight. He's no happier than I am, and yet, what choice do we have? Defying Bryn would be a worthless sacrifice. We need to put distance between ourselves and Perrote to give us time to formulate any kind of plan.

She's not my enemy tonight.

Cadence takes Bryn's offered arm, leaving Tobek and me to eye each other in mutual misery. Reluctantly, I pull myself into the saddle behind him. Monks have begun emerging from their chambers to locate the commotion, and they stare down at us with shadowed faces. Two dozen men—two dozen accomplices, if Perrote spins his lies right.

"Revnik," I finally say. "Lord Inichi. That's where we were going."

Bryn raises an eyebrow. "Then that's the plan."

She takes the lead, and we leave the monastery, crashing through cobblestone streets, forsaking stealth for speed and the most direct route out of the city. People stand back and watch us pass with wide eyes and shouted rebukes, but I keep my eyes locked on Bryn as she expertly maneuvers her horse, urging it faster. Shadow golems materialize ahead of us, not the well-dressed soldiers that Perrote needed to win over a crowd, but misshapen, poorly formed monsters—a spell cast from desperation with no finesse.

Bryn drives straight through them. A flash of heat passes over us before the cold returns, more bitter in comparison. Even with all his stolen magic, Perrote still has no real idea how to use it.

Beyond the city, we ride past herds of sheep and startled goats, bearing west. By the time day breaks, I'm beginning to recognize the uneven scenery and the gold-red ribbon of the Burn that smolders ahead of us, turning the snow to water to steam to fog that banks over the landscape, shrouding everything in an eerie veil. We slow the horses to avoid the gulches and crags within easy misstep of the road.

I almost miss the wagon, its colors muted and dimmed. It remains where it was abandoned, broken wheel crushed and the back end tipped into a ditch. Tobek tenses ahead of me, and something twists painfully in my stomach as we trot past. To see it again is like reliving an old story from years ago, with characters I no longer recognize. Everything has changed since then.

I've changed since then.

The Burn has crept much closer than it was the last time I passed this way, nearly to the road that leads through the Kettich Mountains. Bryn angles toward the pass, but I tell Tobek to stop. After dismounting, I take several wobbly steps forward with a heady mix of fear and homecoming. A thousand second guesses crowd for attention, but there's only time to commit. North needs help, and Bryn could be the difference between a spark or a flame in the fight against Merlock, and every inch of magic needs to count. Whether she was lying or not about only wanting Brindaigel has to wait. North's victory is priority.

And yet, I hesitate, hugging myself against the fog. I have no protection spell to guard my heart; Bryn's amplification abilities will poison me twice as fast as her. I'm being generous in giving myself two days to reach North in Arak, but what if he's not there? What if he's moved on to Kerch, or back to Pilch? What if he hasn't even entered the Burn and is still gathering supplies? Behind me, the Kettich Pass looms, promising an easy way forward. I know Perrote will never find Merlock without help, which only leaves Baedan out there to challenge North's victory.

The others dismount and join me in staring down the Burn. Cadence bends for loose stones and begins tossing them over the edge, where they kick up fresh embers in the ash beyond.

"What are we doing?" Bryn asks, peering through the fog behind us. "We don't have time for inner reflection."

I don't know which choice to make. There's no magic spell pulling me forward, no hidden clues to guide my decision. I watch Cadence throwing rocks, and I think, I'm tired of fighting a battle that someone else started. Two choices, neither one easy. But only one is right.

Releasing a breath, I drop my arms. "Tobek and Cadence, continue on to Revnik. Find Lord Inichi as planned. And then wait there until—"

"No!" Tobek and Cadence protest simultaneously, and I grit my teeth.

"I'm not hiding," Tobek says.

"And I will not be left behind again," Cadence adds, and I inwardly scream at how precariously I balance in her eyes. One wrong move, and I'm condemned again, losing any inch I might have gained since leaving the palace.

"North is somewhere out there," I tell Bryn, pointing to the Burn. "If we have any hope of helping him find Merlock, we need to move fast. So you want Brindaigel? You fight for it."

"You want to go into the Burn." Bryn repeats before her expression becomes incredulous. "Good god. You want to go into the Burn. You know where he is."

"I know where he's going."

"North is still out there?" Tobek straightens. "Then I'm going with you."

"So am I," says Cadence.

"No. This is between Bryn and me," I say. "This is not your fight."

"You have no power over me," Tobek cuts in hotly. "Either of you. Because I intend to fight. First I'll fight Merlock, but then I'm fighting you, Miss Dossel, so be warned. I *am* your enemy, and even if North gives you half of Avinea when all this is done, I won't let you take it."

"Then perhaps you should have listened when Faris tried to teach you how to throw a punch." Bryn snorts, flicking her wrist dismissively. "A limping little boy is hardly a threat."

"Don't underestimate me," Tobek says.

"Likewise," she says, dangerously quiet.

"I can fight too," Cadence says softly. She swallows hard, pale in the misty dawn.

Closing my eyes, I count to ten, fingers clenching into my trousers. "Cadence," I say, but how can I articulate that everything I've done has been to ensure her safety, her freedom? Walking into the Burn negates all of that.

"You have to leave us a horse," Cadence says. "So you can't stop us from following you. You might as well let us ride *with* you."

My hands are now fists, digging against my thighs. Like mother, like daughter, I think.

Like sisters.

And yet, I want to spare her in every way possible, even if it means pushing her further away from me. I hold Cadence's eyes, ensuring she understands the seriousness, that this isn't a game. "The Burn will be painful," I say. "It will not be easy. You will regret every step you take, until you reach the point of no return, when you begin to crave another step forward."

Cadence's eyes widen with fear. Good. I want to scare her so she changes her mind about following me.

"It will feed off your deepest, darkest secrets," I continue. "Whatever weakness you have will be amplified. Whatever fears will be inescapable. You will feel your blood thicken and your heart start to slow. And nobody out there is going to help you. We will be hunted, not just by the hellborne but by the shadows themselves."

"Good god," Bryn mutters, rolling her eyes.

"It takes five days in the Burn to turn hellborne," I say, ignoring Bryn. "And there's no going back from that. Without protection spells, you will become infected and then you will become a monster. And when North succeeds, you will become hunted again."

"It knows my secrets?" Cadence looks at the Burn with renewed fears. "Will you know them too?"

I frown. "No. Of course not."

A soft breath of relief. "Then I'm not scared. But you've already got poison in you."

Bryn arches her eyebrow, and I tense; with her amplification ability and my binding spell, I may not even have half the time they do. Yet Bryn says nothing about it, so I fill the silence with a lie. "I'm protected, remember?"

"Mama's spell."

It's been years since Cadence referred to our mother as "Mama"; it's been years since she referred to her at all. She was barely two when our mother died, too young to know much more than the shape of our mother's face, the hum of her voice, the smell of her skin.

How often does Cadence think of her?

"Right," I say with a flicker of guilt. Cadence never asked me questions, and I never volunteered my memories, selfishly burying all thoughts of our mother behind a wall of accusation and hate. I thought I was sparing her the heartache, but in truth I was robbing her of her chance to make her own conclusions. What would she say if I told her our mother tried to kill a king? And when she failed, she tried again before giving the task to me?

"Well." Bryn flashes me a triumphant smirk. "Looks like we have a new plan."

We return to our horses, but I hesitate before mounting again.

"Last chance to go to Revnik," I say. "There's no shame in being scared. In wanting to be safe."

Cadence chews her lower lip, eyebrows furrowed. She glances at the fire poker strapped to the horse's saddle. "That sword you had at the palace gate would have been better."

I bite back my smile and pull Chadwick's dagger from my boot. "How about this?" I say, offering it to her. "It cuts through shadows," I add in a mock whisper, hiding the truth behind my teasing.

Cadence makes a face. "It's ugly," she says.

Tobek stares at the dagger and then twists in the saddle to give me a dark, questioning look. "Where did you get that?"

I ignore him, watching my sister, waiting for her decision.

Sighing—clearly disappointed—she slides the dagger into her bag and takes Bryn's arm, hoisting herself onto the horse. For a moment there's nothing but silence save for the hiss and whisper of the snow hitting the edge of the Burn and turning to steam. Overhead, the sunrise colors the fog rose and ruby red. A single bird dips toward us with a blur of charcoal before it soars higher. I watch it disappear before I close my eyes.

One step, then another, I tell myself. I've survived the Burn before, I can do it again.

Easier said than done.

Twenty-Five

THE HORSES DON'T LAST LONG. NEITHER DOES OUR LEAD.

We're barely half a day into the Burn before Tobek and I put the poor beasts out of their misery. North refused horses because of the costly protection spells they would require, but Perrote faces no such obstacle, and it's only a matter of time before he overtakes us. Still, it's the growing shadows that unsettle me more. I don't know if we can risk walking at night, even with the candles Tobek thankfully grabbed as he fled the palace, far more prepared than me. But if we don't keep moving, someone—or something—will get us. Birds have been circling overhead for hours, and I've caught glimpses of wolves or worse in the distance.

Cadence watches everything I do with haunted eyes, her arms wrapped tightly around herself. Every shadow that crosses her face is a needle of panic in my spine. Already I feel my own blood thickening in my veins as it absorbs Bryn's reaction to the Burn as well my own.

Five days, I told them. I'll be lucky to have two. Judging from the map North showed me on the *Mainstay*, I'll need every minute of those two days to reach Kerch. I won't even consider what happens if he's not there.

"You all right?" I smooth Cadence's hair back, and she shoves my hand away with a scowl.

"I'm fine," she says, and I take the defiance with some relief. I'll worry when she stops fighting me.

We each shoulder a share of supplies, even Bryn. With the snow melting as it lands in the ash, it thickens everything to the consistency of mud, making it even harder to slog through. By the time we gain a simple rise, I'm winded from Bryn's exhaustion, and I pause, breathless and sweating, looking for cover. We can't outrun Perrote, but maybe we can hide—possibly rest—until he passes. I haven't slept in over a day, and it's wearing on me.

Instead I see Baedan less than a quarter of a mile in the distance. Waiting for us.

Her numbers have diminished since that day in the castle. Only six figures flank her, mounted on hellborne horses with a stillness that frightens me. There's a *nothing-left*-ness, as though the battle in the ballroom scarred them into shadows themselves.

The binding spell, I realize with a sinking stomach. Amplified out here, it'd be a tempting enough beacon to draw out all the addicts from their hiding places. That we haven't been found yet is a miracle.

Bryn finally reaches the top of the dune behind me and wets her lips. This far into the Burn, her dress does not sparkle so much as smolder; the hem is ragged and gray. But she still bears herself with grace and dignity as she glances back toward her father's men, now visible behind us. "Which one is worse?"

"Seven versus an army," I say. "The odds are in your father's favor."

"Give me that dagger," she orders Cadence, hand out.

Cadence hesitates. As ugly as the dagger may be, it's still the first weapon I've ever willfully handed to her. "I want it back," she finally says, giving it to Bryn.

Tobek frowns, pulling a bolt from his quiver and loading his crossbow. "Are we going to fight?"

"*We're* not fighting," says Bryn. "But *they* will."

The monstrous horses strain at their muzzles, but Baedan raises a fist, cocking her head with suspicion as Bryn grabs my arm and pulls me forward, away from the others. Stray hairs cling to her face, and she looks fierce and half-wild. "You have to trust me," she says, voice low.

"No," I say. And then, suspiciously, "Why should I?"

"I know perfectly well you don't have that spell anymore."

My blood chills, and I look at Cadence to ensure she didn't hear. "What are you—"

"Rialdo described it in detail," she says, "and you are not wearing any iron to keep yourself grounded, and you've been following the sun west, not some magic thread." She gives me a pointed look. "You brought your sister into the Burn; obviously you know where North is. But I also know that without your mother's spell to protect you, and with this spell between *us*, you have a day, maybe two, before the infection destroys you. And that's if my father doesn't catch us first." Her voice softens, dark eyes locked on mine. "He will kill you if he has no use of you. And I need you just a little longer."

"What are we doing?" Tobek calls, panicked despite all his former bravado.

Bryn's fingers dig into my arm. "I trust that you know where North is," she says, "and now I'm asking you to trust me when I say I can get you there even faster. I know strategy, Faris. You want to save Cadence? You want to walk out of the Burn alive? Trust me." And then, a single word I've never heard from her before: "Please."

Bryn uses people as ammunition; she uses pain as a motivating force. I can never forgive her for the choices she's made—I can never trust her after what she's done.

But.

It's an insidious whisper, subtle as smoke. It is impossible to reconcile the Bryn who manipulated Tobek, used my life as collateral, and forced a marriage to win her crown, with this girl who now waits for *me* to say yes.

I finally realize how desperate she must be.

There were never any friends at the palace, no confidants. Her own father would kill her without remorse because she was only born as a redundancy to *his* legacy. Bryn has nothing without her crown. No one. And she never will if we're caught.

"What's your plan?" I ask.

She smiles, and it almost looks sincere. "We get captured," she says, raising her voice so Tobek and Cadence can hear.

Tobek stares at her, incredulous. "What?"

"Never fight your own wars if you can find volunteers instead,"

Bryn says, with a pointed look toward her father. "We'll never make it through the Burn on foot; we need to reach North as fast as possible. As it happens, Baedan will want to go in the same direction. If we do this right, she'll play defense to my father's offense and we won't have to get involved."

"It's a feint," I say, heart racing, as Baedan and her men ride toward us.

Cadence stands still, frozen with terror. Without looking at her, Tobek slides his fingers through hers. "Are we even going to try to fight?" he asks in disgust. "Baedan will never believe we were accidentally captured."

I swallow hard and look back as Perrote and his men draw close enough that I can see the color of their uniforms. There are fewer than I expected, two dozen at most, his men and several of Chadwick's defectors. Even now, with victory within reach, Perrote is loath to spare his own people—the font of his power.

Good.

Back in Brindaigel, shadow crows and loyalty spells were the extent of our exposure to Perrote's magic. Most of these men are too young to have seen real, powerful magic in action, only the consequences of such magic dying. When night falls and the hellborne roam and the shadowbred begin to hunt, they'll depend on Perrote for salvation, and his own inexperience will cost him more men than any paltry attack we might try to stage.

"No," I say, "save the ammunition."

Baedan and her men circle us. I edge closer to Cadence and meet Baedan's gaze in silent challenge. There's a new edge to her features, a roughness bred of hunger and manic obsession. The others—four men and two women—stare at us with dull eyes and listless expressions. Interested, but not fully invested. If Baedan has had them searching for Merlock without rest, they've had no time to capture any slaves beyond the Burn. There has been no clean blood to dilute their own infections, to offer them a reprieve from the mud in their veins. They're not at full strength.

"That was too easy," Baedan says.

A warning shot cracks through the air, and the hellborne flinch at the unfamiliar sound, ducking closer to their frothing mounts. A second shot echoes after, and Baedan's expression tightens. "What is that?"

Bryn exhales and adjusts her grip on the dagger. "Let the negotiations begin," she mutters. She hooks me around the throat and levels the blade to my skin.

Cadence startles forward. "What are you doing?"

Baedan scoffs and sits back in her saddle. "What makes you think I care if you carve her open?"

"Because I don't see a crown on your head," says Bryn. "Which means you *need* her and her spell to find Merlock before they"— she nods over her shoulder—"kill all of us." A trickle of blood drips down my throat; Bryn is trembling, and the dagger is sharp. I reach a hand up to steady her grip, already doubting my decision to trust her.

"Yet we don't need *you*," Baedan says, folding her arms across her chest. "We'll take the body bags, though." Her silver eye flicks toward Cadence and Tobek, still holding hands.

Bryn throws out her arm and cuts her palm. The reaction is immediate as I bite back my hiss of pain and clench my hand into a fist. Blood drips between my fingers, and several of the hellborne wet their lips, eyes darkening with unmistakable lust.

"She's been absorbing the poison for both of us since we entered the Burn," says Bryn. "You leave me out here to die, she'll die first. And as we've established, you need her, which means you also need me."

Baedan grins. "Spells can be skinned."

"They can also be destroyed," Bryn says, dipping the dagger to my chest.

Baedan tenses, and Bryn grins. "I'll make you an offer," says Bryn. "I give you Faris; you kill Merlock and inherit Avinea."

"And how does this benefit you?"

Bryn tosses her hair back. "I want Brindaigel."

My breath catches as Bryn tightens her hold around my shoulders. But Baedan looks bemused. "What is Brindaigel?"

"It's a kingdom of no concern to you," says Bryn. "Leave me and my people in peace, and in return I pledge an annual tithe. You'll need fresh blood after Avinea falls. Slaves. I'll provide them in exchange for the safety of my borders."

I run cold at the thought. It doesn't take imagination to guess who would be the first to go in her new kingdom. Scrape out the Brim and free the air for those who live higher.

Just like her father.

But she's only pretending, I tell myself. Right? There's no way Brindaigel could produce enough slaves to keep an addict like Baedan satiated. This is just part of Bryn's plan—her strategy. But the offer sounds too pitched, too planned, too much like everything Bryn really wants. It's exactly as North said. Bryn will always keep a fail-safe. If we fail, Baedan may not, and Bryn could still win.

Baedan frowns as she studies the two of us before her gaze turns toward Perrote. He's not wasting additional ammunition at this distance, but the gunshots have clearly unsettled her. If she lingers, she'll have to fight; she needs to make her decision now. "Where is North?"

"He's dead," Bryn lies smoothly. "The throne has been taken by my father, who needs my blood if he wants to inherit Avinea's magic. He's the one hunting us now."

Baedan laughs, rocking back in her saddle. "Dead," she repeats, relishing the word. "How tragic. He was so very young. Full of potential."

"Do we have a deal or not?" Bryn raises the dagger again.

"Use the spell and tell me where Merlock is," Baedan says at last, leaning forward in her saddle. "And then we'll see if you're as useful as you say."

Bryn releases me, and I stumble in the ash. Baedan has seen the spell; she knows how it works. How am I supposed to fake that?

Adjusting my coat, I cast a sour look at Bryn, drawing a deep breath. As I release it slowly, from somewhere deep down I feel a faint flicker of interest above my heart, some lost fragment of my mother's broken spell fighting to resurface. Pressure begins to build in my head, a warning pain in my chest not to call upon the frayed edges that Merlock didn't remove.

"He's cutting southwest, toward the fields of Arak," I say, tamping down the magic, leaving only a bittersweet feeling of absence.

The hellborne exchange looks of confusion, but Baedan considers my reply with half-lidded eyes. "Are you sure?"

"Yes," I say, frustrated. Perrote is getting closer, and the odds of Bryn's gamble paying off are getting slimmer. "I don't have to use the spell to confirm what I knew an hour ago. If you want me to announce his location to every other hellborne in the Burn, I'd be more than happy to do so. Or you can believe that I'm dying twice as fast as the rest of them because of *her*, and I have no interest in being left out here for the shadows to eat. Lying to you would be worthless."

A third warning shot, close enough to be concerning.

A small smile flickers across Baedan's face. "Let's go," she barks.

We're each pulled onto a mount and Baedan leads the retreat, leaving Perrote at our backs.

Twenty-Six

WE STOP BRIEFLY TO WAIT OUT THE DARKEST HOURS OF THE NIGHT— confirming Gideon's assertion that the hellborne are afraid of the dark. It's a delay I can't afford, and yet Baedan isn't taking orders from me. Perrote does the same in the distance, our two fires a temporary truce against the shadows that slither through the dark and hide beneath the ash. The only positive is that the horses cover far more ground than we could have on foot; already the Kettich Mountains have fallen behind us, replaced with the craggy peaks of the Heralds. If Perrote had given North just a little more magic, we could have brought horses and halved our time in the Burn. It might have made the difference between success or failure.

Baedan reclines on a carpet of animal furs, watching Bryn, who hovers near the fire, warming her hands. I managed a few stolen moments of sleep while riding and now, energized, I sit apart with Tobek and Cadence, watching everything, tallying the weakest among the hellborne, strategizing the best offense. When the time comes, we need to be ready.

"Are you any good with a dagger?" I ask Tobek from the corner of my mouth. We, too, have a temporary truce.

He digs furrows in the ash with the heel of his boot. "Better on a crossbow. How many can you take?"

"Two at best."

"Same," he says with a sigh. "Which leaves three too many, including Baedan. We'd need magic to cut through her spells."

His tone is as defeated as I feel.

Cadence listens, features strained. She's been carrying the fire poker since we left the horses behind, and now clutches it in her lap like a talisman. Baedan hasn't taken any of our weapons, under the illusion of truce, but I imagine she actually sees us as the walking dead, too weak to do much damage.

I resist the urge to smooth back Cadence's hair and ask if she's all right.

"My heart feels funny," she says, as if sensing my question. "Like it's turning into stone."

A quick glance over her hands and face reveals a few warning shadows but nothing like the discoloration of my hand, where the poison has seeped through Bryn's cut. "Your heart will be fine," I say, in that familiar forced voice, all sunshine and hopefulness to hide the dark truth underneath. "You still have four days."

Cadence holds her hands in front of her and examines them, before burying them in her armpits, features screwed up, on the brink of tears. "Can you see it yet?"

"See what?"

She bows her head, curls hiding her face. "My darkest secret."

I exchange looks with Tobek, but he's as bemused as I am. Then confusion gives way to fear. What did Bryn do to her while I was gone? "Cadence," I say, "were you infected before we left New Prevast?"

She shakes her head miserably, but I don't get the chance to press her for more information. One of the hellborne women produces a cloudy syringe, its needle bent from use, and Baedan sits up as the others roar with approval.

"Our first transaction, your majesty," she calls.

Bryn startles, turning to look at her. "What?"

"My men are hungry. We may need you and her, but not the babies," Baedan says, as her smile turns toothy and sharp. She points a finger at Cadence. "We'll start with that one."

"You do not touch her," I say, standing.

"Volunteering to take her place? No, thanks." Baedan's lips curl in a sneer. "I already know what's inside you. Spoiled meat."

"Isn't that what dogs like you eat?" I ask. "Always sniffing the ground for North's leftovers; you can't possibly know the difference between spoiled meat and your own rancid stink."

Bryn stiffens and pinches her thigh in warning: Control your temper, Faris, or you'll ruin everything.

But Baedan snorts, flicking a hand dismissively. "Don't start a fight you can't finish," she says, as two of her men advance toward me. "You don't need that tongue of yours for your precious spell to work."

"No prince to save you this time," one of them says, grabbing for my hair.

I block his arm and twist it back, forcing him to his knees. He tries to lash out with his other hand, but I slam my palm into his nose, tearing loose the thin scab of ash and dirt that formed on my palm after Bryn sliced it open several hours ago. The man recoils with a curse, and I turn for the other man in time to see Cadence strike him in the back with the poker. He pitches forward with a howl, and she straightens, breathless, eyes bright and hair wild.

Tobek stares at her like he might be in love.

"She doesn't need a prince," Cadence says. "She has a sister."

Laughter roars through the hellborne, but my heart wants to burst. Has she finally forgiven me?

My swelling pride costs my attention, and the first man knocks me back, his blade clutched in one hand. I roll out of the way and scramble to my feet, grabbing a broken piece of stone from the ground. When he lunges, I shove him back and pin him down, pinching a hand around his throat. Blistered skin easily parts beneath the slight pressure of my hand, and poison oozes over my fingers, across my bloody palm. My pulse begins to sing, to hunger—blood calling for blood, urging me to plunge the stone through the scarred flesh and rotting blood and brittle bones underneath until I hit ground on the other side. I could carve out his heart, and the temptation is intoxicating.

But I resist, grounding myself with the knowledge that Cadence is watching me, battling her own need for revenge. Giving in like this will only kill me faster.

"Enough." Baedan's expression is unreadable, eyes glittering in the light. "We are allies now, after all."

And she'll need all her men if she expects to survive against an attack from Perrote's army.

Exhausted, I sag back, overcome with delayed pain. "Touch my sister and the deal is off."

"You seem to be outnumbered," Baedan says.

"We had an agreement," Bryn cuts in, hands raised between us in an unexpected gesture of peace. "Nothing has changed."

"I think the price just went up, princess."

"That is not how it works," Bryn says, frustrated. She pulls out the dagger and lets the blade flash in warning. "You need Faris—"

"But not alive," Baedan says. "All I need is the skin that spell is on."

Fear flutters low in my stomach. If she tries to remove the spell and sees it's gone, she'll kill all of us.

"What do you want?"

We all turn toward Cadence, her voice thin but her chin raised high. "Blood? Is that what you eat? Fine." She thrusts a slender arm out, raking back her sleeve. "Take some of mine."

"Cadence, no—" I try to stand, only to stagger, dizzy: too much poison, not enough air. I collapse back onto my knees.

"Finally," Baedan says, as two of the hellborne grab Cadence, dragging her forward. "Someone who appreciates the value of compromise."

"Don't touch her!" Tobek darts forward. "If you want blood, I have plenty."

Baedan's expression sharpens. "Now *that* is a tempting offer. North nearly died to save you once, and it would give me great pleasure to undo all that hard work."

Tobek blanches. "Just let her go."

"Done." Baedan nods and the hellborne release Cadence. Bryn opens her arms. but Cadence runs to Tobek instead. He looks terrified for a moment, before he relaxes, returning her hug. One of the hellborne wrenches them apart and pulls him away; another fits him with a rope around his neck.

"Do something," Cadence demands of Bryn.

"What do you want me to do?" Bryn asks flatly.

Across the fire, Baedan sinks the needle in Tobek's neck and withdraws a syringe of dark blood. She takes the first shot, closing her eyes with an expression of ecstasy.

Cadence looks to me next, and I could kill someone. She finally wants my help, and I'm powerless to oblige.

Tears well up in her eyes as the hellborne fill the syringe a second and third time, passing it among themselves like a bottle of barleywine. Their eyes roll back and their jaws go slack as Tobek's clean blood cuts through the mud in their veins, giving the infection something new to burn through—briefly reigniting the giddy and addictive euphoria of magic.

They could very well be contaminating him with their own blood each time the needle is plunged back into his skin. He was infected once already; it won't take much to make him fall again. But Tobek doesn't resist. His eyes meet mine and he dips his head, a barely perceptible motion, toward the horses tethered nearby.

He wants us to leave him and run while the hellborne are drugged and sluggish.

My chest tightens at the prospect of leaving anyone behind, but this alliance will never last; we need to run, and this may be our only opportunity. But he's coming with us.

"Come on," I urge, pulling Cadence away, back toward the colder shadows where Bryn paces, throwing glances toward her father's camp.

Cadence shakes me off and barrels toward Bryn. "This was your plan. This is your fault. If he's hurt—"

"I didn't hear you volunteering to take his place," Bryn says darkly. "Which is ironic, considering you blame Faris for not doing the same for you when you tried to flee Brindaigel."

Cadence flinches. I squeeze her shoulder—another conversation for another time. "We need to leave while they're distracted," I say, voice low. "We'll take two horses and cut the others loose. You take Cadence; I'll get Tobek."

Bryn stops pacing. "And then what? We outrun my father?"

"Do you have a better idea?!"

"Let them fight it out—"

"North can't fight Merlock, Baedan, *and* your father," I say.

"Corbin is collateral damage," Bryn says, flicking her wrist dismissively. "You're the only one who seems to actually need him."

Cadence looks from Bryn to me and back. "You want to let Prince Corbin die? Isn't that why we came out here? To help him?"

"Plans change and people die," Bryn says. "Surely you know that by now."

Cadence recoils, wounded. The Burn has stripped Bryn of her usual bribes, and gone is the sisterly princess who had dresses and coffees and soft feather beds to buy Cadence's attention. There is only Bryn now, laid bare. And she's not nearly so beautiful as she once was.

Blood ticks in my ears; my vision blurs at the edges, only Bryn in focus. "And you think Baedan will honor your agreement. Brindaigel for Avinea."

"Who knows," she says sardonically. "Maybe Baedan will kill my father and vice versa and I'll inherit them both. Either way, we stick to our plan. And watch that temper," she adds, resuming her pacing. "You'll be hellborne by morning if you keep raging at everyone."

Furious, I storm over and lean into her face. "We're leaving," I say, "and either you're coming with us or you're dying out here on your own. Your choice."

Her eyes flash with warning. "Don't threaten me—"

"You kill me, your amplification ability will kill you out here," I remind her. "You can run to Daddy, but he won't save you and neither will North. As much as it might pain you, princess, we need each other." And then, because I cannot help myself, I add sarcastically, "I'm not the enemy tonight."

Bryn gives me a murderous look to have her own words thrown back in her face, but I refuse to give her an inch. She relents, rolling her eyes and sighing. "All right," she says, pulling my dagger from the folds of her skirt. "I'll get the horses; you get the apprentice."

Satisfied, I release her and turn, nearly colliding with Cadence behind me. She looks as though she wants to say something, and I smooth her hair back. "See, nobody gets left behind," I say, forcing a smile. "And where did you learn to fight like that? You were amazing, Cadence Locke." Digging into my pocket, I retrieve the pearly seashell I picked out for her. "Here. I found this on the beach outside the Burn and forgot to give it to you earlier."

She stares at it, soft pink against the dirt and ash smeared in her palm. Slowly her fingers close around the shell as she straightens, leveling her chin and meeting my eyes. "You were right," she says. "Thaelan did come back for me. And I *wanted* him to. I wanted you to get lost, so that he and I could escape, and then maybe he would finally like me best. And when I saw you that day in the square, and you didn't speak up for me, I—I thought you knew. And you hated me."

My heart cracks open. "Oh, Cade."

"You kept coming back to see me," she continues, voice wavering. "You kept promising to save me, but then one day you didn't come, and I thought—"

I embrace her, as hard as I dare. "I was coming back. I will always come back for you."

Her chin digs into my shoulder, thin arms circling my back. "I know that now," she says at last. "I want to be brave like you, Faris, but I don't know how. I tried to be like Bryn, but . . . I can't do that either."

Bryn stops pacing, eyes meeting mine. She's angry at the implication, of course, but more than that, she's actually hurt. A flicker of resentment crosses her face as she turns her back on both of us.

"You just need to be Cadence, the way you are," I say. "Perrote made Alistair kill Thaelan because Perrote is a coward, and people like us, people like Thaelan, scare him because we aren't afraid to fight. And that's what we have to do now, all right?" I kiss her forehead. "We fight."

Cadence nods, and I kiss the top of her head again, embracing her as hard as I can. "I love you," I murmur. "And I promise your heart will not turn to stone. That's only for trolls in the Wintirlands."

A weak smile at last. I'll take it.

Standing, I reassess the hellborne. Tobek sits, slumped by the fire, balled fists pressed into his thighs. Baedan and the others appear drowsy, intoxicated; it's been too long since they had clean blood, and they seem to have overdone it.

Good.

I cut toward Tobek just as the first shot is fired in the distance, followed by a volley of others. Perrote. His campfire was a decoy, not a truce.

Baedan rouses herself from her stupor, but is slow to retaliate with haphazard magic. It brightens the sky, dimming the stars as I yell at Bryn to get the horses, shoving Cadence after her. In the lull between rounds of fire, I hear the Burn awaken to our noise and the hellborne's spells with a whisper of ash and shadow. This much magic will cause another avalanche.

The hellborne understand the inherent dangers of the Burn and crowd closer to the fire, making easy targets for Perrote's men as they approach. Baedan stands her ground, seeming to awaken again as she casts webbed spells that scorch through armor and skin. She doesn't notice the three of us slipping through the dark to where the hellborne horses are all tethered and saddled several yards away. They grunt, anxious.

"Straight west," I order, swinging Cadence onto a horse as Bryn saws through its rope. "Across the fields. If he's not there, continue west to the abbey in Kerch. Keep the mountains on your left and don't wander."

"Faris!" Cadence reaches for me.

"I'll be right behind you!" I turn back for the camp, cutting off any potential protest. I trust Bryn not to linger.

Tobek still cowers in the ash, tied to a stake in the ground. He flinches when I grab his shoulder in greeting, but soon realizes what I'm doing and tries to help me loosen the rope around his neck. We don't have time to fight with knots, however, and I give up, kicking the stake out of the ground instead. He follows me, sluggish but still moving. I realize—too late—that Bryn has my dagger and I have no way to cut the rest of the horses loose.

I turn to Tobek in question, but he's woozy, disoriented from a loss of blood and the reintroduction of poison. I frisk his pockets, ignoring his indignant protests, and find a small hunting knife. The earth rumbles with familiar warning; dunes of ash begin collapsing around us, kicking up a cloud of debris that cloaks the sky. I work faster, teeth bared against the scorching pain in my bleeding palm. Just as the rope begins to fray, Baedan materializes in front of us.

"No," she growls as she grabs the horse's lead, winding it around her wrist. The horse bucks, fighting for its freedom, but she's stronger. With her free hand she yanks at the rope around Tobek's neck, tightening it until his face drains of all color. "Where are they going?" she demands.

The first wave of ash collides with the camp. The fire flickers, struggling to stay burning, and the darkness creeps close, inhaling with anticipation. But the dunes around us are not nearly as tall as those we encountered more than a week ago; even now, the worst seems to have settled.

"Let him go, and I'll tell you," I say. Wind batters at us, throwing ash into our eyes and hair into our faces.

"Doesn't work like that anymore," Baedan says. She flattens her palm to Tobek's forehead, and poison begins to bleed out of her hand into his skin.

"Stop it!" I clutch the knife in both hands to counterbalance the movement of the earth. My swollen fingers ache with the pressure. Ash begins to sluice around us.

Tobek's eyes roll back; his mouth sags open in a silent scream. The veins across his face flood with poison, but the rope around his neck is acting as a dam, keeping it from spreading lower, toward his heart.

The pistol I took from the guard. Dropping the knife, I pull it from my pocket and aim it steady in my hands. I'm shaking, but my finger folds across the trigger, a gesture committed to my memory from the last—and only—time I shot a gun.

But the shot that tears through Baedan's heart is not mine. She flies back into the ash from the brunt of it. Dead. All her magic was useless against gunpowder and bullets. Apparently a carved-out heart is not the only cure for a hellborne soul.

Tobek is safe, but Perrote's odds of lasting in the Burn just increased exponentially.

Tobek falls to his knees, scrambling to loosen the rope around his neck, gasping for breath. I lower the pistol to help him, but figures emerge from the cloud of ash, drawing my attention. Dirty, blank faces watch us over the barrels of their muskets, features illuminated by small lanterns hanging from each of their saddles, the flames protected by thick plates of glass. More than a dozen men remain, and two more behind. Perrote and Rialdo. Of course they would have survived. Monsters thrive out here in the Burn.

Hiding the pistol in my coat, I raise my hands in surrender. Ash stings my face as it whips past in a frenzied rush, but even with watery eyes I meet Perrote's stare with a defiant glare.

"Shoot her and then skin her," he says.

"The spell is gone," I say. "It has been for days. But," I rush to add, as his soldiers take aim and cock their hammers with a dozen muted clicks, "I know where Merlock is. Bryn is on her way there now."

This, at least, earns a reaction, as he realizes that his daughter is not hiding behind me. Rialdo and Perrote exchange dark glances, and I half-smile, shoving back my coat sleeve to display the binding spell. "Bryn can still inherit," I say, "but if you kill me, she'll start soaking in the poison I've been carrying for her. With her amplification ability, she'll be dead before you find her. And without her blood, you have no chance to take Merlock's magic yourself."

Perrote's smile is thin, forced. "And so you want to negotiate."

"I don't have much time left," I say. I nod to my hand; even in their dim lamplight, the skin is visibly discolored. "I'll take you to Merlock, on one condition."

Rialdo snorts, derisive, but Perrote regards me seriously. "Name it."

My eyes travel down the line of soldiers, and I startle when I see Alistair at the end. Blank, expressionless, armed with a musket but dressed in his waistcoat and cravat beneath the baggy soldier's coat they gave him to wear. An executioner again.

"You kill me yourself," I say, eyes dragging back to Perrote. "I want my blood on your hands, your majesty."

Their horses become unsettled in the deepening ash. Despite the protection spells Perrote's provost must have cast over them, they won't last forever out here. Nothing will.

Perrote wets his lips and considers the request, as if looking for a catch, and then laughs. "As you wish."

"Swear it to me. With all these men as witnesses."

The smile disappears. His men are slaves, but there is a handful of Chadwick's soldiers with no loyalty spells, Elin among them, no doubt swayed by Rialdo's powers of persuasion and the tempting future of an Avinea flooded with magic defenses. These soldiers saw Merlock's betrayal destroy everything, which means Perrote won't be able to risk breaking his word to a worthless servant.

"On my word as king," Perrote says.

"I want your word as a man," I say. "Crowns change hands so easily here in Avinea."

His eyes flash, but he says, "On my word, Miss Locke."

"Then we have a deal."

An arched eyebrow, the return of his smirk. "Like mother, like daughter."

Not that long ago the words would have felt like an insult. Now they feel like a benediction. My mother sacrificed herself to save the ones she loved, and I will do the same. A few days is all North and Bryn and Cadence will need. A few days I can give.

Feeling guilty, I glance to Tobek and try not to think of how I've sacrificed him, too. The look he gives me is proof enough that our truce has ended.

"Merlock is headed northeast," I say, ignoring the way my heart cracks, the way it already mourns those left behind, to whom I never said good-bye. "He's going back to Prevast."

Perrote and Rialdo exchange looks.

"She's lying." Tobek glares at me, finally loosening the rope around his neck and hurling it aside. Weeks of quietly blaming me for everything that has happened surface now, with so much poison in his blood overshadowing all logic. "She's going to drag you across the Burn until all your magic spells dissolve, your horses die, and you're all full of poison."

I turn on him, livid, but he scowls at me, massaging his throat. Poison glows through him. "I'd rather die with North than with you," he says. "And if North has already won? Then bringing them saves North from having to hunt them down."

"And if he hasn't won yet?"

Ignoring me, he says, "We head west, and that's as much as I'll tell you right now."

"Bring them," Perrote barks, and two of Chadwick's former soldiers dismount and march forward. One, a younger, newer recruit, avoids my eyes as he clamps irons onto my wrists, but the other one meets my accusing gaze without flinching.

"Chadwick died trying to save this kingdom from men like him," I say, chin tipping toward Perrote.

The soldier doesn't even blink. "Then I can see why he's dead," he says.

Before I can spit a profane-laden reply at him, Tobek and I are roughly hauled onto two horses, and Perrote gives the order.

We ride, kicking up clouds of ash and displacing hungry shadows in our wake.

Twenty-Seven

THE FIELDS OF ARAK ARE AN UNTOUCHED MEMORIAL TO THE WAR fought more than twenty years ago. Bones shine in the mid-morning light; armor glitters. Skeletal remains clutch corroded pole arms, pitted swords, and the tattered scraps of both Merlock's and Corthen's banners of war. Corthen's are red, like Brindaigel's. The same herald, too: two crows clutching a single eye.

Perrote stole everything from him.

He shows no remorse for the theft and no respect for the dead as we pick our way through the graveyard. Chadwick's former soldiers, on the other hand, wear their questions plainly on their faces as they look from the man leading them to the bones at their feet, wondering how a king they've never heard of could share the same banners as a dead Avinean prince.

The Herald Mountains that were once the walls of my prison in Brindaigel pierce through the fog on our left, craggy and beautiful and already thickly capped with snow. It's surreal to see them from the outside, against a broader landscape. The mountains don't look nearly so tall; they don't stretch nearly so wide. They look passable, not impossible. Waterfalls cascade down the sides of the mountains, kicking up plumes of ash, disappearing into unknown riverbeds. They awaken some intangible longing inside me, some distant need for *home*.

"Which way?" Perrote asks.

Tobek looks worse than I feel, his eyes swollen with exhaustion. The skin on his face is beginning to crack, and ash settles in the edges. He surveys the fields, but there's nothing to see but death, destruction, and the occasional cairn erected in memory. If one of them is Merlock's, he's been gone long enough that the stones have all turned black again, hiding his presence. We've missed him. And North as well.

"Continue through to Kerch," Tobek says wearily.

"And then?"

"I'll tell you then," he says, closing his eyes.

We make a pathetic pair, our hands shackled and our blood turning black. How can we possibly fight anyone, man or monster or Merlock, like this? Tobek's logic was flawed: In no way will leading an army to North be a benefit. We should have led them into the Burn to die.

The ruins of Kerch appear just after noon, half-swallowed by ash and rubble. Only one building was spared destruction, and it rises above the rest at the center of the village.

The abbey.

The first warning shivers of adrenaline spike down my back; my hands turn clammy. If North isn't here, he'll have continued on to the next marker on his map. I'll never make it that far. But how do I get into the abbey without Perrote following?

The narrow, clogged streets force us into a single file. The abbey looms above the broken roofline, but Tobek doesn't know where North was going in Kerch. He's only guessing now, his head swinging left to right as he scans every possible nook and cranny for some sign that North is still here.

Ahead of me, a soldier falls from his horse, hitting the ground with a grunt. I assume it's an accident—exhaustion, no doubt— but then I see the arrow protruding from his throat and the blood spreading beneath him, turning the ash to mud.

More hellborne?

Perrote rears his horse and calls for his men to take cover, but nobody can move until the person ahead or behind moves first, which causes a logjam. Some try vaulting the half-walls around us, but others are penned in, and one, two, three more men go down. Perrote's soldiers fire blindly, heads thrown back to scan the jagged roofline for targets, while Perrote twists in his saddle to find me, eyes narrowed.

"Get her out of here!" he shouts.

But there's nowhere to go. The soldier at my back tries to squeeze his horse between others, but we're stuck. Swearing, he dismounts and yanks me down between the bucking horses and panicked men, toward a cavernous doorway leading into the remnants of an old shop. I wait until we're out of sight and then swing my shackles at the soldier's head, colliding with his face in a rattle of iron. But I'm not nearly strong enough to topple him, and he retaliates with the hilt of his sword struck across my temple. Stars explode and I stagger, breathless, as he spits out a wad of blood at his feet.

There are no other easy exits, nowhere to run. Straightening, I even my breathing and mentally chalk out the lines of the fighting ring. The soldier's tired too; Perrote has been riding them for a day and a half straight with barely any rest. I don't have to be stronger; I just have to last longer.

The soldier levels his sword in warning, only to recoil in surprise when I call his bluff and launch myself directly at him. Circling my iron shackles around his neck, I twist behind him and pull.

He struggles to loosen the shackles, dropping his sword as his fingers scramble for purchase at his throat. My heart slams in my ears, sluggish and thick, and I close my eyes, feeling sick with apology—and a more insidious, poison-fueled satisfaction.

I loosen my hold. The soldier slumps to my feet, choking for air, his hand pressed to his throat. Ropy bile floods out of his mouth, and he tips his head to the floor, a position of defeat.

The fleeting satisfaction is gone, replaced with repulsion toward myself. Feeling sick to my stomach, I lurch toward the door, to the chaos of the fight still raging outside. Details are shrouded in dust; faces are mostly blurs of light and shadow. I see someone on the rooftop above me, leveling a crossbow toward my heart, before they withdraw the weapon in recognition, pointing behind me instead.

Tieg, Davik's brother. Directing me to the abbey.

North is still here.

Darting back into the street, I press myself along a rough stone wall, dodging horses and ducking stray arrows. I reach an alley and brace for a run, but rough hands grab me by the arm, holding me back. Rialdo. His dark hair is white with dust, his features strained but determined. He presses something cold against my lower back. A pistol.

"Where are you going?" he asks.

The gunshot is like thunder, too close to my head, filling my nose with the acrid smell of smoke and gunpowder. Rialdo's grip on me slackens, then releases as he falls back. Dead.

I twist, scanning the rooftops, until I see Cohl.

In that instant I forgive her for leaving us out in the Burn.

She quickly turns back to the fight, and I break into an uneven run. A slurry of footsteps mars the snow along the broken stairs of the abbey, and I follow them inside with my blood still pounding like a rhythmic drum of war.

The footsteps turn to damp water marks and then disappear. I slow, surveying the open nave, my ragged breaths bouncing back from the vaulted ceiling. Rows of pews have been overturned or rearranged into haphazard piles in between stone columns. The tiled floor is cracked and choked with debris and dead bracken. A balcony forms a U above me, the balustrade sagging in places, gone in others. Thick velvet drapery hangs in tatters, hiding the aisles and the banks of arched windows on either side of the nave. The outer structure may have survived the Burn, but its innards have not been spared.

My attention is captured by a tomb that sits nestled in the apse, raised on a dais atop a rotted carpet with fraying threads of black and silver. A cairn of stones is balanced at its center; there's a dampness in the air, the smell of rot.

And then, a voice.

Merlock kneels at the altar, his hands pressed to the ground. His tone is rushed, furtive, as though he's running out of time.

He's praying, of all the inexplicable things.

Still breathless, head aching, I pull the gun from my pocket and raise it at his back, striding silently down the nave. Each step is a new rush of poisoned anger, and I welcome it even as I fear it, allowing it to burrow through my blood, to warm the chill from my skin. It's a mindless, exhausted fury, a simple thought that killing him will end everything. Baedan went down with one bullet. Why shouldn't a king?

"Don't," a voice says, soft. Broken.

I stop; the gun wavers. A bullet won't kill him because the gods protect him with their legendary caveat: Only royalty can kill a king, and my bullet is not forged with North's blood. And my dagger is with Bryn.

I'm finally here, and I'm useless.

Turning, I scan the church for the broken voice, until I see him, propped up by a stone column only a few feet away.

"North," I whisper.

North stares at me, eyes hooded, haunted, his face mapped with blood and bruises. Dirty cloth is bound around his leg for some unknown wound. A dagger hangs in one hand. The blade trembles, and he tips his head back, swallowing hard.

He's been too long in the Burn, I realize with a sickening lurch. The poison has eaten through his defenses and he's barely holding on.

"He's almost done," North says, eyes turning back to his father.

Merlock's prayer continues, uninterrupted, as if we are inconsequential, unimportant, no threat. Magic flickers around him, remnants of some long-ago memory. I catch glimpses of an open tomb, of a young man nestled inside, of a weeping man bent over him, fingers curled against the edge of the tomb. Thin tendrils of poison bleed through the stone, reaching the edges of the young man's funeral garb and staining the cloth black.

Corthen.

The gun is dead weight against my leg, but North has the means to end this. Surely the gods will forgive an unfinished prayer in this instance.

But ever the gentleman, North will not kill a mourning man whose back is turned to him. I love him, but Bryn was right: His nobility may condemn this entire kingdom.

Bryn. I search the abbey again for some sign of her or my sister. Or are they with Davik's brothers, hidden away on the roofs?

"You came back," North says in a voice full of broken glass. Then, with a weak smile, "How did you get here?"

My eyes return to him. "It doesn't matter. I'm here."

His smile fades and he nods, closing his eyes. "You're here," he repeats, sliding an inch lower down the column.

The gunshots outside sound louder, closer; we don't have much time. I shift the pistol to my opposite hand and wipe my palm dry against my trouser leg. The iron shackles rattle with every move I make, and the sound echoes back from the walls. Merlock has to know we're standing here, *waiting*.

He finally finishes his prayer, kissing the backs of his hands before he sits back on his heels. He's a portrait of Avinea, framed at the altar: The craggy Herald Mountains are his knotted spine through his coat; the Burn is the ash-gray tangles of his hair; the birch tree forests we passed in North's wagon are his slender frame, skin mottled by poison and age.

And even the heartbreaking hope that remains in Avinea is momentarily there in his eyes as he turns away from the tomb, still mourning his brother. Then hope fades and his expression hardens as he looks at us.

"You do not learn from your mistakes," he says.

"Nor do you," I say. "You can't change the past, no matter how much you try."

He half-smiles in acknowledgment before he steps up onto the dais to press his hand against the tomb. It cracks beneath the pressure, as though made of flimsy paper instead of solid stone, weakened by too many years absorbing the Burn. As he turns back, my pistol is torn from my hand by an unseen force and skates up the nave to his feet. The abbey doors slam shut behind me, and pews fly back, hitting the walls and columns and splintering apart. I duck, hands over my head, but he strides toward me, calm and unruffled, his demeanor contradicting the sorrow still carved in his face.

North staggers forward, but Merlock locks him in place with one raised hand. North's fingers peel apart, one by one, until his dagger is released. It flies toward me, hovering an inch above my heart.

"I can't change the past, but I can alter your future," Merlock says. "So what do I? Do I show mercy, or do I cut out your heart?"

North edges forward. "Your fight is with me."

Merlock flicks his hand, and I'm thrown aside. North's dagger clatters to the ground. "You mistake me," Merlock says. "I have no fight with you, my son. Only every possible hope."

I can't breathe; I can't think. My heart is slowing down, but my lungs are gasping for air, and I suck in shallow, rattling breaths that don't satisfy my need.

North stares at his father. Trembling. "What do you mean?"

Merlock spreads his hands and cocks his head with a chilling smile. "I want you to continue our legacy," he says. "Give our people the future they deserve. The future that they've *earned* but that I have so selfishly cheated them of. Not destroying this kingdom entirely is the one mistake I can still correct. Through you."

North shakes his head, battered features twisting into a look of absolute loathing. "You are a coward," he says. "You were too weak to find another way, but I am not."

Merlock's smile vanishes, and he lowers his hands. "Do not presume that I'm weak. I am still the king, and you are the bastard son of a whore. You cannot kill me unless I allow myself to die. And I will not die until I see this kingdom in hell, where it belongs."

North strikes with precision, finesse—no showmanship, only efficiency. His magic collides with his father, who loses a fraction of his footing. With a growl, Merlock casts a spell that calls shadows from the floor. They emerge like spindled demons that separate and race toward North. More shadows drip from the walls and the vaulted ceiling, as viscous as poison as they congeal into monstrous forms, with serrated spines and sharpened claws and heads too heavy for their malformed bodies.

I lunge for the dagger as North casts a spell that ignites every candle left in the iron brackets along the nave, on the altar, in the balcony. The shadows recoil from the bright light, but he's already weak and getting weaker. Merlock easily knocks him onto his back and pins him to the ground with magic. Shadows wind around North's arms and legs, holding him hostage.

North struggles against their grip. His own magic collects into his fingertips, but shadows envelop them, blocking any attempt at attack. More shadows ring his chest, inching higher, toward his face.

Frantic, I rush for Merlock, dagger raised, but before I even reach him, I fly back, into a broken pew. Pain brightens my vision as I roll onto my stomach, gasping.

"Stop fighting it," Merlock says. "Accept your fate, my son; accept your death so that you may truly live. Claim your sins and bear them with honor. You are human and you are fragile, and you," he breathes, crouching beside North, "are broken beyond repair. Like me."

"Not yet," a cold voice says.

Bryn steps out from behind a column, Cadence at her side, both of them clutching candles dripping with wax. Merlock sits back, head cocked, but Bryn wastes no time, burning the shadows wrapped around North's hand before her fingers thread through his.

It is a moment of beautiful despair as the shadows retract and North's magic surges with Bryn there to amplify it. Merlock is bowled back, and North rises to his feet, hand in hand with Bryn: the prince and his wife.

They will be legend after this day, if they survive.

But I won't survive, not at this rate. North's infection trans-fers through Bryn into me, stronger than ever. My head ignites, and I double over, retching, fingers splayed against the broken tile floor. My heart beats once and waits forever before it beats again.

"Faris!" Cadence runs for me, diverting North's attention. He releases Bryn's hand to spare me, and Merlock presses his advan-tage, shoving North to his knees as Bryn is cast aside in a tumble of skirts.

"Our people are parasites. They crave magic and they crave power, and nothing you do or say will ever satiate their greed. So give them what they want." He cradles North's face, a temporary image of paternal affection. "Let them rot with desire and bleed with hunger and starve to death by their own wicked hearts." He tightens his hold on North's face, poison-stained fingers digging furrows into North's cheeks. "We can't save anyone. We never could. Surely you see that."

North cries out, teeth bared in agony as his father's poison rips through his flesh. Dark blood drips from his nose, but his eyes shift past Merlock, to me. Trembling hands reach up and grab Merlock by the forearms. A gesture of subservience, of submission—but I know better, because he did this once before. He's holding Merlock in place, using the last of his power, the last of his strength: all or nothing, no second chances.

But unlike the first time he did this, this time I'm ready.

"Having a heart is not a weakness," North says, the words heavily slurred. "You didn't save your brother, and you can't save yourself." His eyes shift to me again as shadows crawl down Merlock's back, around his arms, over North's skin. "I'm willing to die for this kingdom, which is far more than you ever would."

"Now!" Bryn shouts, placing her hand on North's exposed arm, doubling his power—and the poison inside me.

I strike.

The dagger sinks between Merlock's shoulder blades, and he twists, incredulous, releasing North to face me fully. North collapses against Bryn as Merlock takes a step toward me, then another, only to falter, hesitate, stop. His eyes widen as the blood forged in the blade begins to eat through his skin and the magic threaded through it. He laughs in disbelief before sagging to his knees. Breathlessly I wrench the dagger out of his back, dizzy as I stare him down.

He rattles with laughter, eyes watering as they focus on me. His skin is almost completely gone, and with it, every spell protecting his heart.

"He will regret this," he wheezes, "and he will resent you for burdening him with the impossible task of hope."

"He'll survive," I say, and drive the dagger through his throat before he can say one more poisoned word.

There's not much time before Merlock's heart will stop, and yet I spare a second for North, who lies, unresponsive, in Bryn's arms.

"Don't touch his skin!" I say, waving her away. "You'll only make it worse!"

She doesn't argue, easing him onto the tile floor. She stands and backs away, staring at him with a strange, unreadable expression. Cadence joins me as I pocket the dagger and wipe North's sweat-stained face with the sleeve of my coat, then press my ear to his chest, listening for a heartbeat.

Slow and getting slower. He's alive, but only barely.

"Don't you dare, not again," I whisper to him. "I need you, North. Do you understand me?"

His eyelids flutter, but there's no response.

"Here," I say, pulling Cadence closer. "Use your coat sleeves to cover your skin. Then keep his head up and listen. Don't let his heart stop."

"How do I do that?" she asks, terrified.

"Talk to him," I say. "Let him know he's not alone. All right?"

Her eyes well up but she nods, gently easing his head onto her lap. Her blond curls are stained with ash, and we all look like nightmares today.

"Hurry," she begs.

Turning back, I confirm that Merlock is no longer moving. Gracelessly I pull back his coat and rip open his shirt to the broken skin beneath. Bracing myself, I plunge the dagger through his chest, gagging on the feel of muscle and bone and sinew giving way like damp sand choked with algae. And then I feel it collide with the blade, hard as a stone and hot as a pyre.

The heart of a king.

Merlock goes limp when I tear out his heart, and I turn away, fighting down a rise of bile. Thread, I think. Bind it tightly. I yank the lace from my boot and begin to wrap the still-beating heart, my own a slow echo against my ribs, scattering my thoughts. Brief flashes of darkness interrupt my vision; I can hear myself gasping for every aching breath, but they never seem to be enough.

Bryn kneels beside me, watching. "I need the dagger Cadence gave you," I mumble, and she pulls it from her cloak and unscrews the hilt, revealing the hidden vial of North's blood tucked inside. My fingers are too slick for traction, and I have to uncork the vial with my teeth. I upend its contents across the leather, before I stop cold.

How did she know there was blood hidden in the blade? I never told her what the dagger was, where it came from, or even why I had it. Frowning, I roll the vial in my hand. Merlock's blood from my hands smears the glass and outlines the broken wax seal.

The Dossel coat of arms.

I drop the vial. It bounces once against the tile before rolling away. My stomach sinks as I meet Bryn's eyes.

"This isn't North's blood," I say.

She offers me a wincing smile, a cruel facsimile of apology. "I was raised to be a queen," she says. "Anything less is a waste of my time."

Rialdo, I realize. If he was her father's proxy, she would have known about blood-forged blades. She knew exactly what this was when she asked Cadence for the dagger.

I shake my head, fire igniting in my veins. "No. That's impossible. You can't even bleed—"

"How do you think I was going to kill my father and inherit Brindaigel? When I actually believed he was a king, at least." She scoffs at my naivety—or maybe hers. "I needed a blade forged with blood. One of Pem's vial's worth was all I needed, long before I ever met you."

The heart already feels heavier in my hands, not a muscle so much as a stone, a burden I cannot risk bearing much longer. If it's not unbound soon, it will be absorbed into my body, and North will have to cut it out of my skin.

Bryn reaches for the heart, but I cradle it to my chest, revulsion warring with fury. "You're bloodbound to North. He can still inherit even with your blood on the bindings—"

"I will kill you if I have to," she says, and all apology is gone, replaced with the familiar look of war. "I won't need you once I become queen."

The injustice of it cuts too deeply—to have come this far, to have lost so much, to have finally *trusted* her, when all along she did intend to take Avinea for herself. With her amplification ability, there'd be no fighting her.

"You could still be Queen of Brindaigel," I say desperately. "You don't know how to use magic. You need North—"

She stares at me. "I have always intended to rule alone."

The flashes of darkness are getting longer; her face flickers in and out of view. "I can't let you do this."

Shouts and gunfire outside are a shocking reminder that Perrote is still fighting. A moment later, he shoves through the abbey doors, flanked—protected—by only five of his original two dozen. It's a relief to see Alistair among them, and Tobek, too, held captive by Perrote as one last bargaining tool.

Perrote surveys the damage before his eyes settle on me, still holding Merlock's heart even as I feel its power begin to bleed through my skin, an intoxicating lure for the poison in my blood. Possibilities begin unfolding through me as my greed awakens. I could be powerful. I could be unstoppable. I could be—

No. This magic was never meant for me.

Perrote strides forward, leveling his pistol at me. "Give her the heart," he commands. When I don't move, he changes direction, releasing Tobek and grabbing Cadence by the arm, yanking her to her feet. North's head hits the floor with a dull thud, but he doesn't move. The soldiers sweep through the abbey, muskets trained on Bryn and me.

"Give. Her. The heart," Perrote repeats.

I look to Bryn, but it's not hate that squeezes so tightly in my chest. It's pity, that for every choice she's made, there was an alternative. In another life, this could have been our shared success. We're not so different, after all. We are both willing to fight for what we want, no matter the cost.

But she chose a path paved with vices that she will be doomed to circle for years to come as she tries to understand why her heart can hurt so much when she never offered it to anyone. Because a weak heart breaks, a broken heart bleeds, and blood can be poisoned.

"I forgive you," I say, and Bryn frowns, bemused. "And I hope that one day you can forgive yourself. Because greed costs, your majesty."

Dropping the heart, I grab North's dagger and plunge it through the bindings, striking stone on the other side. A pistol fires, its sound swallowed by a blast of heat that bellows through the abbey, knocking me onto my back. I roll onto my side, watching as Bryn tries to salvage the heart with frantic, panicked gestures. The knotted leather lacing begins to fray, unravel, and rot, turning to ash before spinning away in a rising eddy. Bright white light splinters the air, fragmenting my view of her features, and I close my eyes, turning away. I feel knots of magic unraveling inside me—the binding spell, the remnants of the spell my mother cast—all dissolving like a thousand sunset skies melted into liquid starlight.

Sounds come caving back in with a rush of air and adrenaline. My ears ring, and I open my eyes. My vision clears to see Perrote standing over me, furious, pistol aimed at my face. "What have you done?!"

But then a single shot, a single gasp, and the world inches further off course.

Perrote sags back, pistol dropping. His eyes slide to Bryn with open accusation as the hole in his heart widens and turns a bright, blinding red. He falls to his knees and then slumps over. Dead. The loyalty spells that protected him were unraveled the way my spells had been, and his men now watch with wide, startled eyes and a choice to make. Who is their real enemy?

Bryn stands, fierce, unflinching, furious, holding the gun I stole from the guard in New Prevast—the one Merlock swept aside. Her eyes meet mine, and I see the anger behind them before she turns, angling for a dark doorway at the back of the altar.

I roll onto my knees and then my feet, growling with pain as I stagger after her, down a short hallway and into an outer courtyard. The Herald Mountains beckon from above the abbey walls, and I stop.

She's going home. She didn't kill her father to spare me; she did it to ensure her contingency plan. With her father dead, her husband victorious, and her power over me dissolved, she has no hope of taking Avinea.

Bryn spins to face me from several yards away. "I owe you nothing now," she says.

"Bryn—"

"Do not come after me," she says. "Do not make this war, Faris."

"You can't survive in the mountains forever," I say, slumped against a column for support. "That was your father's mistake."

"I am not your enemy now," she says, "but I will become one impossible to defeat if you test me. I will fight, and I will never stop. Remember that." Her eyes flick past me, back inside. "Both of you."

My legs buckle, and I slide down the column in a smear of blood as she crosses the courtyard and vanishes beyond the walls on the other side. The cold air is blistering against my face, and I close my eyes, rocking my head back, swallowing a mouthful of bile.

North. Is he even alive?

But I can't muster the energy to move.

"Here! She's out here!" Cadence. I turn toward her voice, full of words I can't articulate. Her slim hand slides into mine and squeezes hard as footsteps surround me.

"Sofreya!" a familiar voice shouts. Alistair? "She needs to be excised immediately or she'll never make it home!"

Home.

And then callused hands on my face, my throat, my arms. "Faris," Alistair says. "Hold on. This is not your last fight."

Bright white stars dot a curtain of black behind my eyelids as I'm lifted into someone's arms.

For the first time in months, I look to the stars and I make a wish.

Twenty-Eight

IT SNOWED AGAIN LAST NIGHT.

The harbor is now frozen from the Bridge of Ander all the way to the quay, and most fishing boats are moored off the bridge pilings, closer to the open water and the thinner ice. A few skiffs remain at the dockside. Every morning their crews carry them on their shoulders along the beachfront before casting off. It's almost surreal. A whole war was fought in the Burn, and while the city remains ignorant of most of the details, the basic facts are all they needed to know: Merlock is dead, and so is the magic. And in spite of knowing that magic will never return to Avinea, the city still survives.

We all do.

I press my forehead to the frosted glass, watching Cadence and Tobek in the courtyard below, throwing snowballs. Alistair stands on the sidelines, hands plunged into his pockets and a lit cigarette dangling from the edge of his mouth.

It's the first break he's taken in days. Our blood was so thick with poison when we returned from the Burn, he's been buried in his lab for more than a week, conducting transfusions. Little by little—needle by needle—Alistair is cleaning the infected blood, a heretofore impossible feat. Science triumphing over magic, just like he promised.

I bite my lip, tracing the dark veins in my arms. Having absorbed more than the others, it's taking longer to replace my poisoned blood. Sofreya excises what she can every few days, which dulls the headaches and mutes the call of my vices, but my heart still beats twice as slowly as it should, and it leaves me tired. Too tired to risk going outside or exerting myself in any way. So from the safety of the library, I watch my sister laughing, with a shawl pulled tight around my shoulders and a fire roaring behind me.

It feels strange to stand still after a lifetime of running, and yet I don't feel trapped in the palace anymore.

Finally I feel safe.

Alistair glances up and sees me through the window. He raises his hand with a hesitant smile, and I press my palm to the glass in return, exposing the pale scar around my wrist—a permanent reminder of the spell that once linked me to Bryn.

Cadence notices Alistair and twists, breaking into a grin as she waves. I smile more broadly this time, still giddy over our new relationship: sisters again, but something more, something that grief and tragedy have made stronger. After returning from the Burn, she swore off swords and soldiers, and Alistair promised her an apprenticeship. Now she spends every night snuggled beside me in bed, burning a candle down to a nub as she reads books from his laboratory.

She doesn't understand most of it yet, but that doesn't stop her from trying. Hearing her voice stumble over words that neither one of us has ever heard is a better lullaby than anything else I could imagine. A better victory than any in the fighting ring.

The fire pops behind me, and I close my eyes, exhaling slowly and steadily, fogging the glass. Turning, I look back to the wide table spread with maps, ready to resume my work, before I realize I'm no longer alone.

North stands in the doorway, leaning into the jamb for support, one hand straining on a wooden crutch. Darjin winds between his legs before padding over to the fire and throwing himself down with a soft *whump*.

I stare at North, paralyzed by his appearance. He's gaunt and unshaven, his shaggy hair still more gray than black. His dark clothes hang off him like blankets, his shirtsleeves rolled up to show his skinny forearms. Puncture wounds freckle the skin where Alistair withdrew poisoned blood and returned it back clean.

But then the shock wears off and I cross the room, throwing my arms around him. I hold him for what feels like forever.

"You shouldn't be out of bed," I say at last, muffled against his shoulder.

One arm circles my waist, his chin on top of my head. "You don't come to see me, so I came to see you."

I don't go to see him because it scares me to see him so weak, with blood and bandages and needles scattered across his bed.

That he even made it back to New Prevast alive is a blessing—and a testament to Sofreya.

"Here." Releasing him, I pull a chair out from the table, and he dutifully limps toward it, sitting down with a grimace. I take a seat across from him, nervous beneath his intense gaze.

"You killed Merlock," he says at length.

"And all the magic," I say. When he doesn't reply, I lower my head and pick at the edges of the maps. "I'm sorry. I thought I was doing the right thing by destroying his heart. It was the only way to keep it from Bryn."

"It *was* the right thing to do. I don't know that I could have done it, no matter how much I wanted to."

"But magic will disappear now," I say softly. It already has, in the area around the abbey. With no heartbeat to feed it, the Burn has begun receding on its own.

"It'll take time," he agrees, shifting in his seat. "A few years, maybe longer, depending on how quickly it's used. But at least if it's gone, it can never be abused again. We'll have to learn how to solve our own problems now. And I admit," he adds with a ghost of a smile, "knowing that my children will not have to kill me to inherit their futures is something of a relief."

I force a smile only to realize he's staring at the scar on my collarbone, an ugly, puckered welt of shiny flesh and innumerable stitches, each one ringed with yellow bruises. I adjust my shawl to hide it again. For some reason I can't look him in the eye, and my nerves are on fire, kicking my heart into frantic motion.

"Your mother would be proud."

"So would yours," I say.

North acknowledges me with a dip of his chin before he pulls the maps closer, expression guarded. "Are you leaving?"

"In the spring."

His fingers tighten along the map. He tries to mask his hurt, but it colors his voice. "Where are you going?"

I push back from the table with a screech of wood and join him on his side, shoulder to shoulder as I lean over to point. With no more magic in our skin, there's nothing for the poison in either of us to respond to—no danger in a touch. No darkness, no vice underneath, only a soft blooming pleasure that makes my heart race.

A tantalizing, promising *maybe.*

"We'll start here in Cortheana," I say. "And from there we'll go north, toward the mountains. This marsh here"—I tag it with my finger—"turns into a river. We'll follow it to a cavern, and a tunnel, and a staircase carved from marble that will lead us into the dungeons."

North stares at the map, incredulous. "You're going back to Brindaigel?"

"The Burn now encompasses two thirds of Avinea, and Bryn is sitting on the largest hoard of magic left on the continent," I say. "Merlock is dead, but you are far from saving Avinea, your majesty. We could wait a few years for the magic to dissolve on its own, but I say we press our advantage. Force an agreement. You are the rightful king, after all, and your people know it now."

North turns, watching my profile with a look of amazement.

"She'll want land," I continue with a flush, gratified by his expression. "Resources, trade routes. She'll also want protection for her borders, which means she'll be willing to compromise on her demands."

"Or it could mean war," says North.

"Yes." I swallow, fingers curling into a fist. "There's a possibility that Bryn will fight. In fact, I know she will. But we have all winter to prepare. It'll give you time to prove yourself to your people, to prove that they need *you* more than they needed your father's magic. You are strong, North, and we'll show them that. So that when the moment comes, they'll finally be willing to fight for you."

"We," he says, turning to face me.

I smile, but it quickly fades as I stare at the maps until the edges blur out of focus. "Offer me a seat on your council," I say. "And then treat me as an adviser and nothing more. Avinea needs its king, and the king still has a wife."

He rubs his mouth, looking away. Like all the other spells, the bloodbound spell linking his heart to Bryn's was dissolved in Kerch, but marriage proclamations have already been received by dozens of courts around the Havascent Sea—not to mention across his own kingdom. Until a suitable dissolution can be presented, he must play the part of scorned husband. "Of course," he says, strained. "But—"

"But," I say.

North looks over, lips parted.

My hand slides over the map until my little finger hooks through his.

"Thank you for coming back to me," I finally say, forcing myself to meet his eyes.

"I held on as long as you did," he replies, just as softly.

The fire crackles and hisses from the other side of the room as North lowers his head. "Not that long ago I offered you and your sister the best rooms in the palace."

"And all the books I could read," I say. "There was also a promise of tarts, which has yet to be delivered."

"And of a kiss," he says quietly. "That offer still stands, and more. So much more. You were the seedling that Avinea needed. But this"—his finger tightens around mine—"is all *I* have ever needed. You are my greatest weapon, Faris Locke, and I need you in the months ahead. Name your price for staying until I'm free."

My stomach tightens, and I feel the threads of poison that still linger in my blood that have yet to be excised. Desire, greed, and some unnameable longing. *Home.*

"Time," I finally say.

"I can afford that," he says with a smile. "As much as you need. But these belong to you in the interim." Sitting up, he pulls several small rocks from his trousers pocket.

"How?" I ask as he laughs, dropping three of them into my cupped hands. "You've been in bed for ten days! Did Tobek bring these to you?"

"Anonymous sources," he says, his crooked grin suddenly shy. He retrieves the first stone and sets it down along the edge of the map. "This is for that night we spent after Prevast," he says. "A night of great willpower, Faris; you have no idea."

My breath catches as he reaches for the second stone, fingertips ghosting across my skin. "This one is for the moment you entered the abbey with your gun raised, ready to kill my father for me," he says. "And this one"—he touches the final stone before curling my fingers around it—"is for this moment right now." He's all serious-ness now as his hand brushes across my cheek, then slides into my hair. "Keep these until the time is right, because I love you and I will wait as long as I have to." His expression softens. "But not a moment longer."

"But what are they for?"

His gaze softens, and my stomach somersaults. *Oh.*

As tempting as the future sounds, we deserve a moment of weakness now. I reach forward, moving hair out of his eyes. "Just one," I murmur, brushing my lips across his.

"Just once," he adds with a smile, pulling me closer, deepening the kiss.

Apparently I didn't destroy *all* the magic left in Avinea.

When he finally pulls back, he picks up one of the stones and brandishes it toward me. "But I advise you, Faris Locke, to hoard these like gold, because I fully expect you to trade every last one of them in at the same time, and when you do, I am going to kiss every single inch of your skin. Bruises and scars included."

"But until then," I say, flushing with heat. Sweet, steady North has a spark of the wild within him.

Good.

"Until then," he repeats softly, still watching me with that smol-dering grin. A moment later he stands, and Darjin rolls onto his feet to join him. "Did you know there are secret passages in this palace?"

"Cadence has mentioned them."

"One of them goes directly to my rooms from this library," he says, arching an eyebrow as I scan the room on reflex. He grins again, before he turns, heading for the door. "It never hurts to have a fail-safe, Miss Locke," he calls over his shoulder.

I watch him disappear, biting back my own grin. From outside, Cadence's and Tobek's laughter carries through the glass, and I begin to straighten my maps, feeling more at peace than I have in weeks.

Ten years ago I believed my mother to be a murderer and my life to be a mistake. But now I know there is nothing else I would rather be: Brim-raised and battle-worn, with a scar above my heart and an insatiable need for more that carried me under a castle, over a border, and across a kingdom riddled with decay, so that one day I would finally be here:

Home.

Acknowledgments

Authors often speak of their second contracted novels in whispers of horrified despair, underlined with the nagging fear that they will be unmasked as imposters along the way. For me, an amazing support system was the difference between weeping under my desk—or hitting my deadlines despite all the doubts.

So thank you to Alexa Pastor for keeping Faris focused on the task at hand—and for being an editorial wizard. This book would have perished in the Burn without your guidance. The entire team at McElderry/Simon & Schuster continue to provide the best home Faris could hope for. Thank you for another beautiful book.

From deadlines to trade reviews to hospitalizations: the debut road has been rocky, but my family has been steady. Mom and Dad, thank you for letting me grow up a little wild and a little weird and for always believing I could do this (twice!). Audrey, I owe you so much more than a dedication. Nicole, thank you for being the first to buy my book in the store, and to Alex for being right there with her to take the photo. Cathy, I truly appreciate how you celebrate every one of my successes, no matter how small.

Debuts are often lost in the crowd, so a shout-out to the book bloggers and bookstagrammers who've promoted Faris and her misadventures, and to anyone who's ever written a review. Authors may not thank each one of you personally, but we see you and appreciate every ounce of support you provide. I want to say thank you especially to Morgan from Take Me Away To A Great Read, Austine Decker from NovelKnight, and Christen from Whimsify. Thank you for the enthusiasm and generosity with which you embraced this strange story I wrote.

A special squish and a cuddle to my son, Jacob, who missed the start of this journey but has kept me going to the end.

Finally, Eugene. No matter what I try to say here, it always comes down to the same simple truth: I love you.